THE
PHOTOGRAPH

A Detective India Hargreaves Mystery

L.E. LUTTRELL

Beaten Track
www.beatentrackpublishing.com

The Photograph

First published 2021 by Beaten Track Publishing
Copyright © 2021 L.E. Luttrell

Paperback ISBN: 978 1 78645 507 9
eBook ISBN: 978 1 78645 508 6

Cover design by PixelStudio
Male model photograph licensed from iStock

Beaten Track Publishing,
Burscough, Lancashire.
www.beatentrackpublishing.com

For my son Simon

THE
PHOTOGRAPH

1

HE STARTED THE minute she opened the door, his cranky complaints echoing down the long narrow hallway. Was she imagining it? Was she simply recalling the irritating whines that had followed her out of the house this morning? She closed the door and stood outside for a moment. Could she face this after a long working day?

She'd taken extra care as she'd approached, cutting the engine and lights as she swung onto the tarmacked driveway and closing the door with a gentle click. Surely, he couldn't have heard the car? It had only taken her a few seconds to walk up to the house. She'd left the fly screen clipped back this morning, and she'd oiled the lock on the front door, so the key slid in and opened it silently. So how could he be aware of her return?

It sounded as though he was still sitting in the dining room at the back of the house; exactly where she'd left him this morning. He couldn't see the front door from there, so how did he do it?

Unless, of course, his confinement to the wheelchair *was* all an act. Had he spotted her car turning into the driveway through one of the front bedroom windows and raced back to his wheelchair to take up his favoured position at the table? He could have used his wheelchair, she supposed. It was electronic and might just about give him time to make it back, but it wasn't that fast.

For some weeks, she'd suspected he was more mobile than he was letting on. Her strategy this evening was to see if she could catch him out. Returning from work an hour earlier, she'd hoped to find him strutting around the house, thinking she wouldn't be home yet. Well, that hadn't worked.

She must have been imagining the sound of his voice. Even able-bodied, she doubted he could have moved so fast. Perhaps he was voicing his complaints out loud. Practising his litany of demands. He was certainly accomplished in that respect, and there was nowhere in the house she could escape to for sanctuary. With the door shut in both the bathroom and her bedroom, she could still hear him. Would he ever stop? She didn't know how much more she could take.

Slipping the key back into the lock, she paused to listen. She hadn't imagined it. His voice boomed down the hall and had progressed from muttered complaints to one of his rants. Taking a deep breath, she stepped inside.

"Hello, darling," she called out. "How was your day?"

2

A T SIX FOOT, Doctor Greer Hamilton towered over her female colleagues and, even in one-inch heels, was taller than most of her male colleagues. She was the senior practitioner in the accident and emergency department, and staff bustled around her cautiously. It didn't do to upset Doctor Hamilton. She demanded one hundred and ten percent efficiency; woe betide anyone who slacked off, as she was quick to lash out with her tongue. Not that everyone could understand what she was saying. Her gentle Scottish accent seemed to thicken as she angered, but they could gauge her mood by the tone and volume.

One of the department staff had looked up the name 'Greer' that morning and quickly spread the results of her findings amongst colleagues in the canteen at lunchtime.

"It's a *unisex* name that means 'watchful and vigilant'," the nurse told the small group. "Also, the name is a female derivative of Gregory."

"That'd be right," one of the male nurses said. "She's Amazonian—I reckon she has quite a lot of testosterone in her. And she's certainly watchful and vigilant."

"I think she's great," one of the nurses piped up. "Everything runs smoothly when she's on duty."

"You would think that, Nicole, because you're shaping up to be just like her," the male nurse said. "Things run

3

smoothly when she's on duty because she's got the old whip out. I reckon she'd look *really* sexy in one of those tight latex outfits wielding a whip. Just thinking about it makes me—"

"Enough!" Nicole snapped. "You're being disrespectful."

***

THERE WAS ONLY one member of staff who was never on the receiving end of Doctor Hamilton's tongue lashings: Sister Marion Fisher; a fellow Scot who had the same expectation of efficiency.

Sister Fisher had lived in Australia for almost thirty years, moving to Sydney as a young, married woman after qualifying as a nurse. Marion had taken to Greer Hamilton as soon as they'd met. Greer was thirty-eight to Marion's fifty-three years, not quite enough of an age gap for Marion to be her mother, but she was inclined to mother Greer at times, admonishing herself on many occasions about it. She preferred to be Greer's friend. Marion had never managed to carry a child to full term, and with her childless status, she'd felt socially isolated from her neighbours and peers. Developing a friendship with Greer, whose marriage was also childless, had given Marion a renewed social life. Until Lachlan's accident.

With so many staff off ill with their first sniffles of the season, Doctor Hamilton and Sister Fisher hadn't had a break all day. At three in the afternoon, Sister Fisher managed to slip off to make them both a cup of tea.

"Here, Greer," she whispered. Marion was the only one allowed to call her by her first name. "Come and take five. I've brought you a cuppa."

"Oh, you're a darling. And here was me just thinking I could kill someone if it meant I could sit with a cup of tea in peace and quiet."

They moved into Greer's small office, and both sank with exhaustion onto chairs.

"How's Lachlan these days?" Marion asked Greer.

"He's a lot better, thank you—now that I've promised him we'll return home. He's been very homesick since the accident. But he's smiling more these days, grumbling less and not so irritable. In fact, he's so laid-back he's almost horizontal."

Marion laughed. She couldn't imagine a 'laid-back' Lachlan. Not that she'd ever seen the couple in their home environment. On the occasions they'd socialised, the three of them had met at the cinema or in restaurants, but Lachlan always had an air of irritability about him. He was impatient and downright rude at times, although all that seemed to change once he'd downed a few whiskies.

"Are you talking about going home permanently or just for a visit?"

"I'm not sure. We'll need to—"

Their conversation was interrupted when a nurse entered the office after a quick knock.

"Sorry to disturb you, Doctor Hamilton, but we have an emergency admission and need you."

"No rest for the wicked, eh, Sister Fisher?" Greer said, standing and stretching for a moment. She gulped down the last of her tea before striding off.

***

SHE WAS GREETED with blissful silence when she opened the door that night.

"Hi, honey, I'm home," she called out, putting on her best American accent while removing her jacket.

He didn't reply, but he was grinning at her as she walked into the dining room.

"You liked that, huh? It's good to see you smiling for a change. How was your day? Mine was hectic as per usual.

5

I didn't even manage a lunch break—just a quick cuppa and time to make a few calls. I'm absolutely famished. I don't suppose you've cooked dinner?"

She bent over to look more closely at him; he was still grinning stupidly at her.

"No, I don't imagine you did. Cooking is not exactly your strong point, is it? Looks like it's going to be a microwave meal again tonight, darling. I think that's all we have left. I'm off work for the next three days, so I'll do a big shop tomorrow. It's going to be a busy few days in all, sorting everything out. I managed to phone Miguel this morning, and he's going to help us sort things out at his end. Right, let's see what we can have for dinner."

She turned and walked into the kitchen, opening the fridge to inspect the contents. There was a choice of a fish dinner or roast beef.

"Roast beef, I think, don't you?" She turned to her husband, who didn't reply.

"You're not sulking, are you? It's not because I phoned Miguel, is it? I thought he was the one best placed to help us, given the circumstances. Or are you upset because you know I'm about to have a glass of wine and you're not allowed to drink alcohol? It messes with your medication. You know that. I'm sorry."

After setting the microwave, she poured herself a glass of red wine and returned to the dining room. She caught an unpleasant odour as she passed him.

"I tell you what, you're a bit whiffy tonight. You haven't showered again today, have you? I'm not sure I can sit through another meal with you smelling like that. I think I'm going to eat in the living room tonight. You can stay here by yourself."

3

"E STAS LISTOS, SENORITA?"
"Casi, senor."

"Did that sound better?" Sonny asked Chrys.

She turned away so he wouldn't see her smiling and set about washing up her breakfast bowl and mug. She didn't want to correct him either. He should have said 'esta lista', not 'estas listos', but Sonny was becoming more and more insecure about his Spanish, and she didn't want to inhibit him from practising.

"Chrys?"

Realising he expected a reply, she nodded and said, "Your accent is marginally better, but you used a more formal address, so I replied in the formal. A husband wouldn't address his wife like that."

"Well, we're not married yet, miss, so it was okay to use it, wasn't it?"

"Watch it, smarty pants," she said, turning back to him with a fake scowl.

"I just can't get my head around all these verb variations where it's a different spelling and pronunciation if it's 'I', 'he', 'she', 'we', 'they' and different words for 'you'. And masculine and feminine words? That's crazy. Why can't it be simple like English?"

7

"Spanish speakers would no doubt think our language very strange and complex."

"But dress is *masculine*, shirt *feminine*. How did they decide that? And we don't say things back to front, like 'she bought a dress red'. Placing the adjective *after* the noun makes no sense."

"Only to us."

"I suppose. But really, Chrys, can you still tell my accent is like an Aussie attempting to speak Spanish?"

"Mm-hmm."

"I didn't quite catch that."

"Yes. We both sound like that. We're still only beginners, Sonny, so stop beating yourself up about it."

"But your accent sounds okay to me."

"Maybe because I learnt another language as a kid. You know my maternal grandmother was Hungarian. I think once you are bilingual, it's easier to pick up other languages and accents. When Pop died, Nagyi came to live with us. I was only two at the time. Little kids soak up languages like a sponge, and she spoke Hungarian to me all the time, although my mother kept telling her to stop it. Mum wouldn't speak Hungarian to her at all. Not unless she wanted to say something to her so Dad wouldn't understand."

"You wouldn't ever do that to me, would you?"

"What?"

"Speak to *your* mother in Hungarian so I won't understand what you're saying."

"Chance would be a fine thing. They're not even coming to our wedding. 'We can't leave the animals,' Mum told me."

"So they're definitely not coming?"

"Nope."

8

"When did you last speak to her? You didn't mention it."

"I spoke to her last night, and you were out until late, so I haven't had a chance to tell you. I'm telling you now. Come on, we need to leave or you're going to miss your train. Do you want me to drop you at the station?"

Sonny had been standing at the edge of the kitchen peninsula all the time they'd been talking. Meanwhile, she'd washed the dishes, wiped the counter, washed and dried her hands, walked out to join him and picked up her handbag ready to leave. He'd be cutting it fine to make it to the station now.

"No, it's too much of a hassle to get my bike in your car. I'll cycle," he said, finally making a move.

"Okay, see you later then." She pecked him on the cheek.

Sonny followed her out of the house, slamming the door behind him. He double-locked it and closed and locked the fly-screen door.

She paused before climbing into the car. "Will you be home at the normal time this evening?"

"Yes, and I know, it's my turn to cook," he said as he wheeled his bike out of the car port.

"What's on the menu?"

"You'll have to wait and see, it's a surprise." He grinned.

"Right. In other words, you haven't decided. I'll look forward to whatever it is, anyway. See you then."

With that, she started the car, backed out and drove off, waving out of the window.

***

SONNY'S DEPARTURE WAS delayed; he couldn't find his helmet. Had he taken it into the house last night?

He never did that, but he'd been out drinking late, and Tony had dropped him home, his bike stashed in the back of the ute. Perhaps the helmet fell off at some point without him noticing.

He rushed back into the house, but as he suspected, the helmet was nowhere to be seen.

Damn! He'd have to take his chances and cycle to the station without it. He'd been meaning to buy another helmet for weeks after his best one had rolled off the bike and Chrys had accidentally backed over it with the car. He'd been using his old helmet, and now that seemed to be missing. He made a mental note to buy another one later.

He left the house again and grabbed his bike. After mounting and pedalling to the edge of the roadway, he checked to see it was clear both ways before crossing and cycling off. He'd have to get a move on if he was to make his train.

***

CHRYS MENTALLY COUNTED the days as she drove. Just nine more days until she and Sonny married. She couldn't stop grinning every time she thought about it. Two days after their marriage, they were travelling to Spain. A week in the Costa del Sol lazing about in the sun—something they seldom did in Australia. From Malaga, they were flying to Santander in Northern Spain, and from there, after two nights in the city, they were travelling to Oviedo in preparation for a pilgrim trek to Santiago de Compostela. They were walking the 'Camino Primitivo'—or 'the original way' as it was more commonly known—from Oviedo to Santiago de Compostela. It was only a little over three hundred kilometres, and they'd allowed twelve to fourteen days to complete it. There was no particular hurry, as they'd both booked five weeks' leave from their jobs—a combination of holidays and long-service leave.

They'd been planning this trip for the past eighteen months, ever since their engagement. Chrys did a mental calculation and worked out that it was two years and three months since she'd met Sonny at Spanish classes. At the time, she'd been thinking of visiting South America and wanted to learn some basic conversational Spanish. Sonny had intended to travel to Spain to complete the walk they were doing on their trip. There had been an instant attraction between them, especially when they discovered they'd had similar childhoods—silly names imposed on them by their parents that had led to them being on the receiving end of constant jokes. They'd also grown up in 'alternative' towns not far from each other in Northern New South Wales. They both shared a common love for walking and spent much of their leisure time and holidays exploring hiking trails in remote parts of Australia. The Spanish trek would seem like a piece of cake in comparison.

After attending classes for a year, they both dropped out, taking up other individual pursuits, but in January, they'd resumed lessons, hoping to improve their Spanish in time for this trip.

Chrys was looking forward to the wedding, which was to be a low-key affair with friends and a few members of their families attending. Money was tight, due to the hefty mortgage they'd taken on last year, and they'd opted for a celebrant to marry them in a local park, followed by a reception in their own sprawling backyard. She hoped the weather would stay fine for it—they'd hired a large marquis, which Sonny and his mates were planning to erect two days before, but guests would have to tramp in and out of the house for the bathroom. She had planned to set up all the tables with their dressings, but Sonny quashed that notion.

"You can't be here when we erect and set up the marquis."

"Why not?"

"I want it all to be a surprise."

"But what about the tables and decorations?"

"I've got it all under control," he'd said, wiggling his hand at her. "Trust me on this. I want you to go and stay with Casey."

"That seems a bit silly, Sonny. We already live together, and it's only the night before the wedding we shouldn't see each other."

"I want it *all* to be a surprise, Chrys, so no arguments. Let me deal with all this."

"All right, all right," she'd conceded.

At least they would only have one set of parents to monitor on the day. She was secretly relieved that her parents weren't coming. Sonny's would be more than enough to cope with. She just hoped they wouldn't start rolling joints at the reception. Sonny had warned them not to bring any of their homegrown grass with them. Some of their straight friends would take offence, and neither Chrys nor Sonny wanted the smell of it permeating their house; they'd experienced enough of that growing up.

As she pulled into a vacant spot in the car park at work, a shiver ran up her spine. She sat for a moment in silent alarm, questioning the cause. Excitement, she decided, and turned off the engine.

4

"I'D LIKE TO report a missing person," Chrys told the police officer on duty.

"Right," he said. "Name?"

"Do you mean my name or the missing person's name?"

"I need both."

"My name is Chrys Waters."

She watched as the policeman began writing down her name, as usual spelling it incorrectly.

"Is that short for Christine?" he asked. "Only we need your full name if that's the case."

"My full name is Chrystal. Here's my driving licence, which will show you the correct spelling and my address."

"*Chrystal Waters,*" he said with sarcasm. "Now what kind of name is that to give someone? I bet you get some digs about it. What were your parents thinking?"

She sighed. Some things never changed. She'd been receiving jibes about her name since she'd started school as a five-year-old. Ignoring his comments, she passed him Sonny's driving licence, which she'd taken from the drawer of their hall stand before coming to the station.

"This is the person I am reporting missing," she said.

"Sonny Day!" the officer exclaimed, picking up the second licence. "You've got to be kidding me. Chrystal Waters and Sonny Day. Is this some kind of joke?"

"No. It's not. Our parents are hippies."

"I suppose it could be worse. They could have spelt Sonny with a 'u' instead of an 'o'."

She just nodded. Sonny said much the same when introducing himself to new acquaintances—before they could get the jibe in.

"So how long has Sonny been missing?"

"He didn't arrive at work yesterday morning. He didn't come home last night, and he didn't turn up for work again today. He's not answering his phone, and none of our friends have seen or heard a word from him. So two days really."

"If you last saw him yesterday morning, I make that a little over twenty-four hours, as it's only ten-thirty now. It's a bit premature to be reporting him missing. He might have just gone on a bender with some mates."

"Something's happened to him. I know it. You need to take this seriously. Sonny wouldn't take time off work like that. He's never *not* come home. We're due to marry in just over a week, and we're having five weeks off work then. There's no way he'd go on a *bender* as you've suggested."

The officer shrugged. Clearly, he didn't believe her.

"So was yesterday morning the last time you saw him?"

"Yes. I left him outside our door. He was about to cycle to the train station."

"And how did he seem?"

"Fine. He seemed fine. We were running a little late, as we'd been practising our Spanish."

"Spanish?"

"We're travelling to Spain on our honeymoon and have been learning Spanish. We practise speaking a little every morning and evening."

"And how was he the night before?"

"I...I didn't see him the night before. He had a night out with some of his friends."

"There you go then. He's probably off with some of them now. Grabbing the opportunity while he's still a *single* man."

"No!" Why wouldn't this fool take her seriously? "I'm telling you something has happened to him," she said, raising her voice. She was feeling distressed enough as it was. He was making things worse.

Chrys felt a tap on her shoulder and turned to see a blonde woman flashing identification at her. There was something familiar about her, and Chrys was momentarily distracted trying to remember where she'd seen her before. Apart from a couple of local policemen she'd met in her hometown, she'd never had any contact with or met anyone who worked for the police, so she couldn't think where she knew her from.

"Is there a problem here?" the woman asked.

"Yes, there is," Chrys said. "I'm trying to report my fiancé as a missing person and this..." *fool* she wanted to say but corrected herself in time. There was no point in antagonising the police. "This officer doesn't think it's a serious matter. But I know it is."

"I can see you're a little upset. Why don't I take..." The woman turned to the officer on the desk.

"Miss Waters," he said, passing the woman the driving licences and the paperwork he'd started. "Be my guest.

I'd be more than happy for you to see to *Chrystal Waters, Detective Inspector* Hargreaves."

"Thank you," Chrys said, bristling a little at the man's sarcastic dig, which seemed to be aimed at both women. Finally, someone more senior was going to take her seriously. A detective.

"Would you like to come with me?" The detective turned towards a door and punched in a code to open it.

Chrys followed her down the corridor to an interview room and sank gratefully into a chair. Her legs were shaky.

"You might have heard from our desk sergeant that my name is Detective Inspector Hargreaves. Would you like a cup of tea or coffee?"

"I'd love a cup of tea, please—milk and one sugar. I've been up since the early hours and already drunk several cups of coffee. I'm jittery, and my nerves are a little frayed."

"I won't be a moment." The detective left the room.

Chrys had been holding back tears out in the reception area but now let them flow. She was so worried. She'd woken at three a.m. to discover that Sonny still hadn't come back. He was supposed to be home at his normal time from work, cooking their evening meal. When he hadn't turned up by eight p.m., she began phoning him with no response. At nine-thirty, she'd heated up some leftover curry from the meal she'd cooked the previous night. At eleven-thirty, she'd collapsed into bed, tossing and turning with a mixture of anger and worry. Where was he? She must have dropped off at some point but then woke in the early hours and had been up and pacing ever since. Deciding to go into work late today, she'd phoned Sonny's work only to discover he hadn't been in the previous day and hadn't turned up again this morning. They'd also tried phoning him, getting no answer.

It was then she began phoning around his friends she had listed in her contacts. No one had seen him or heard from him. They offered to phone other friends she didn't have numbers for but had soon called back saying they'd had no success. Sonny hadn't been in touch with anyone. Chrys knew something was really wrong.

***

INDIA RETURNED TO the interview room with two cups of tea. Chrys Waters was crying but quickly wiped her face with a tissue and sat up.

"Sorry to take so long." India handed her one of the cups. "I thought it might be useful to phone around the local hospitals to see if your fiancé or any unidentified males had been admitted."

"I tried the hospitals this morning before coming here. Sonny would've had his wallet and phone on him anyway, so he would have been identified."

India nodded. She didn't add that she'd run their names through the system to see if either of them was known to the police. They weren't, and the woman sitting in front of her seemed quite genuine. Although she was distressed, she didn't appear to have any mental health problems—none which were apparent anyway— and she didn't look like she was on drugs. There were bags under her eyes, maybe from a lack of sleep, but she was dressed in a smart outfit, a red skirt, black blouse and cream jacket, indicating she worked in an office or as a professional somewhere. Her neat, brown, shoulder-length hair had golden streaks in it, as though it had caught the sun, and apart from her tiredness, the woman had a healthy glow about her.

"So, take me through everything again from the last time you saw Sonny."

***

CHRYS SPENT THE next fifteen minutes going through every single detail she could recall that might be significant. Their last morning together. Where Sonny had been the night before he disappeared. The meal he was due to cook. Their forthcoming wedding and trip to Spain. Their house purchase. The detective scribbled down some notes as Chrys talked but paused every so often to look at her.

"Where does Sonny work and what is his job?"

"He's a bespoke kitchen cabinet maker. He works for a company down in Penrith. As I said, he was out with Tony and Marcus—his friends from work—two nights ago. It was Marcus's birthday."

"I'll need the company's name—and address if you have it. And Tony's surname. You said Tony dropped Sonny home that night?"

"Yes, he did. The company is called Custom Kitchens. I'm not sure of the formal address, but I have their phone number." Chrys scrolled through her contacts and passed the phone to Detective Hargreaves.

"Tony's surname is Bellini. I don't know Marcus's surname."

"And you? What is your job?" the detective asked her while still writing.

"I'm a librarian. Well, actually, I'm a primary school teacher as well, but I work with all the local primary schools in the library at Richmond."

More notes were written. Chrys was feeling exhausted and wished she could just lie down and go to sleep, but she was too worried to sleep.

"Did you and Sonny always leave the house at the same time each morning?"

"No. I usually leave about an hour after him—unless it's one of my school-visit days. Yesterday morning, I had a class coming in, so I left early to finish all my preparations."

"Did you actually see Sonny cycle off?"

"No. He was just about to leave when I drove off. I offered him a lift, but my car is too small for his bike. We have to mess about with the back seats so much to squeeze the bike in, and it doesn't save much time. Sonny needs the bike when he arrives at Penrith because the workshop is quite a way from the station."

"Have you checked his belongings to see if anything is missing? Clothes, passport?"

"I did that this morning when I discovered he hadn't been in to work again. Nothing is missing as far as I can see. All his clothes are still there, and his passport is in a desk drawer with mine—as was his driving licence. He hasn't run off, Detective Hargreaves."

"We need to check all possibilities in these situations. You've had no recent disagreements, nothing that you'd fallen out over?"

"No, nothing. Sonny and I never fight. We might have the odd difference of opinion, but we always work things out amicably. For example, he wanted to paint our bedroom walls a dark green. I didn't like the idea, so we compromised by having one dark green feature wall and the remainder an off-white. He might want to go hiking in the mountains somewhere and I'd rather hike on more level ground. Little things like that. We've *never* had any blazing arguments."

The detective looked at her with a blank expression. Chrys couldn't tell if she believed her.

"No, really, we're both quite laid-back people. Don't get me wrong, we're passionately in love, but we have a very easy and comfortable relationship."

The detective nodded. "I know what you mean."

"Sonny and I are due to be married tomorrow week—on the twelfth of April. I *know* something terrible has happened to him, Detective Hargreaves. He wouldn't take off like that. Anyway, where would he go? None of his friends have heard from him, and— Oh, I forgot to tell you. I checked with his parents this morning. They haven't heard from him either. What can you do to help me?"

"Well, we've ruled out him being admitted to hospital. We can check CCTV at the station to see if he caught his regular train or a later one. Can you describe what he was wearing yesterday morning? Also, I need a more accurate description of him—height and build. His driving licence only gives me a head-and-shoulders shot. You wouldn't have a full shot of him on your phone, would you? I'm also going to need his mobile number and a contact number for his parents."

"Yes, I have a photograph of him taken on our hike a couple of weekends ago. I'll open it up for you in a minute. Sonny is about one metre eighty-eight tall. Or six feet two if you prefer. He's not skinny, but he's slim and fit. Yesterday, he was wearing a navy-blue jacket over navy cycling pants and navy-and-white trainers. He keeps work clothes at the workshop that he changes into when he gets there—boots, jumper, jeans and an overall.

He brings his jeans home every Friday for washing. Hang on a minute and I'll find that photograph of him."

"Can you send it to my mobile? My name, number and contact details are listed here." Detective Hargreaves handed Chrys a card.

After sending the policewoman the picture of Sonny, Chrys asked, "So apart from checking at the station, what else can you do?"

"We need to search around the house and grounds, then along his cycle route to the station to make sure he hasn't met with an accident and is lying injured in a ditch somewhere. I'll see if I can pull in a few uniformed officers to help do that now."

"Thank you so much for taking Sonny's disappearance seriously. I can tell you now, Sonny's bike is not at home. Not where he normally leaves it anyway. I had a quick look along the road as I drove into town, but it would be best to walk every metre of it to be thorough. I'd like to help you with that."

"Why don't you go home and wait for my officers and me to join you? We can cover both sides of the road. I know where you live is semi-rural. He wouldn't have walked off into the bush, would he?"

"I doubt it very much. If he had, then his bike would be there, and it's not."

"What make and model is his bike, do you know?"

"It's black and blue with silver swirls. That's all I can tell you. I haven't a clue what the model or make it is. I've never been a cyclist. Where I grew up in Nimbin, it was too hilly for cycling."

"Nimbin?"

"Yes. You might have heard me tell your sergeant my parents are hippies, which is why I have this name. It's the same for Sonny, but he's from Mullumbimby."

"Right. Well, I think we'd better make a start. I'll go and see how many uniforms I can muster. You head on home."

***

INDIA WAITED UNTIL she saw Chrys Waters leaving the station before turning to speak to the desk sergeant. Sonny Day did not sound like the type of person who would take off out of the blue. She hadn't even found a parking ticket in his name. Was he too good to be true?

22

5

THE DESK SERGEANT had assigned two uniformed constables to India, who'd returned to the station while she'd been talking to him. A further pair were to be diverted from a patrol car. She also roped in Detective Senior Constable Aaron Jacko, who worked with her on more serious investigations.

Jacko had joined her at Windsor a couple of years back, and they had an instant rapport that made working together easy. Windsor had been his first posting after being promoted. He'd been based in Tamworth before that but had told her that he'd spent his childhood in the Windsor area. He had a few aunties, uncles and cousins who lived nearby. When she'd told him colleagues in her small team addressed each other by their first names away from the public, Jacko had objected. "No. That won't work for me. I don't use my first name. I prefer to be called Jacko *all* the time."

Although she'd been curious about why he didn't use his first name, she hadn't asked him about it. He seemed friendly enough, but there was something guarded about him. He was a man who seemed to value his privacy. He very seldom called her India either, preferring to use 'boss' in a friendly manner. Being a nosy person, though, she'd asked him a few questions about his background. Jacko had been willing to reveal that several generations back, his great-grandmother had given birth to a daughter, who was fathered by a white man. The couple had never married. That daughter, Jacko's grandmother, had married an indigenous man called Bernie Jacko.

Anyone looking at Jacko could tell he was of indigenous origins, but he was light-skinned compared to many who lived in the region. India thought Jacko was a good-looking man; he was solidly built, of medium height—about 175 cm tall. He kept his dark-brown hair cut short, claiming he didn't like the curls it produced when he let it grow. He was only in his late thirties, but odd grey strands had started to appear above his temples. Women seemed to like him, but for the most part, he didn't seem interested. She suspected somewhere along the line a woman had broken his heart.

On the drive out to Chrys Waters' property, she filled Jacko in on the details.

"I'd like you to have a look through Sonny Day's personal belongings. As long as Ms. Waters agrees, of course. Check out his passport as well. See if you can find details of any bank accounts he has. We'll need those. Also, something with his DNA on it. A used toothbrush or something like that. Ask Ms. Waters for Mr. Day's mobile number and a contact number for his parents. I asked her for them earlier, but I didn't realise until she'd gone that she hadn't given them to me. While you're in the house, try ringing his phone to make sure it's not there."

"So you think something has happened to him?" Jacko asked.

"Something has definitely happened to him. But exactly what is the question."

"Do you believe her version of events?"

"She seems credible, but we need to check everything. Remember that case last year where the husband reported the wife missing?"

"Yeah. He'd stuffed her in a large drum dumped out in one of his remote outbuildings. You think she's done something like that to him?"

"Not really, but we need to be thorough."

"You don't think he's done a runner? Got cold feet about the wedding at the last moment?"

"He may have, but from the description his fiancée gave of him, it doesn't sound like the kind of thing he'd do. We'll go and talk to his employers and work buddies later. They might give us a different story."

***

CHRYS WAS HAPPY for Detective Jacko to look through Sonny's clothing and personal papers. Anything that might help shed light on what had happened.

"Are you sure nothing's missing?" Jacko asked.

"I haven't noticed anything. As you can see, his drawers and his side of the wardrobe are pretty full."

"No bags missing? Like a small holdall or anything?"

"No." She shook her head. "Only the small rucksack he takes to work with him every day with his packed lunch and water."

"Is his toothbrush here? I'd like to take it away with me if it is."

"It's in the bathroom. I'll get it for you. Do you want it so you can pick up some DNA from it or something?"

"Yes. Now, can you show me where you keep his passport?"

She led the detective into the smallest bedroom where there was an old writing desk.

"We keep them in here," she said opening one of the drawers. "Both of our passports are fairly new. Neither of us have ever been overseas before. We only applied for them late last year."

She handed Sonny's passport to the detective, who scrutinised it and took a shot of it with his phone.

"Okay, thanks." He passed it back to her. "What about bank statements? Where would I find those?"

Pulling some files down from a shelf, she said, "We each have our own accounts, and then we have a joint account as well. You'll find everything you need in these files."

"Toothbrush?" he reminded her.

She left him and returned a minute later with an electric toothbrush. He bagged it before turning his attention back to the bank statements.

"I need his mobile number. Can you give me that?"

Taking her mobile out of a pocket, she opened it to Sonny's contact number, holding out for him to see. DC Jacko tapped the number into his phone.

"I'd also like his parents' phone number."

She scrolled through her contacts to find the right number; he tapped that into his phone too and made a note of Sonny's mobile provider.

"If that's everything you need, I'm going outside to see if they've found anything," she said. "Can you put everything back on the shelves when you've finished."

***

"There's no obvious sign that any of Day's personal belongings are missing," Jacko told India when he met up with her outside. "The passport's there, and I've looked through their bank records. Nothing out of the ordinary showing there either. I rang his mobile when Miss Waters left the house, but it just rang out. I'd say it's run out of juice and is not set for messages. I rang it a few times just in case and walked around, listening carefully, but couldn't hear any ringing or buzzing anywhere. Unless we search the whole house, there's no way to tell if it's there."

"Okay. Make contact with Dale back at the station. Get her to put in a request for his phone records and where the phone was located the last time it was switched on. We haven't found anything on the property grounds either. I've sent a couple of the uniforms over the fence to check out the paddocks at the back. There're two more uniforms out the front. I'm going to start the road search. Join us as soon as you can."

The road dropped off into shallow ditches at various points. Jacko found what looked like drops of blood on a small rock underneath a bush in one of the ditches. The bush also showed evidence of broken branches. He called out to India, who was searching on the opposite stretch with one of the uniforms and the Waters woman.

"That looks like blood to me," he said quietly when the women joined him. "It rained last night, so if there was any on the road, it could have been washed away. These bushes might have prevented the rain washing away any blood from this rock."

"Bag it up and take it in. We'll send it off to the techies for analysis."

The fiancée pushed past them to see what they were talking about.

"You think that might be Sonny's blood?" The woman looked like she was about to burst into tears, so Jacko jumped in to reassure her.

27

"It's a remote possibility," he said. "But it's more likely to be from some animal. We'll check to make sure, though."

***

APART FROM THE 'bloody' rock, the roadside and the home property searches drew a blank. Jacko sent the rock off to the forensic technicians for analysis. India asked Dale, the key support worker in their department, to go down to the railway station and trawl through their CCTV footage. India had uploaded the photo Chrys Waters had sent her of Sonny onto their computer system and printed out a copy. Dale had ordered Sonny's phone records, and they were waiting for them to come through.

A call to Sonny's parents confirmed they hadn't heard from him since the previous week. Unlike Chrys, they didn't seem concerned.

Late in the afternoon, Jacko and India travelled down to Penrith to interview Sonny's work colleagues. India had phoned earlier and spoken to the company owner to make sure all staff remained at the workshop for them to talk to.

***

"CAN YOU TELL me how Sonny was when you were out with him two nights ago? Did he have a lot to drink?" India asked the two men sitting before them. The owner had given them space in the company's offices to talk to Sonny's closest friends, Tony and Marcus, as the machinery in the workshop was so loud.

"He'd had a few beers, which is why I drove him home in my ute," Tony said.

"You hadn't been drinking yourself?"

"I'd had a couple of beers earlier in the night, but after our meal I switched to coke, as I knew I'd be driving. Sonny wasn't drunk or anything, but he would have been over the limit for cycling. His helmet fell off the bike in the back of the ute, but neither of us noticed it. I only saw it the next morning after I arrived at work. I phoned him to say I had it, but he didn't answer. It just rang out. I don't think Sonny has ever set up his phone for messages."

"Right. Did he have another helmet, do you know?"

"I don't think so. His newer one was damaged a few weeks before. He kept saying he needed to buy another one."

"Did he talk about his impending marriage and trip abroad to either of you that evening?"

"Yeah. He was looking forward to it," Marcus said. "Neither of them has ever been out of the country before, so it was going to be a huge adventure for them."

"He didn't appear to be having second thoughts?" Jacko interjected.

"Nah. He and Chrys are a tight couple."

"You didn't invite Chrys to your little birthday celebrations?"

"Nah, it was just the three of us. Tony's wife couldn't make it, and I don't have a partner at the moment."

"Were both of you invited to the wedding?"

"Yeah. Everyone here was planning on going. Sonny's been working here for just over ten years. We're not a big outfit. There's only eleven of us, not counting the boss and his wife."

"So no one here has heard anything from Sonny since your night out together?"

"No," Tony said. "Do you think he's had some kind of accident? It could only be something like that to keep him away from Chrys."

"We're looking into all possibilities. Well, thank you for your time," she said, standing.

Their inquiries with the owners, Mr. and Mrs. Richards, confirmed everything Chrys Waters had told them. Sonny Day had booked five weeks off work commencing two days before his planned wedding. Mr. Richards opened Sonny's locker, where they found the work clothes Chrys had described. Sonny had a large photograph of himself and Chrys pinned to the back of the locker door. They certainly looked like a happy couple, and Mr. and Mrs. Richards reiterated that Day had been really looking forward to the wedding.

***

"The CCTV at the railway station shows no sign of Sonny Day making it to the station on Thursday," Dale confirmed with India after returning to the police station. "And his mobile was last located close to his home address."

"So where do we look next?" Jacko asked.

"We'll make door-to-door inquiries along his cycle route. If that brings in no results, I'll ask the chief if I can do an appeal through the press."

6

WHILE INDIA WAS all business-like at work, at home she was Mrs. India Ellis, married to Detective Superintendent Rob Ellis, who was now based down in Penrith. A visit to the ladies' at the station this afternoon had confirmed her worst fears. She wasn't pregnant; again. She'd shed a few silent tears before pulling herself together and leaving. Now she had to face Rob tonight and break the bad news.

She and Rob had been married for more than twelve years. At first, they hadn't wanted children, but for the past nine years, they had been 'trying'. She'd had three miscarriages that they were aware of—two of them in the fourth month of the pregnancy. India believed there'd been more pregnancies where, before she could complete a pregnancy test, she'd started bleeding heavily.

She hadn't sought any further promotions since her advancement to detective inspector, not wanting any greater responsibilities. There was no DCI located at the Windsor station now—a role Rob had previously filled—making her the senior detective on site. Her superintendent, the person she answered to directly, was based in Richmond, although he retained an office on the floor above their small squad room and regularly popped in to see them, often unannounced.

She'd made contact with Superintendent Havering in Richmond that afternoon, apprising him of the Sonny

Day situation. He'd agreed that the circumstances warranted a full investigation and gave her the go-ahead to contact the press if further investigations shed no light on Day's disappearance.

India was stirring the pasta sauce when she heard Rob's key in the front door.

"Good evening, Mrs. Ellis," he said, planting a kiss on her forehead and embracing her when she turned around to greet him. It always gave her a bit of a thrill when he called her that. "Anything new to report?"

"You mean regarding us or what I'm working on at the moment?

"Both."

"My period started this afternoon, so I'm not pregnant."

"I'm sorry, darling. Are you feeling okay about it?"

"I was upset at first, but I'm fine now."

"You seemed so optimistic this morning. It's probably better to stop thinking about it altogether. You tense up every month and then become excited if your periods are a day or two late. You're placing too much pressure on yourself. The last time you fell pregnant, you didn't even realise until you were well into it."

"I know." She didn't want to be reminded about last year's pregnancy. She'd not long become involved in a new investigation when she realised she was pregnant and soon after miscarried. It had given her hope, though, that she could still fall pregnant after a lengthy gap from the previous one.

"It's just time is rolling on now. In another few years, it will be too late."

"If it's meant to be, it will happen for us. I've told you endlessly that it makes no difference to me whether we have children or not."

"You say that, but we both know it's not true. You want children as much as me."

"I would like to have a child, India, but having children is not the most important focus in my life. You are. And if it doesn't happen, well, that's okay."

Rob held her closely, and she relaxed. He was right. She was too stressed about it all. Everything she'd read about couples who'd had difficulty conceiving was that stress or pressure appeared to prevent it happening. Doctors had assured her there was no medical reason why she couldn't carry a baby to full term.

"Dinner smells good," Rob said, releasing her. "How long before it's ready? Do I have time for a quick shower?"

"If you're really quick. I'm just about to put the pasta on."

"Okay, I'll be back in a jiff. Then you can tell me about your workday while we're eating."

***

"ARE YOU WORKING on anything new?" Rob asked her as he paused to take a sip of wine.

"Yes, I am as it happens."

She filled him in on the Sonny Day case, explaining everything that had happened so far.

"So, this Sonny Day appears to have vanished into thin air?"

"Yes, except we know there's got to be a plausible explanation."

"Do you think someone might have accidentally knocked him down and killed him, then taken the body away to cover it up?"

"It's one explanation."

"Or—he could have gone off with someone willingly."

"He might have, but from everything I've heard today, that seems unlikely. But you never know. Perhaps the vision Sonny Day portrayed to the rest of the world about his relationship was an illusion."

7

DOCTOR GREER HAMILTON was enjoying a quiet break in her office. A few minutes before, Marion had left her office visibly distressed. Greer had told Marion that she and Lachie had decided on a permanent return to Scotland and she'd handed in her notice. Normally, the hospital would expect a few months' notice, but given Lachie's circumstances, she'd told them she needed to leave immediately after the Easter break. She'd booked a flight for them in late April, travelling first class. Only the best for her and Lachie. Her last day of duty would be on Friday 25th. She had things to organise. Most of the packing was already done; there were just tiresome things like informing the power company and giving the place a good clean. She'd already given notice to the agents, their place being a rental.

When they'd moved into the house three years ago, Lachie hadn't wanted to purchase a property. They still owned a house back in Scotland, where they'd lived briefly before Lachie accepted a position in Australia instead. The economic climate in the UK had not been favourable to selling; they would have lost money after making major improvements, so Lachie insisted they rent out their house until the market picked up. They'd still not done anything about the house when Lachie had had his accident. Greer thought that was a good thing, as they'd have a home to return to. She'd informed the agent who managed the property for them of their return, and they had given notice to the tenants. The problem was they wouldn't be able to return to the house until mid-June, as the tenants required two months' notice. She was going to have a well-deserved break until then. She'd booked a short-term let until the house was free: now that the compensation from Lachie's accident had been paid out, money was not an issue.

A knock at the door interrupted her thoughts.

"Sorry to disturb your break, Doctor Hamilton, but do you think you could come and deal with a patient? I can't understand the language he's using."

"Do you know where he's from?"

"He's Scottish—I think. It's difficult to tell. His accent is unlike any I've heard before."

"Ah. I see why you've asked me to deal with him then. What are his injuries?"

"He has a minor head wound and abrasions on both hands. From what I can gather, he had a fall. I have to warn you—he's been drinking."

"Okay," Greer said, standing. "You'd better take me to him."

She could smell the alcohol as she approached the cubicle. *Another drunken, loutish Scot,* she thought. Penrith seemed to have their share of them. She'd had to administer minor surgery to numerous Scotsmen over the past three years. Australian men weren't much better with their attachment to beer, but this one was a whisky drinker if her nose was serving her correctly.

"Good evening, young man," she said as she entered the cubicle to see a dark-haired, bearded man sitting on the bed. "Can you tell me what happened to you?"

"I'd been havin' a wee dram wi' me mates, you ken," he started, "an' as we was leavin' the pub, mi pal pushed me ower. Joost in fun, like. I lost mi balance and fell. I was oot for a bit, I tink. Next I ken, I was 'ere."

"That looks like a nasty bump you have there. I don't think you need stitches, but we'll have to admit you overnight to observe you. You might have sustained concussion. How long were you unconscious for?"

"I dinna ken. I wasna drunk, joost caught by surprise."

"Let me see your hands."

The man held out his hands, and she could see they didn't require stitches either.

"I'm going to clean you up a bit, then we'll see if we can find you a bed for the night."

As she was cleaning his wounds, she asked, "Where are you from?"

"Scotland," he said, looking at her with a shifty expression.

"I gathered that, but I thought I detected something else in your accent."

The man looked at her for a moment before saying, "Weel, I moved oot here from Glasgow. Where are *you* frae?"

Greer could hear a hint of a Glaswegian accent, but she also knew he wasn't being completely honest.

"Elgin originally," she told him, "but I moved to Aberdeen for my training, then Edinburgh. My husband and I moved out here three years ago, but he had a serious accident last year and we're going to return home soon."

"I wish I coul'. I canna git on wi' the lassies 'ere, and I miss 'ome. I ha' bin 'ere three year too."

"Why don't you go back then?"

"I canna afford it."

"Hmm."

She carried on cleaning his wounds in silence, glancing occasionally at the young man. When she finished, she asked him if he could stand. He launched himself off the bed a little too quickly.

"Careful," Greer said, reaching out to steady the man. He was surprisingly tall. After a moment's hesitation, she said, "You know, if you really want to return home, I know someone who might be able to help you. I'll come and find you later and we can talk more."

8

"WE RECEIVED QUITE a few responses to our media appeals and door-to-door inquiries but nothing that could take us any further forward with the investigation. I'm sorry," India told Chrys.

"Today is supposed to be my wedding day!" Chrys said, tears sliding down her face. Her friend Casey was comforting her on the couch.

"I know, and I'm really sorry. Did you manage to cancel everything?"

"Yes. I helped Chrys with all that," Casey said. "Notifying all the guests. Cancelling the marquee."

Chrys wiped her eyes and added, "The airlines only gave me a partial refund, but the hotels in Spain fully refunded me. We'd paid a bit extra to cover last-minute cancellations."

"Apart from the fiasco with Alex, what did you learn from *your* appeal?" Casey asked.

India was sure that Chrys was fully aware of the disaster that ensued when Sonny's friend Alex had stepped in for her at the last minute at the press conference making an appeal to the public. She didn't think this was the appropriate time to mention it. Chrys probably blamed herself.

"It seems a number of neighbours down the road regularly saw Sonny cycling to the station but not on that particular morning. Commuters who caught the same train as him each day recognised him, but again, no one recalled seeing him on the day he disappeared. We'd already ascertained from the CCTV that he didn't make it to the train station. And as I told you the other day, his mobile signal was last picked up in this location."

"But you've searched the whole house and it's not here!" Chrys said in frustration.

"I know. It suggests his phone was switched off immediately after leaving here. We've found no trace of his bike either."

"I don't understand," Chrys wailed. "Someone must have seen him! Someone must have picked him up. Do you think he was knocked down by a driver who's taken him off somewhere? Injured or…"

"It's one possibility. Chrys, there's no point in torturing yourself with different scenarios. We don't know what happened to Sonny."

"Do you think we'll ever know? Isn't there anything else you can do?"

"Not unless some new leads come to light. Some people disappear and are never found. Others are found again with a range of circumstances to explain their disappearance. Occasionally, we discover a tragedy has occurred but we're still unable to find them."

"Like that little boy who was kidnapped last year?" Casey asked.

India sighed. She wished Casey had not mentioned the boy. *Joshua.* It was a case which still haunted her dreams at night.

'Yes, like him," she said.

"Sonny would have to be badly injured or dead. That's the only thing that would prevent him from being in contact and missing our wedding."

"Someone could be holding him against his will," Casey speculated. "He wouldn't be able to contact you then."

"Do you think that's a possibility? That someone is holding him against his will?" Chrys asked with a hopeful expression. This scenario could result in Sonny returning to her alive. India could understand why Chrys might prefer this option.

"We've taken that into consideration, but our inquiries have brought no results so far."

"What about his phone records?" Casey asked. "Had he received any strange calls?"

"They've already told me that," Chrys said. "No. His last call was to me on the Wednesday just before he left work. But what about the blood you found on that rock?" she asked India. "You haven't told me what your results showed on that. I assume it wasn't Sonny's."

"No. That turned out to be animal blood. I'm sorry, Chrys. If we hear anything else, I'll be in touch. I need to be going now. Don't get up, I'll see myself out. Thanks for the coffee."

***

INDIA DROVE AWAY from the house with a heavy heart. She hadn't wanted to visit Chrys today of all days, but her friend Casey had pleaded with her to come this morning to give Chrys an update on the investigation. She hoped it wasn't going to be another one of those cases they were unable to resolve.

***

THE TWO TEENAGE hikers were skirting the side of the stream when one of them stopped.

"Look, Jason, that looks like a bike. What on earth is it doing up there? You can't cycle anywhere around this place."

"Someone must have thrown it over from the top," Jason said. "Let's have a look."

They scrambled up the slope to where the bike's fall had been halted by a large gum tree.

"It's a bit damaged but looks repairable," Craig said. "What do you reckon? Should we take it with us?"

"How do you propose we do that, Craig? The terrain we've been hiking in would make it impossible."

"But it's a bloody good bike. Better than my one. It's a shame to leave it here. Someone must've dumped it."

"Maybe, but I'm not lugging it back. You can if you want."

"Nah. Like you said, it'd be too much of a hassle."

"Come on, we need to get going if we're gunna make it back before it gets dark."

9

"WE'RE READY TO take you and your husband in now, if would you like to come with me," the air stewardess told Greer.

She pushed a groggy Lachie along the walkway into the aircraft. Another air stewardess greeted them, showing Greer to their comfortable first-class accommodation. She'd booked one of those new suites some airlines had installed where they, in essence, had their own room and wouldn't be too disturbed.

"My husband is sedated," she told the stewardess. "I plan to keep him that way throughout the flight. Otherwise, things could be very difficult. He can't talk properly and will make a lot of strange noises. Please don't be alarmed by them. He has a catheter and colostomy bag fitted. You do know about his injuries, don't you?"

"Yes, we were made aware of everything. Don't worry. We'll make sure you're comfortable and not disturbed too often. Would you like me to help you move your husband onto the bed?"

"Yes, thank you. That would be most helpful. I might be tall but I find it difficult to manage him on my own."

***

Overall, the journey back to Scotland went without any major hitches, but the delays in flight connections from Manchester to Edinburgh had been an absolute pain. Greer couldn't understand why the airline couldn't run a flight directly into Scotland. When she'd asked one of the air stewardesses, she'd been told the company were planning to do exactly that. In a few months' time, she would be able to catch a flight from Abu Dhabi into Edinburgh. Today, though, they'd had to change at Manchester for the connecting flight. Greer congratulated herself on her decision to pay the extortionate first-class rates—it had certainly made life a lot easier on the first leg of the journey. They hadn't had the luxury of their own room on the flight into Manchester, but everything had gone well.

At Edinburgh International Airport, Greer collected their rental, a special vehicle that could accommodate a wheelchair passenger in the rear just like the one she'd had to purchase in Australia after Lachie had his accident. She had a long-term hire on the car until they were back in their own home. She then intended to purchase her own vehicle.

"Well, Lachie, we're home in *sunny* Scotland. Mind you, it's not so sunny today but I'm hoping the weather will pick up while we're at our cottage. Then we can send some nice postcards and pictures back to all our friends in Australia, can't we?" Greer laughed.

The only reply she received from Lachie was a few grunts.

10

Sue Liston was busy washing up the breakfast dishes when she was startled by cursing and screeching from her son, who was outside under the covered back patio.

"Muuum," he called, "Betsy's bloody puppy has chewed through one of my tyres! Can you drive me to school? I'm gunna be late."

Sue sighed. She also had to get to work, and she wasn't ready.

"I'll have missed the school bus now, and I've got a mock exam this morning."

"Okay, Craig, but you'll have to wait. I've got a couple of things to do. Give me two minutes."

Sue pulled the plug out and stacked the remaining dishes beside the sink. She'd tackle them tonight. After removing her rubber gloves, she hurried off to the bathroom. It would be a relief when this year was finally over. With Craig in his final year of his Higher School Certificate, her emergency school-run duties would finally be over. Since she'd returned to work six years ago, there'd been constant issues of dropping Craig or his older brother Brad at school because they'd missed the bus, or having to collect them early after a phone call from the school to say they'd been injured at sports or were ill. Their eldest, Brad, was now living in Parramatta with friends and was a qualified electrician. She couldn't wait for Craig to decide on his future. He was talking about going to university, depending on his HSC results, and had already applied to a few universities up in Queensland. If he moved to another state, he wouldn't be bringing his dirty washing home of a weekend like Brad had when he'd first left home. Much as she loved her boys, she and Pete had had little peace in their lives since the rascals were born. She was looking forward to the day when the house wasn't subjected to blaring music (that you couldn't even dance to) and troupes of Craig's friends wandering in and out leaving their dirty plates strewn around the kitchen. Craig's bedroom was an obstacle course of clothes and other discarded paraphernalia. She'd refused to continue cleaning it for him since he'd turned thirteen. She'd trained the boys from a young age to take responsibility for their own messes, but with a poor role model in their father, it was like banging her head against a brick wall.

It was an absolute pain dropping Craig off in the morning. His school, Hawkesbury High, was in the wrong direction for her work, meaning she had to double back, sometimes arriving late.

"I'm ready," she called out to Craig. "Go and get in the car."

Craig had his music blaring by the time she joined him; some hideous sound. She turned it off, switched on the radio and fiddled with the dial looking for the news.

"Aw, Mum, why do you always have to listen to the news? It's boring."

"I like to hear what's going on."

They rode in silence for a minute with Sue listening to the newsreader. She sometimes struggled to separate the different news items. It was as though the newsreader had been told she was on a strict time clock and wasn't allowed to pause for a breath in between. The result was that the items ran into one long report and sometimes included advertisements. One moment she'd be listening to a serious report about someone being arrested for a murder, and the next — without a pause — she'd hear "… and you can get all your hardware supplies at…"

It was very confusing sometimes. Television news was far better, but she often missed it with so much to do. They had a DVD player, but Pete would not entertain having a digital recorder so that she could record programmes and watch them later, claiming she'd just record all those 'stupid property shows' and the kids 'some violent zombie film'. Once their antique video recorder had broken and purchasing a replacement was no longer an option, he'd thrown all their videos out, saying, "No more recorders."

It was no wonder Craig spent much of his time at his friend Jason's house. It was filled with all the latest technology, and Jason's parents subscribed to one of those pay-to-view systems that Pete also refused to consider. The only thing Craig could offer his friends was listening to CDs in his bedroom. He owned a compact stereo, which produced an alarmingly loud, good quality sound. It had cost a fortune, so it ought to, but Sue often regretted giving him the extra money he'd needed to purchase it.

She turned the sound down after the broadcast had finished. "What's your exam this morning?"

"Maths."

"Well, you should be fine with that. You're not nervous, are you?"

"Not really. I just don't want to be late. I wish I'd carried back that bike I found the other week. Then I would have had a spare."

"Hmm. What bike are you talking about?"

"When Jason and I were hiking a couple of weekends ago, we found a bike that had been thrown down into the gulley. Someone had obviously dumped it. It didn't look too bad. I could have fixed it up easily—it only had one damaged wheel. But Jason didn't want to help me carry it out, and it would have been difficult to do it on my own."

"You don't need another bike. I'll ring your father and see if he can pick up a tyre for you today, then you can fix it tonight. You'll have to put up a hook on the shed wall to stop the puppy getting at it."

"Yeah, I suppose, but I would have liked that bike."

Sue had a niggling thought in the back of her mind. Hadn't she heard something about a missing bike? What was that in connection with?

***

"THEY NEVER FOUND any trace of that man, did they?" one of Sue's colleagues mentioned at lunchtime. "You know, the one that cycled off to the station and was never seen again?"

"I don't think so," she said before making the connection with her conversation with Craig this morning. That was it! The Windsor police had launched an appeal for any witnesses who might have seen him on his bike. Could the bike Craig and Jason found be anything to do with the missing man?

"Trev thinks he got cold feet and ran off."

"Hmm."

She excused herself and went out to the recycling bin in the yard. There hadn't been a collection since she'd dumped a pile of newspapers in there the other day, and she was sure the paper with an article about the missing man was still in there. Rummaging around in the bin, she finally found the one she was looking for. She scanned the article and yes, there had been an appeal for anyone to come forward who might have found the man's missing bike. Craig had not described the bike in any detail, but she thought it was worth making a call. If it had been Pete who'd disappeared, she'd have wanted people to come forward with any little crumb that might lead to discovering what had happened to him. She recalled thinking the poor man's fiancée must be out of her mind with worry.

She pulled out her phone and rang the number listed in the article.

"Hello," she said when the phone answered, "I'd like to speak to Detective Inspector Hargreaves. It's about that missing man, Sonny Day. My son found a bike that might be his."

***

"You DIDN'T HAVE to pick me up, Mum. I'm not a little kid anymore," Craig said when he spotted her waiting outside the school gates that afternoon. "I planned to catch the bus. Shouldn't you be at work anyway?"

"I arranged to leave work early. The police are coming around to the house to speak to you. They wanted to collect you from school earlier, but I said you had exams on. I didn't think you'd be too happy about the police coming into school, and I thought it would be better if I came."

"What do you mean, police are coming to speak to me? I haven't done anything!" Craig stepped back with a look of horror on his face.

"Go and get into the car, Craig. I'll tell you all about it on the way home."

"No, tell me now."

"Trust me, it's fine. Come on, or they'll arrive at the house ahead of us."

Craig reluctantly followed her to the car and climbed in. She could see he was frowning.

"Stop worrying. It's nothing to do with you and your friends smoking marijuana."

"Whaaat?"

"Oh, you think I didn't know about that?"

"You've never said!"

"I have. A few times you've come in and I've said, 'You've been smoking—you reek of it. Go and change your clothes and clean your teeth.' What did you think I meant?"

"I thought you meant I smelled of normal cigarettes."

"I've never smelled normal cigarettes on you—only grass. It clings to your clothes and your breath."

"Oh. You're not mad at me about it?"

"I'm not happy about you smoking, and you need to be sensible about it. No smoking before any of your exams this year. You'll fail if you do. I watched it happening to someone I knew at school. People believe their mind expands when they smoke grass, giving them the answers to everything in the world, but in reality, they spend so much time contemplating endless trivia that they can't focus on what's in front of them. An ex-boyfriend of mine smoked a joint just before his science exam and barely answered any questions. Every time I looked over at him, the silly idiot seemed to be lost in daydreams. He failed, when he could have passed with flying colours, and had to do a re-sit."

"Did you ever smoke any yourself?"

"A few times. It made me cough too much, though, and I didn't like the taste. Most of my friends tried it at least once. Just don't let it become a habit."

"Does Dad know I smoke it?"

"Of course he does. I wouldn't keep something like that from him."

"He's never said anything either, but he did give me a lecture about the evils of drugs a few months back. Was that because he knew then?"

"Yep, and he's been keeping a close eye on you. You'll be eighteen in a few months, Craig. You're old enough *now* to make sensible choices, but once you're eighteen, you're considered an adult. If you were caught in possession of any drugs—and grass is considered a drug—you could be sent to an adult prison, and it would ruin your life."

"I know. I don't really like it all that much anyway. I doubt I'll be smoking it anymore. It's just that everyone expects you to have a drag or two at parties. I'd rather have a beer."

"Well, that's good to hear—as long as you don't drink too much of that either. Everything in moderation, Craig. You know once you get your provisional licence it's zero tolerance."

"I know. Hey—they're not going to search my room, are they?"

"I wouldn't have thought so. You haven't got anything in there, have you?"

"No, but if they brought sniffer dogs, the dogs might detect traces of grass from joints Jason and I have been given, which I've had in my pockets, or smell it on my dirty clothes like you claim you can."

She laughed. "That'll teach you to leave your dirty clothes lying around."

"So why are the police coming to see me? You still haven't told me."

"It's about that bike you found when you were hiking."

"What? Why would they want to talk to me about that?"

"If you ever read the papers or watched the news, you would know about the man who disappeared some weeks back over in Windsor. He was cycling to the station when he vanished. The police have been looking for him—and his bike. After you told me about it this morning, I decided to call them. You never know, it could be his bike."

"Oh, yeah, I did see something about that bloke on my phone. People don't buy papers anymore, Mum. They use their phones."

"Not everyone, Craig."

"They still haven't found him?"

"No, and the bike you found *might* be his. I want you to tell them everything you can remember."

11

"THE POLICE ARE here," Sue called out to Craig. Since arriving home, he'd been scurrying around his room scooping up all his dirty clothes and putting them into the washing machine. She heard him start the machine a few minutes later; he was still in the laundry when the police car drew up. At least this police visit had motivated him to clear up his room a bit. Now he could see the carpet, perhaps she could persuade him to give it a vacuum.

"Good afternoon, I'm Detective Inspector Hargreaves and this is my colleague Detective Senior Constable Jacko," the woman standing at the door told her while they produced their identification.

"Yes, hello, come in. I've just called Craig. Would you like a tea or coffee?"

"No, we're fine thanks," the female detective said.

Sue showed them into the lounge, where a red-faced Craig was already sitting on one of the chairs.

"This is my son Craig," she said, introducing him to the detectives.

***

THE WOMAN WHO'D greeted India and Jacko at the door seemed too young to be a mother of an older teenage boy. Sue Liston, with her light-blue eyes, red hair, freckles and fair complexion, only looked about thirty.

She must have had her son when she was very young, India thought. She introduced them to a young man, who clearly hadn't taken after his mother, as he had light-brown hair. He had the same pale-blue eyes, though. If his red face was anything to go by, he was uncomfortable and embarrassed. The living room was quite cosy, and India chose to sit on a couch very close to Craig, keen to hear what he had to say.

***

"HELLO, CRAIG, I believe you and your friend found a bike while you were out hiking the other week," the female detective said. They had sat on the couch opposite him, and Craig was distinctly uncomfortable with the way they were both looking at him. He felt like he was a suspect or something. He cleared his throat before answering.

"Yes. It looked like someone had intended to throw it towards the creek, but it had landed against a tree and hadn't gone all the way down."

"What day was this?"

"It was a Saturday. The first weekend of our Easter school holidays."

"Can you describe the bike?"

"It was a Malvern Star mountain bike by the look of it."

"Do you remember what colour it was?"

"Yeah, it was blue, black and silver. A real beauty. I was tempted to bring it home, thinking someone had dumped it, but it was too difficult to take out of there."

"When you say there, can you tell us exactly where you saw it?"

"It was along Tin Gulley. We were following the edge of the creek along there."

"I've brought a map of the area, Craig. Do you think you could show us exactly where you found it?" the male detective asked, spreading a map on the coffee table in front of him.

Craig bent down and, using his finger, traced the route he and Jason had taken. "We came out here, at Argents Road. I would say it's probably at least half a kilometre back along there, maybe more. I think someone had been walking along an upper trail and then just threw the bike over."

"If you will excuse me, I have to make a call," the male detective said, standing and leaving the room.

"Did either you or your friend touch the bike?" the woman detective asked. He couldn't remember her or the man's name.

"Yeah, we both did," Craig said, his cheeks reddening again. "We didn't know we shouldn't."

"Can you give us the name of the friend you were with that day? We'll need to speak to him also."

"Why? Do you think *we* dumped the bike there?"

"No. I don't think that. It's just that *if* this is the bike that belonged to our missing person, we need to have everything carefully noted for our records. We will need to take your fingerprints and those of your friend. For elimination purposes only, of course."

He was startled at the idea of having his fingerprints taken.

"The police will only need fingerprints from you and Jason *if* it is the man's bike. Isn't that right?" his mother asked the detective, who nodded.

"And once you've taken them and matched the boys' fingerprints on the bike, you won't need to keep them on record, will you?"

"If it is the bike we're seeking, we wouldn't need to keep the actual fingerprints we've taken, but a report would be written up to explain the prints found on the bike."

"So, can I just clarify, Craig and Jason's prints would be destroyed?"

"That's right," the detective said.

"That's okay then. You'd better tell them about Jason then, Craig," his mother said, nodding at him.

He cleared his throat. "His name is Jason Ferguson. We go to school together. He lives in Wilberforce as well. On Macquarie Road, just near the public school. It's an egg farm, and the property is called Craigmere. Nothing to do with me. The name is a coincidence."

"Also, for elimination purposes, Craig, can you verify where you were on the morning of Thursday the third of April?" the detective asked him.

"Why?" Craig asked.

"He was at school, of course," his mother jumped in to say. "I watched him cycle off myself, around eight o'clock. He leaves at that time every morning when he cycles—give or take a few minutes either side."

Of course, his mother believed that's what he'd done. He wished now he'd never laid eyes on the bike. The detectives were bound to find out what happened that day.

"You normally cycle to school? Hawkesbury High, isn't it?"

"Um, yeah, that's right. I cycle in unless the weather is too bad. If it's freezing cold or raining, I usually catch the school bus. Occasionally, Mum drives me—like this morning."

"Craig doesn't cycle anywhere near where that man disappeared outside Windsor. His school is over towards Freeman's Reach."

The male detective walked back into the room and nodded at the other detective, who stood. It looked like he was off the hook—for now. He felt his body relax with relief.

"Right. Well, thank you for all the information, Craig, and thank you for contacting me, Mrs. Liston," the female detective said, turning to his mother. "We're going to see if we can find that bike now before it gets too dark. Then we'll be calling in on Craig's friend. We'll need to arrange for you to come down to the station to give us a statement and your fingerprints if this is the bike we're seeking."

"A statement? As in a witness statement?" he asked.

"Yes. But only if we believe it's necessary. We'll let you know."

"You'll need a couple of people to haul that bike out of there. If the bike doesn't belong to that missing man, what happens to it? Is it possible for me to have it?"

"If it's not his, we would need to look at our records to see if anyone has reported a bike theft," the male detective said. "Not just in this area."

"That means no, I'm guessing. You'll hang on to it then?"

"For the time being, yes."

Craig nodded. It was worth a try. The bike he'd found was a much better one than his. He needed to phone Jason as soon as they were gone to warn him about the police visit.

12

"I'VE ALERTED THE uniformed constables, who've been on standby with the utility van," Jacko said as they drove away. "They said they'd head straight over there. I said we'd join them as soon as possible. I'm not sure we'll be able to find it today—we haven't got a lot of daylight left."

"I'd say we have about an hour available. It might be enough."

"It could take us longer than that."

"Let's see."

"You don't think those kids had anything to do with Day's disappearance, do you?" Jacko asked.

"No...but we need to check them out all the same. We wouldn't be doing our job properly if we didn't."

"This is the turning—take a right here."

India cruised down Argents Road until she spotted the police van, pulling over onto the gravel shoulder behind it. Jacko stepped out of the car and walked up to the front of the van. A few seconds later, he returned to speak to her.

"They're not in the vehicle. They must have headed off. Are you coming?"

"No, I'm not exactly dressed for hiking in the bush in my skirt and shoes. You go ahead. I'm going to go and see this Jason Ferguson. I won't be long, and

I'll drive back down here afterwards. Ring me if there's any problems."

"I doubt there'll be any signal down in the gulley. I can't get one here, and in there—" he pointed up the gully "—it will be the same. There was only a very weak signal at the Liston house, and that was on higher ground."

"Okay then, I'll aim to be back in an hour's time. If for any reason I'm delayed and you're back with the bike, get the boys to drive you up to the school, where there should be a signal, and phone me then."

"Will do," Jacko said, saluting as he walked off.

***

INDIA ARRIVED BACK at Argents Road just as the group were approaching the climb back up to the road.

Daylight was fading fast now; she could make out faint lights and heard a few choice curses as they finally emerged, Jacko guiding them by torchlight with the two uniformed constables shouldering the bike between them. They had it wrapped in plastic and wore gloves.

"We found it exactly in the spot young Craig showed me, and it fits the description of Day's bike," Jacko said.

"We can call in to Chrys Waters' place on the way back, see if she's home and ask her to identify it."

"Shouldn't you phone her first?"

"No, I'd rather just call in. She told me she had someone staying with her, and if she identifies this bike, she'll need some support. If she's not there, I'll phone her and ask her to come down to the station with her friend."

"How did it go with the other kid?"

"He confirmed his friend's story. But like Craig, he was red-faced and shifty when I asked him where he'd been on the morning of April third. I suspect there's something they're not telling us."

***

A WOMAN INDIA had not seen before answered the door at Chrys Waters' house.

"Good evening, I'm Detective Inspector Hargreaves," she said. "Is Chrys at home?"

"Chrys!" the woman shouted unnecessarily, as Chrys appeared at that moment, her face full of hope.

"Do you have some news?" she asked.

"We believe we've found Sonny's bike and we'd like you to come and have a look at it to verify if it is his."

"Where is it?" Chrys cried, pushing past the woman who had answered the door. "Sorry, Roxy," she said, turning back. "Detective Hargreaves, this is my cousin Roxy. She's staying with me this week."

Roxy nodded at her and followed them out to the van.

Jacko was waiting for them with the van doors open and a powerful torch shining in on the bike. Chrys peered closely at it without saying a word, then backed up a few steps.

"Where did you find it?" she asked almost in a whisper. "Have you found Sonny?"

"No, Chrys, only the bike. Can you confirm whether this is Sonny's bike?"

"Yes. It looks like his bike. Where was it?"

"On a bush trail over at Wilberforce?"

"Wilberforce? What would Sonny be doing there?"

"Sonny may not have been there. But someone dumped his bike there."

"Oh God!" Chrys cried, doubling over as if in pain. "He's dead, isn't he?"

"We don't know that, Chrys. Roxy, could you take Chrys back into the house? I'll join you in a minute."

Placing an arm around her cousin, Roxy led a tearful Chrys back into the house, leaving the door open.

Turning to Jacko, India said, "Can the boys squeeze you in to take you back to Windsor? I need to speak to Chrys. The bike needs to be sent to the forensic team to see what they can get off it. Also, first thing tomorrow morning, I'd like at least six uniformed officers to do a wider search of the area where you found the bike. Did you cordon it off?"

"Yes, but only a short perimeter around where the bike was."

"Okay. Can you put a team together for the morning? There might be more to find there...including Sonny."

"Right. Leave it with me," Jacko said. "Will you be heading home after you've finished here or coming back to the station?"

"I'll head home. You should too. I'll be in first thing. I'll see you then. Thanks guys," she called out to the uniformed officers. "Goodnight, all."

***

INDIA FOUND CHRYS curled up on the couch, her face blotchy from crying. She could hear her cousin moving about in the kitchen, but she reappeared moments later carrying a small glass, which looked to contain spirits.

"Here, Chrys, get this brandy down you."

Chrys took the proffered glass and downed it in one swig, shuddering after swallowing it.

"Urgh. Disgusting, but thank you, Nurse Roxy."

L.E. Luttrell

"It'll make you feel better," Roxy said.

"Nothing will make me feel better—apart from Sonny walking through our door alive and well."

"I wanted to let you know, Chrys, that tomorrow, we'll be carrying out a wider search of the area where we found the bike. It was too dark to start searching today, but we'll be heading out at first light. We're sending the bike off to forensics to see if we can pick up any evidence from it."

"What do you hope to find there tomorrow?"

"Something that may shed light on what's happened to Sonny."

"Do you think he's lying out there somewhere?" Chrys asked, tears beginning to slide down her face again.

"I don't know, and as I've said before, there's no point in tormenting yourself with thoughts of that possibility. We might find nothing at all."

"I know. I just can't seem to help it. I keep imagining all sorts of things."

"But imagining him lying injured or dead doesn't help you," Roxy said. "What might help is if you could imagine him in the arms of some other woman. Then you could get mad at him—get mad at the woman. I hate seeing you like this. You're normally a fighter, Chrys."

"I...I feel so weak at the moment."

"But why do you feel weak? Because you're tormenting yourself with things you don't know. It's awful not knowing what's happened to Sonny, but that's just it. You *don't* know. So hang on to the wonderful memories you have of him and hope that you might build some more in the future. You've put your life on hold. How long are you going to do that for? What if the police

62

never find out what happened to him? Are you going to give up on life? Sonny wouldn't want you to do that."

"No, you're right, he wouldn't," Chrys said in a quiet voice.

"Have you been back to work at all?" India asked.

"I cancelled my leave and went back to work the week after our supposed wedding. But I couldn't focus. Couldn't cope. The doctor's signed me off sick with stress. When Roxy found out, she took a week's leave and came to stay with me."

"Do you live in Sydney, or have you come down from Nimbin?" India asked Roxy.

"It's only Chrys's immediate family who lives in *Nimbin*," Roxy said, pulling a face. "You wouldn't catch my parents up there. Chrys's father is my uncle—the Waters clan came from Baulkham Hills, and some of them are still around there. My mother was a Waters. So, I'm not. My name is Carr. My parents live in Castle Hill, but I live in Northmead. Do you know it?"

"Yes. I used to work out of the Parramatta station. Are you really a nurse or was Chrys joking?"

"I really am a nurse. I work at Westmead Hospital."

India nodded. She was about to stand to leave when Roxy shouted, "I've got it! I told Chrys you looked familiar to me, and she said she thought that when she first met you. You look like that actress, what's her name…"

"Cate Blanchett!" Chrys cried.

"My husband says that, although I can't see the resemblance myself," India said.

"I think you look a lot like her," Chrys said. "I *knew* there was something familiar about you when I first laid eyes on you."

"No, it's not Cate Blanchett I was thinking of," Roxy said. "It's another actress. Her hair isn't as blonde as yours or Cate Blanchett's. I can't think of her name right now. I saw her in something not long ago. She is Australian, though—I think. It's difficult to know these days when actors from Australia, America, Canada and the UK drop in and out of television series and films, changing their accents."

India had no idea who Roxy was talking about and didn't feel comfortable with the conversation, although it seemed to have distracted Chrys. "Right, well, I'd better be off, Chrys," she said, standing. "I'll be in touch tomorrow after the search to let you know whether we've found anything."

"Okay. Thank you," she heard Chrys say as she moved towards the door.

13

DRESSED APPROPRIATELY FOR the search this morning, India was wearing her hiking boots, trousers, a winter shirt, jumper and jacket. She met up with the team Jacko had organised at the station.

"We need to block off a section of Argents Road," she told the assembled group. "One officer will need to remain with the vehicles while the rest of us walk through the terrain. It looks like the bike was thrown down from a higher position than where it was found." She pointed to the spot on the map pinned to the board. "I want all this higher ground searched thoroughly, and we need to move further along the creek bed as well. If you find anything, don't touch it. Stop, call out and make radio contact. If your radio fails for any reason, blow your whistle. Any questions?" She looked around at the team, which consisted of four men and two women, plus Jacko.

When no one spoke, she said, "Right, let's get going then."

***

INDIA WAS PLEASED to note that neither of the female constables were selected to remain with the vehicles. She had arrived at the cordoned-off area and was moving leaves and rocks, looking through the undergrowth. There would have been insufficient light for yesterday's

65

group to notice anything in this thickly wooded area. Looking up, she spotted Constable Partinger, whom she knew was keen to become a detective, higher up, covering a section alone. With the density of the bush and grey, threatening clouds overhead, the light wasn't great now. She hoped the rain would hold off for the search.

"Up here," she heard someone call. It was Partinger, her voice echoing down the valley as she repeated herself. India abandoned her search and scrambled up the slope.

"What have you found?"

"A phone. I almost missed it—it's so dark here. I was poking around with a stick when I turned it over. You can see the screen is cracked—probably from where it landed on those small rocks. Otherwise, it looks all right. I can see it's a Samsung. Is that the model you were looking for?"

"Yes." India nodded. "It could be Sonny Day's. Well done, Partinger. Place a marker here and cordon it off."

She waited for Partinger to act and then took a couple of photos of the phone. After putting on some latex gloves, India carefully sealed the phone in an evidence bag.

"What's that you've found?" Jacko asked, joining her.

"It was Constable Partinger who found it. A phone which could belong to Sonny Day. I'm going to head back with this now. You're in charge, Jacko. Carry on searching. I suspect this is all we're going to find out here, but we need to make sure."

***

"WE DIDN'T FIND anything else," Jacko told her later that afternoon when the team returned. "The whole gully was surprisingly clean—no dumped rubbish. Not even one plastic bag."

"That's good to hear, but it doesn't help our investigation. By the way, I discovered something interesting today as well."

"Hmm. What was that?"

"I spoke to Craig Liston's school. Neither he nor his friend Jason Ferguson were in school on the third of April. Their parents had phoned in to report them as being sick, according to school records."

"So, Sue Liston lied to us—or the boys were wagging school and got someone to phone in for them. Could it have been Sonny Day? Were the school able to tell you whether it was a male or female who phoned in?"

"I asked that question, and no they weren't. Just had a note in the log that a parent called in. The time frame is wrong for Day. He left the house—or, I should say, Chrys believed he left the house at around seven. That was the time he left each morning."

"Day *could* have met up with the boys later."

"Maybe. I don't think so, though. There's no connection between the families. I suspect the boys were bunking off school with some other agenda. I noticed Craig turned red in the face when his mother was talking about the time he would have left that day."

"Have you arranged for the boys to come in for their statements yet?"

"Not yet. I was waiting on the results from the bike. The bike has Sonny Day's prints on it along with two other sets, which I imagine are the boys'."

"How about I wait outside their school tomorrow and question them informally about the third of April?" Jacko suggested.

"You could do that, but we could also question them when they come in to give their statements and fingerprints. I was going to phone their parents tonight to arrange a time."

"Let's see what they have to say first. Any news on the phone yet?"

"No. I only dropped it over to the labs this afternoon. The techie told me it looked like there was only one set of prints on it. I was curious to see if the boys' prints were on it as well, but it doesn't look like it. I should hear the full details tomorrow morning, they told me."

*****

"IT IS SONNY Day's phone," India told Jacko after hanging up from the lab. "There were a couple of distinguishable fingerprints on it, the rest were smudges. They match the ones we picked up from Day's house. We're not going to learn anything from the phone. There is nothing on it which indicates Day had contact with any other women—or men—we don't already know about."

"He could have had another phone, as we discussed."

"Yes, but we looked at all the providers. There was nothing registered in his name. I know he could have got a mate to pick one up for him, but somehow, I doubt it. Either he dumped this phone himself or someone else did. I suspect the latter."

"I've been thinking about it," Jacko said, "and I think we should head off to the school to talk to the boys now instead of meeting them after school. They can have one of the staff sitting in. We need to clarify what they were doing that day."

"I agree. Okay, let's go."

***

"WILL YOU HAVE to tell my parents?" Craig Liston asked when they confronted him with the fact that they knew he'd been off school the day Sonny Day disappeared.

"That depends on what you tell us, Craig."

Craig glanced around at the member of staff, who was sitting a discreet distance away. He lowered his voice before saying, "We went back to my house with a couple of the year twelve girls. We spent the day there. Both my parents are out at work all day."

His face reminded India of someone who had spent too long in the sun. He was quick to blush, giving himself away. He needn't have worried; she wasn't about to pry into his sex life—unless their inquiries revealed something untoward. All parties involved would be of legal age. If he'd met up with girls in lower years, it would be a different story. They'd need to be asking more probing questions.

"And you stayed there all day?"

"Yeah, just about. The girls had to leave to head home for the right time, of course. They had their bikes with them."

"I'll need the names of the girls, Craig. We'll need to verify the information you've given us."

"Oh, come on. We had nothing to do with that bloke going missing. The girls will be really upset if they knew I told you about them spending the day with us."

69

"But you haven't told us any *details* of how you spent the day, Craig. All we need to know is whether they were with you and Jason on that date."

***

"WELL, THAT WAS fun!" Jacko said after leaving the school.

"I felt a bit sorry for the girls, although I thought they handled it quite well, acting all innocent. I would have died with embarrassment if a policeman asked me questions like that when I was their age," India said.

"Did you bunk off school with boys, though?"

"That would be telling."

"Spoilsport! I didn't get the impression they were couples as such. Just looking for a bit of fun, but they seemed sensible types. Are you going to tell the boys' parents when they come into the station?"

"I don't think we need to. It's up to them if they want to confess their sins, but I doubt they will. The school might say something to the parents about the kids being questioned. If Craig's parents query it, I'll have to tell them the truth. He's not eighteen yet. Jason has just turned eighteen, so we don't have to say anything to his parents. The girls' parents might contact us, though. Both are still under eighteen."

"Rather you than me."

"By the way, while you were visiting the gents', I phoned Chrys Waters to let her know about the phone."

"How did she take the news?"

"As you would expect. Tears and more questions that I couldn't answer. Apart from searching every metre of the bush for miles around—which we don't have the budget or resources for—there's nothing more we can do really. Sonny Day's disappearance will remain a mystery unless something else turns up."

14

SOMETHING ELSE TURNED up in the first week of June. A dead body. India received a phone call from the desk sergeant to say a naked body had been found on a property in the Wilberforce area. The super wanted India to attend the scene with her team. She'd had one heart-stopping moment for the few seconds it took for the sergeant to clarify it was the body of an adult male. Not a child. Not Joshua—the boy who had been kidnapped last year and never found. This news was almost as bad, as she suspected it was going to be Sonny Day. She put the phone down and walked out to speak to Jacko and Naomi.

"The body of an adult male has been unearthed on a building site out on King's Road in Wilberforce."

"It'll be Sonny Day. What's the bet?" Jacko said.

She nodded. "It could be. It's a property where the husband murdered his wife and then shot himself more than twenty years ago. Apparently, it was sold recently, and the new owners demolished the house. The builders have dug footings for the new house and were excavating the area where the pool will be installed when they discovered the body."

"Is it a body or a skeleton?" Jacko queried. "It's nothing to do with that old case, is it?"

"I doubt it. I was told 'body', not skeletal remains."

"So it could be Day?" Naomi asked.

Nodding, India turned to Naomi Partinger, who had been posted to the detective team less than a week ago. Naomi had a look of excited anticipation; the idea of a seeing a body was clearly not unsettling her.

"Can I come with you?" she asked.

"Yes, of course. We'll all go."

"Ever seen a dead body before?" Jacko asked Naomi.

"A couple of times. Road traffic accidents."

"This will be a *murder* victim," Jacko said. "A completely different kettle of fish. Expect to be—"

"All right, Detective Sergeant Jacko," India said. "No need to wind our new detective constable up. We don't know what we're going to find."

Jacko's promotion to detective sergeant had been in the pipeline for some months before it became official, and he'd been strutting around the station like a pompous peacock over the past week, on several occasions attempting to intimidate Partinger without success.

"Let's go. *I'm* driving," she said, grabbing her keys. She wasn't partial to Jacko's driving style.

***

THEY FOUND THE forensic pathologist already at the scene where all building work had ceased. The excavated area had been cordoned off, and India noticed beyond the house footings the builders were huddled around a fire in a large drum, drinking tea or coffee. A temporary building had been erected on the edge of the site; presumably housing a makeshift office and kitchen facilities. A portable toilet stood some metres away towards the back of the site. She sent Jacko and Naomi off to talk to the builders to find out who was operating the digger and whether they'd uncovered anything else of interest.

She had suited up before going onto the site and, after obtaining the pathologist's permission, jumped down into the hole next to her. Despite wearing several layers under her disposable suit, India was shivering from the cold.

The body, she could see, had been wrapped in a blue plastic tarpaulin—the type you could buy in any paint, hardware or DIY shop. The pathologist was obscuring her view of the face, but she could see the body was naked.

"What can you tell me?" she asked the doctor.

"It's a male. Estimated age between thirty-five and forty-five years old. Quite tall—well over six foot I'd say. I can tell you more once I have him on the table."

That *could* fit Sonny Day. He'd turned thirty-four on his last birthday and was six feet two.

"How long do you think the body has been here?"

"A couple of months. It's showing considerable signs of deterioration."

Again, that would fit with Sonny Day. It was a little over eight weeks since his disappearance. India leaned over so she could see the victim's face and head and was shocked at what she saw.

"Is that a *smile* carved into the face?"

"Yes. Grotesque, isn't it? It was done post-mortem, I'd wager."

"Have you established cause of death?" she asked, although she could see the victim's throat had been cut.

"It looks like his common carotid artery was severed. I'll know more when I do the post-mortem."

"We have a missing person who would fit the description of this victim. How long before we could obtain a DNA match?"

"I can take a sample and send it off today. You'll have to chase them up on the results."

***

"WHAT DID THE builders have to say? India asked Jacko when they wandered over to look at the body. She'd seen both Jacko and Naomi grimace at the slit throat and mutilation of the victim's face.

"They haven't found anything else of interest on the site," Jacko said, readjusting his features to their usual bland expression. "I've asked both the bloke who was operating the digger and his mate who was directing him—he was the one who spotted the body—to come into the station to give a formal statement. They're going to pop in early this afternoon, seeing as they can't carry on working."

"Good. You can deal with that. I'm going to drive across to Richmond to inform Chrys Waters of this body find. I don't want her hearing about it on the news. I can see there are a bunch of reporters and news vans here already. Someone must have phoned them. One of this lot, I suspect." She waved her arm towards the builders. "I'll drop you two back in Windsor. I'd like you to dig into records and find out who the new owner is, which agent sold the property and when, who the previous owners were and the names of anyone who lives in any nearby properties. The body was buried by someone who knows this place has been empty for many years but didn't expect it to be sold so soon afterwards."

"It's not conclusive that's it's Sonny Day, though, is it?" Naomi asked. "I mean, you can't really tell who he was."

"No, and it will be a few days before we find out, but I have to prepare Chrys Waters for the possibility it is Sonny. The face is too disfigured for me to compare it with the photographs we have of Day. The age, height and build look about right, though."

***

AT RICHMOND LIBRARY, India asked Chrys if there was somewhere quiet they could go.

"Just tell me."

"It would be better if we did this in private, Chrys—"

"You've found his body, haven't you?"

"Chrys. Please." India turned to address another staff member. "Can you manage on your own for a few minutes? I need to speak to Chrys."

The woman nodded, her worry for her colleague clear on her face as a nervous Chrys led the way through to the kitchen, where India suggested they make a cup of tea.

"No. No tea. Just tell me what you need to say. It's about Sonny, isn't it?"

India took a deep breath. She hated this part of her job. "The body of a man was found this morning on a property in Wilberforce. We don't know if it's Sonny. It didn't look like him to me. However, I needed to tell you, as the media are all over the site and it will be on the news soon—if it isn't already. The media will assume it *is* Sonny and will start bothering you."

Chrys dropped into a chair. Her face had taken on a deathly white pallor. "What do you mean, the body doesn't *look* like Sonny? Have you seen it?"

"Yes, and as I've just told you, it doesn't look like the man we've found is Sonny, but we won't know any more until the post-mortem is carried out."

"Why couldn't you tell if it's Sonny? Is the body deteriorated so much or is there some other reason?"

"I'm not able to tell you that, Chrys, but I will let you know as soon as we have the results."

She'd been thinking about the body on the drive over to Richmond. Although the height, age and hair colouring roughly matched Sonny, there was little resemblance to the man she'd seen in the many photographs Chrys had shown them. The body was extremely pale all over, as though the person hadn't been exposed to the sun for years, whereas Sonny Day had a tanned complexion in the recent photographs Chrys had snapped of him. Could a tan disappear in such a short time? Surely there'd be at least faint markings where his arms and legs had caught the sun against parts of the body which hadn't?

"Can I see him?" Chrys asked. "I could soon tell you if it is Sonny."

"I'm afraid that won't be possible. We have Sonny's DNA and can make a comparison. I can't tell you any more at present. Now how about that cup of tea?"

***

"I'VE SPOKEN TO the selling agents," Naomi told India after she returned from her visit to Chrys. "They said the property had been on their books for a little over *nineteen* years. A lot of potential buyers didn't want to touch it when they heard about the murder. Others thought the house needed too much work." Naomi paused to look at her notes. "It was surviving members of the wife's family who inherited the property. The agents said they'd never been near the place. They live in Brisbane. The new owner is a Michael Chen, son of the owners of a Chinese restaurant in Penrith, called The Chinese Dragon. He doesn't work at the restaurant. He's a senior lecturer in Traditional Chinese Medicine at Western Sydney University, based at the Cambletown Campus. His wife is a lawyer and works at a small practice in Penrith."

"Cambletown is a bit of a trek to travel for work from their new house," Jacko butted in. "Are they intending to live there?"

"People commute a lot further than that each day," Naomi threw back. "My father commuted from Lithgow to Sydney every day." Turning back to India, she added, "According to Mr. Chen, he didn't know about the murder from twenty years ago. The agent failed to mention it. He was told the house had remained in the same family and had fallen into disrepair, which, of course, is true. The sale went through just under two weeks ago, and he had builders on site the day after completion. He wasn't happy to find out about the old murder, and he had a pink fit about the body we've found. He was going on about it being 'bad Feng Shui'."

"Where does Mr. Chen live now?" India asked.

"Just off the Northern Road outside Penrith."

"I can't see him having any connection to the victim."

"Mr. Chen mentioned poor weather had delayed work on the site, and he *was* planning to move there, *Jacko*—" Naomi gave him a sidewards glance "—although I gather from what he has told me, he won't be doing that now. He didn't say, but I suspect he will build the house and then sell it. He wants to know when the site will be released so he can get on with the building."

"Tell him we'll get back to him tomorrow. I need forensics to go over the burial site first. The pathologist told me they were on their way when I left her. Chase that up will you, Naomi? Find out when they'll be finished. We can't release the site until they've completed their work. Also, can you look through missing persons case files and see if there is a description of anyone who matches our man?"

Naomi nodded and returned to her desk.

"You don't think it's Sonny Day then?" Jacko asked.

"I don't think it could be," India said before explaining why.

"That makes sense," Jacko said.

"Have you completed the builders' statements?" she asked.

"Yes. All done and dusted. I also have a list of all the nearest residents to the property. Are we going to interview them?"

"We're too busy—can you arrange a team of uniforms to do that? We need to know who lives in their households, whether they knew Sonny Day or anyone of a similar age and build to him. The victim was either killed somewhere else and his body moved to the site, or he was killed in the old house and buried later. So, the officers need to ask whether they saw anyone on the site or entering the derelict house going back a few months. They may have seen Mr. Chen and the agent, but that's fine. We need to know about *anyone* they saw. Distribute copies of Sonny Day's photo to the team for them to show the householders. If anything interesting crops up from those inquiries, a follow-up visit will be made, but probably not by us. If this is a murder, and it's looking like it is, we'll have to call in the homicide team. But I'd like to get the investigation underway before we have to hand everything over to them."

***

"HE DIED FROM a cerebrovascular accident caused by a massive cerebrovascular haemorrhage," the pathologist told India.

"What's that in plain English?"

"He died from a massive stroke."

"What? He died of *natural* causes?"

"Yes."

"So what was all that business with the slit throat and carving a smile into his face? And why bury him?"

"The slit throat and face carving were done post-mortem. As to why it was done, it will be up to your team to answer that. Dead bodies tell us many things but not, I'm afraid, those kinds of details."

India smiled at the pathologist's statement. She hadn't really been addressing the questions to her, just thinking out loud.

"Have you done a tox screen?"

"Yes, but I'm still waiting on the results. They'll be sent through to you as soon as they're completed."

With the man dying of natural causes, it meant her team would need to continue with the investigation. They wouldn't be calling in the homicide division. Of that, at least, she was grateful.

***

"IT'S NOT SONNY," India told Chrys three days later. Chrys was staying with her friend Casey to avoid the press, who had been hanging around her house and workplace since the body of the unknown male had been found.

"Oh, thank God!" Chrys collapsed onto the lounge chair. "Do you know who it is? And do you think the person has any connection with Sonny's disappearance?"

"I'm afraid I'm unable to tell you anything. Not only because it is an ongoing inquiry, but because we simply don't have those answers. We haven't been able to identify the victim. He doesn't match anyone we have listed as a missing person, and there's no match to his DNA or fingerprints on our databases. We'll be giving a press conference this afternoon appealing for information with a sketch we've compiled."

***

"AS WELL AS ascertaining that the cause of death was a massive stroke," India told her team, "the post-mortem revealed that the victim sustained head and spinal injuries and a number of other healed fractures a good while before death. The toxicology report revealed opioid analgesics in his system. Testing of his hair indicates that our dead man has been taking these opioids for some time. Forensic analysis of the victim's teeth showed that he was likely to be of British origins."

"So the old injuries were still causing the man pain?" Naomi asked.

"It would seem so. He was an otherwise healthy man—not under or overweight for his age or height—although the pathologist believes he may have had trouble with mobility."

"We've received the computer-generated sketch of the dead man now," Jacko said, pointing to an image pinned to the board, which showed a man without the grotesque carved smile.

India nodded. The sketch didn't particularly resemble Sonny Day, although there were similarities between the two men.

Addressing Jacko, Partinger and Dale, she said, "We need to get on to all the hospitals in the Sydney metropolitan area to find out whether they treated someone with these types of injuries in the past year. Also local GPs. Someone must know this man. He's not been reported missing, but a neighbour or relative might identify him. The media are issuing the computer-generated sketch of him today. Let's hope that brings some results."

***

MARION FISHER'S HUSBAND, Murray, studied the image on the television screen in front of them.

"He looks a bit like Lachlan, doesn't he?"

"Hmm?" Marion looked up at the screen from her knitting to see a body being carried out of a building site.

"The man they just showed a sketch of looked a bit like Lachlan," Murray repeated. "Perhaps Greer killed off her old man before she left Australia? He was always a miserable bastard."

"Don't be ridiculous, Murray. I told you I saw them off at the airport."

"I was kidding. It was probably someone who clashed with some gangsters."

"I wouldn't know," Marion said, thinking back to that day at the airport. Traffic had held her up, and she arrived as Greer had been about to wheel Lachie through the departure gate. She'd parked Lachie and turned back after Marion called out to her.

"What a lovely surprise!" Greer had said, coming up to give her a hug.

"I couldn't let you go without a final goodbye. How's Lachlan?"

"I've sedated him for the journey. You know what he can be like."

They'd spent a few minutes chatting before Marion reluctantly turned and left. She was going to miss Greer, but she understood why she would want to return home, where she had family who could support her with Lachlan's care.

15

TEN DAYS AFTER the body had been discovered on the building site, India was called out to the reception desk to find a tearful Chrys Waters.

"I've received a letter from Sonny. Although, it's not right. I think he's trying to send me a message in it. I knew something bad had happened to him, and now I have the proof."

"Slow down, Chrys. I'll take you through to an interview room and you can explain it all to me. Did you bring the letter with you?"

"Of course I did."

"Come on then. Let's go and have a look at it."

She took Chrys through to the same interview room they'd sat in back in April when they'd first met.

"Would you like any refreshments?"

"No. Thank you. I just want to show you this letter." Chrys dug into her bag and pulled out an envelope. "See, it's postmarked Stockholm in Sweden. Sweden of all places!" Chrys passed the letter to India.

"Can you confirm this is Sonny's handwriting?"

"Yes, it's definitely his writing, but it looks a bit spidery, like his hand wasn't very steady."

"Okay, let me just take a moment to read it."

Dear Chrys,

I am so sorry for not being in touch with you sooner. The truth is I felt so ashamed I didn't know where to start. As you can see, I am in Sweden. I met the most beautiful girl in the weeks before I went away and just couldn't help myself. I fell head over heels in love with her. Birgit was on holiday in Australia, and we had a whirlwind romance. The idea of her leaving and never seeing her again was too much for me.

I followed her over here, and we are now married. I'm so sorry, Chrys, for all the pain I must have put you through. I know when I proposed to you while we were camping in the Pilliga Forest, I said we would be together forever, but meeting Birgit was so unexpected and took me by surprise. I hope you can forgive me. I am making a new life for myself here in Stockholm now, so the house is yours to do with as you wish.

With very best wishes for the future,
Sonny

"How did he travel to Sweden without his passport?" India asked, surprised by the contents of the letter.

"That was the first question I asked myself after the initial shock of receiving this. I went to get Sonny's passport out of the drawer, and it's missing. His driving licence is also missing. None of your officers took them, did they?"

"No. Detective Jacko examined the passport then gave it back to you. I took copies of the driving licence when you first came into the station."

"Well, I put both back in the drawer, and now neither of them are there. Your forensic officers were the last ones to search through the house. Either one of them removed them or someone came into the house and took them."

"Surely that would have been Sonny? After he decided to go after this Birgit or whatever her name is."

"So you might think. But I don't believe that. See where he says about us camping in the Pilliga Forest?"

"Yes."

"Well, we've *never* camped there. We talked about it and decided it was a place we'd like to see one day. But we haven't *ever* been there. That is not where Sonny proposed to me. It's a clue, I'm certain of it. He'd know I'd realise details of the letter aren't true. Someone must be holding him against his wishes.

"There's a photograph that came with the letter." Chrys pulled it out of the envelope and passed it to India. "This is Sonny, and the date stamp on the photograph says May this year—after he disappeared—so he *is* in Sweden. But I think someone forced him to go there."

India examined the photograph. It showed Sonny standing against a wall. He was wearing sunglasses, and his face looked very pale compared to the photo Chrys had given them. Where the wall ended at the side of the picture, there was a lake in the background, and in that lake, she could see a small island. The surrounding mountainous terrain looked rugged in sections, while others were covered in trees. The scenery was familiar in some way, most likely something she'd seen in a film or on television.

"Another thing—Sonny is wearing a black jacket in this photo. He hates black and would never choose to wear it. He says it reminds him of his grandmother who, after her husband died, wore black clothes for *thirty* years until her death. This is all the evidence I need to know that Sonny is being held against his wishes by someone."

India suppressed a compulsion to laugh at Chrys's reasoning. He hadn't taken any of his own clothes with him, so his choices might have been limited.

"Could Sonny have substituted the Pilliga in error for some other place you've been together? Somewhere he made the same promise to you?"

"No. When Sonny proposed to me, we weren't camping anywhere. We were on holiday up at the Gold Coast. He proposed to me in a restaurant."

"What about this promise he refers to. Did he make a similar promise to you *anywhere*?"

"No." Chrys shook her head. "We did talk about our future, having a family, but not in the way he's described the promise in this letter. I'm telling you, he's being held against his will!"

"Yes. Okay, Chrys. Can I have the letter and photograph? We'll need it—"

"I want to keep both the letter and the photograph. Can't you make a copy of them?"

"Okay. I'll copy them both and give *you* the copies for now. We need to see if we can pick up fingerprints from the originals, and we'll need your fingerprints to isolate others. I imagine forensics will already have your prints from their search of your house. Now we have this information, we can make some inquiries with customs and see if we can pinpoint when Sonny travelled to

Sweden. Do you have any idea when the passport could have been taken from the house?"

"No. As I told you, I showed it to your detective when he was looking for Sonny's phone. That was the last time I saw it—back in early April. I haven't needed my passport, so there was no reason to look at them again. I don't think I've even opened the drawer where we keep them."

"Okay. I'll just go and make these copies and be back with you in a minute."

India left Chrys, returning to the squad room. As well as making photocopies, she took a shot of the photograph and letter on her phone camera to upload to her computer. This was an interesting twist of events. If Chrys was correct, then there was certainly something suspicious going on. If Sonny was being held captive and forced to write a letter to Chrys, the letter would have to look genuine so his captors wouldn't know it held a secret clue. Smart thinking—if that was the case. They hadn't checked with customs for any sign of Sonny leaving the country, as his passport had been in his house. Now they had new lines of inquiry to follow.

16

INDIA FILLED JACKO and Naomi in about the letter and photograph Chrys had received. She'd made additional copies of the letter for them to examine.

"So he did take off after another woman," Jacko said after reading it. "And where the hell is this Pilliga Forest?"

"I don't think you were listening to me, Jacko. I said Chrys Waters claims the business about the proposal and promise made at the Pilliga is not true. The Pilliga is an ancient inland forest between Coonabarabran and Narrabri. I checked it out. They've never been there. He proposed to her in a restaurant up on the Gold Coast. She believes Sonny has deliberately given her a clue to indicate that the rest of the letter is false."

"Well, how the hell are we supposed to verify that if he's in Sweden?"

"First of all, we need to find out when he travelled to Sweden. Can you get on to customs, Jacko, and see if you can find out what day he left the country? Also ask them whether it is possible to trace a young Swedish woman called Birgit who might have entered the country.

"Naomi, can you get on to the Swedish Embassy and find out if Australian citizens need a visa for travel there? Also, while you're talking to them, ask how we might go about looking into someone with the first name of Birgit in Stockholm. I don't know if it's a common name there, but I recall citizens' tax records and personal details are freely available for anyone to look at. Find out how we might do that. I'll send the letter and envelope to forensics."

"What about our unidentified victim?" Jacko asked. "Do we stop working on that? We're still sifting through information that's come in."

"We need to do both. But prioritise the Day investigation first. I'll also carry on looking through the house-to-house inquiries, and I'll need to phone the super about this latest development with Sonny Day."

***

NAOMI KNOCKED ON India's office door just as she terminated a call with Rob. She'd sent him their photo-fit image of the buried man and now this new photo of Sonny. Rob had confirmed that local inquiries in Penrith had brought no results on the unidentified man. She'd also spoken to the super earlier, updating him on the letter and photograph Chrys had received. The super confirmed that he wanted her team to continue pursuing their lines of inquiry related to Day and the unidentified body.

She asked the super for more admin personnel to assist them, as Dale was the only administrative staff member attached to their team, and she was still making hospital and GP calls in the greater Sydney region along with other tasks she'd been allocated. The calls were proving to be a lengthy and laborious task, which so far had brought no results. There were a couple of other admin personnel based in the station, but they were generally allocated to other duties and not part of their team. The chief agreed to temporarily send an extra pair of hands over from Richmond to assist Dale.

India waved at Naomi, inviting her to sit. "What did you find out from the Swedish Embassy?"

"I picked up this information from their website. Australian citizens can visit Sweden without a visa for up to ninety days. If they wish to stay longer, they have to make an application for permission to remain."

"Okay. We need to contact the Swedish authorities and find out if Sonny Day has made that application. It might be a little premature—his ninety days wouldn't be up yet—but if he'd planned on staying, he may have put in an application earlier." Naomi scribbled some notes while India continued. "It's worth finding out exactly where the application would be lodged so we can remain in touch with them. If he's being held unwillingly, there may not be any application made. Has Jacko managed to pick up any names from immigration?"

"I'm not sure. Shall I ask him to pop in to see you?"

"Yes, please—when he finishes his call. I can see he has his head down out there. Then come back in as well, and we'll discuss what to do next."

***

IT WAS A further seventeen minutes before Jacko and Naomi returned to India's office. She'd been reading through some of the information the team had collected from neighbouring properties near the burial site, finding nothing of significance that could help identify their body. The two detectives settled down and Jacko launched into his findings.

"Sonny Day flew out of Sydney late on Sunday twenty-seventh April on an Emirates flight that terminated in

Dubai. From Dubai, he would have picked up a flight to take him on to Arlanda Airport in Stockholm. He would have landed in Stockholm the following day—unless he had a stopover in Dubai. I don't have those details. I haven't made any contact with Swedish Immigration yet. I wasn't sure if you would want me to."

"Yes, I do. Find out exactly when he arrived in Stockholm. Do you know if he was travelling alone?"

"Yes, he was—well, he left Sydney alone anyway."

"How did he pay for his ticket if he hasn't accessed any of his bank accounts or credit cards?" Naomi asked.

"I was wondering that," Jacko said. "Perhaps he had another account or credit card he never mentioned to Miss Waters? I didn't find any evidence of a different card or account at the house, though. Maybe his new girlfriend paid for it."

"Any luck with anyone by the name of Birgit entering Australia?" India asked.

"There were three Swedish Birgits entered the country between January and April. One a child, one an elderly woman and one who could be the right age. Her name is Birgit Martinson, born on eighteenth February 1989—so she'd be twenty-five. Birgit Martinson arrived in Sydney on twenty-sixth February and departed again on twenty-eighth March, so she was in the country at roughly the right time. She apparently travelled out to Australia with friends but listed a relative as a contact point in Sydney for her destination. I was able to track them down, speaking to her aunt who lives in Caringbah, a suburb just before Cronulla." Jacko paused and made a sidelong glance at Naomi.

"And what did the aunt say?" India asked.

Jacko shifted uncomfortably in his chair before he resumed talking. "She told me Birgit stayed with her and her family for a few days before joining up with her friends. Birgit met up with the family again for a final lunch date in the city before she left but made no mention of having met someone. In fact, her aunt thought it highly unlikely, as she had the impression Birgit was involved with one of the women she travelled with. She'd brought the woman in question—a Kristina Hansson—to lunch with the family. Kristina spelled with a 'K', that is, and she preferred to be called Kris. Although Birgit hadn't said anything, the aunt said Kris was quite butch, and the two women were very touchy-feely throughout the meal. She doubts Birgit would've started a relationship with any men during her stay here."

So that was why Jacko had paused. He believed *Naomi* was a lesbian.

"Well, that sounds like it might be a dead end, but we need to follow it up, just in case."

"Sonny Day might have met the women and not realised Birgit was a lesbian," Naomi said. "Some women don't like to make big announcements about their sexuality."

Jacko scowled at Naomi. He often made remarks alluding to her sexuality—out of Naomi's earshot. So far, Naomi hadn't revealed her sexual orientation, and India hadn't probed—it wasn't any of their business—but she'd had a private word with Jacko a couple times when she'd heard him make unnecessary comments about gay men.

"I have no issues with gay men," Jacko had said. "It's only those who deceive their partners who bother me.

They cause unnecessary heartache and confusion for their partners and children."

They'd debated at length, and it was during that discussion he'd revealed his sister's husband had left her and their two children for a man and moved to Melbourne.

"Maybe he didn't realise he was gay when he married," India had argued on behalf of Jacko's ex-brother-in-law.

"Oh, he knew, all right. Turns out he'd lived with a man in Sydney before he married Sonia—as a couple, not just housemates—and had numerous other relationships prior to that."

"Well, perhaps he didn't want to be gay and simply wanted to marry and have a family."

"But he should have been honest with Sonia so she could have made the choice. He denied her that option. She took an HIV test after he left her—just to make sure. It was clear, thankfully, but it could have been a different story."

"You're right about that," she'd told him. "Over the years, I've come across a few cases where people with HIV knowingly had unprotected sex—both gay *and* straight individuals."

She'd made sure Jacko understood that and didn't use his sister's experience to justify what appeared to be a prejudice against the LGBT community. It was important to India not just on a professional level but also a personal one. Her and Rob's close friend Brian, who worked in forensics, was gay. When things became serious with his partner Ronnie, one of the first things they did was have HIV tests to show they were clear of it. The latest news from them was that they'd decided they wanted children, so they were in discussions with a lesbian couple about the possibility of shared parenting arrangements. It wasn't ideal, but surrogacy—their only other option to have a blood-related child—was illegal in New South Wales.

Hearing all their problems always made India sad for the limited choices Brian and Ronnie had. It wasn't that far removed from her and Rob's situation. If they couldn't have their own children, adoption was their only other real choice.

She was suddenly aware that Jacko had said something she hadn't caught.

"Sorry, can you repeat that?"

"According to the letter Chrys Waters received, Sonny Day and this Birgit are now married. A lesbian wouldn't marry unless it was an *arrangement* linked to citizenship—or having children."

"We don't know if the Birgit you checked out *is* a lesbian," Naomi argued.

"Perhaps the lesbians are keeping him captive," Jacko said, winking at her. "Perhaps they lured him to Sweden so that they could—"

"Enough, Jacko!" India shot him a warning glance, as she could see Naomi was about to react. "Get back on to immigration and see if any more Birgits entered Australia in the few months leading up to December last year. The letter mentioned she'd been here on a holiday, but we have no idea how long that holiday was—or indeed if the woman even exists. The whole letter might be a pack of lies to put us off the scent. Naomi, you follow up on applications linked to Sonny Day and any record of a marriage registered in his name."

"I'm having trouble reaching anyone to speak to at the Embassy in Canberra, but I'll keep trying," Naomi said.

"Right. Contact Emirates Airways as well and see if you can find out how the ticket Sonny Day travelled on was purchased. Was it purchased directly through them at the airport, online with them, through some other online company or at a travel agent?"

"Okay, will do."

Twenty minutes later, Naomi was knocking on her door.

"I managed to get through to the Swedish Embassy and have some answers for you. Sonny Day hasn't lodged an application to remain in the country—as yet, anyway. And there are no records of a marriage registered in his name. Swedish citizens can access information about their fellow citizens, but we can't. The member of staff I spoke to told me we'd need to contact the police in Stockholm, who might be willing to trace this Birgit—if we have her full name and date of birth."

"Okay. Well done. I'll see if I can contact the police in Stockholm and ask them to check out this Birgit Martinson and Kristina Hansson. Jacko should have Birgit's date of birth. It's four p.m. here now— only six a.m. there. I'll wait until later tonight and try them from home."

17

INDIA SAT LOOKING at the two folders of the cases they were currently investigating—the one on Sonny Day and the one on their unidentified male victim. Rob was away in the city tonight and was staying in some plush hotel. NSW Police seemed keen on holding conferences for those of Rob's rank and above, although he was a reluctant participant. He was never enthusiastic about attending and seldom had any positive comments to make when he returned home.

If nothing else, Rob's absence gave India the opportunity to go over both cases while waiting for a suitable time to call Stockholm. She opened the file on their male victim. The sight of the dead man's image with his grotesque grin sent shivers down her spine.

"Who are you?" she asked, speaking out loud to the photograph. "And why would someone want to mutilate and then bury you?" The starting point was always with the victim—if they knew who he was, but they had no clues and were no closer to finding out. Dale's contact with local GPs and hospitals in the greater Sydney area had so far drawn a blank. There were a number of men in the right age range who had been treated for head and spinal injuries, but none matched the height and description of their victim. His identity remained a mystery.

Their appeals in the press had resulted in the usual crank calls—people accusing their neighbours of killing a family member, or claiming their neighbour was a drug dealer and suggesting the victim had been killed when a drug deal had gone wrong. India and her colleagues had checked out a few calls where the person in question had moved or not been sighted for some time, but all proved fruitless. Each person was tracked, and in one instance, the neighbour had been correct. The man was a drug dealer who was now in prison on remand. He hadn't looked anything like the victim, but as the neighbours only ever saw him wearing a hoody, his tall, lanky build was the point they latched on to, as well as the fact that he'd disappeared.

She sighed and closed the file, opening the one on Sonny Day instead. This was proving to be another mystery. Was he really in Stockholm? Jacko had ascertained that he'd landed in Arlanda several days later than expected, on 2nd May. He'd had a stopover in Dubai. Why would he do that if he was keen to get to Sweden? Perhaps he'd been unwell or was shopping in Dubai for presents. From accounts she'd heard, it was a great modern city with lots on offer.

She stared at the photograph of Sonny—the one Chrys had received with the letter—then picked up a separate image. One of the computer technicians at Richmond had cut out Sonny and enlarged the image showing the lake or fjord in the background. She'd trawled through her memory, trying to recall where she'd seen similar scenery before. She'd shown the photograph to Rob last week in the hope he might recognise the setting from something they'd watched together. He had no idea. She'd even dug out her three DVDs based on

Stieg Larsson's Millennium series and sat through each film on consecutive nights hoping they might reveal a location depicted in the photograph. They hadn't.

It was hopeless. Nothing was coming through.

Forensics had analysed the letter and envelope. Only three fingerprints had been found on it: hers, Chrys's and presumably Sonny's. As expected, numerous prints had been found on the envelope but none that were in their system. She sighed again and looked at her watch. It was nine p.m. now, making it eleven a.m. in Stockholm. She'd made a note of the number of the police headquarters in Stockholm before leaving the station. She picked up her phone and tapped it in now.

**

THE FOLLOWING MORNING Naomi was in Penrith seated on a bench near a Flight Plan shop. She'd found out that this was where Sonny Day had purchased his ticket. She'd sent a text to DI Hargreaves telling her where she was and that she'd return to base as soon as she had made her inquiries.

Spotting a man and a woman approach the shop, unlock the shutters and enter, Naomi waited a few minutes before following them.

"Good morning, I'm Detective Constable Partinger from the Windsor Police. I'm looking into a ticket purchase made here by a man named Sonny Day a few months back."

The two workers looked at her with blank expressions.

"The ticket was purchased on the twenty-fourth of April, for a single flight to Stockholm in Sweden."

She showed them a photograph of Sonny.

"I don't remember him," the woman said.

"I do," the man said. "We don't get too many bookings for Sweden, and it was the day before Anzac Day. Remember—" he said to his colleague "—he's the one who turned up here with cash, only he had a moustache and beard," he added, pointing at the photograph.

"Oh yeah, I remember," the woman said without looking away from her computer screen. Naomi would've bet the woman was looking at a social media site, checking out her friends' updates.

"He paid for the ticket in cash?"

"No. Yes—well, sort of. We aren't allowed to take cash, but he claimed he had closed his bank accounts because he wanted to leave Sydney as soon as possible— to be reconciled with the love of his life or something. He said they'd broken up and she'd returned home, and he wanted to follow her, so he'd left his job, given up his flat, closed his bank account and was wanting to take off. He had all his luggage with him and everything."

"So you took the cash from him?"

"Not exactly. He was ranting on and on about it all in his strange accent, and in the end, I offered him a solution. He came with me to my bank, I deposited the money, and then we returned here and I processed the ticket for him using my own card."

"Are you allowed to do that—" Naomi checked the nametag on his shirt "—Ryan?"

"We've never been told we couldn't. It's not something I would normally do, but I felt sorry for the bloke. I couldn't get him a seat for a flight until the twenty-seventh, though. He said he'd bunk in a hostel in Sydney until his flight date."

"Can we go back to what you said about his accent? What kind of accent was it?"

"I'm not sure. Swedish, I assumed. I couldn't understand everything he said. His English wasn't very good."

"He didn't sound Australian?"

Ryan laughed. "Not in a million years."

"Did he use any Swedish words that you picked up?"

"When he was waving his damaged bank card around after I told him that was what he needed, he said something like 'nay bra'. I thought he was talking about women's bras or something. I couldn't make sense of it. Then he corrected himself and said, 'No goot.'"

"Right, that's helpful," Naomi said, making notes. "His name didn't ring any bells with you?"

"No. Should it have?"

"The name 'Day' doesn't exactly sound Swedish, does it?"

"His mother could have married an English or Aussie man. We get all sorts in here. People from all over the world who can barely speak English but have very *English*-sounding names."

"Okay, fair enough. Didn't he have to show you his passport to purchase the ticket?"

"No. He only needs his passport for checking in. I just sold him the ticket."

"Did he show *any* form of identification?"

"Yes. He opened his wallet and pulled out his old bank card, which he must have bent in half after closing his account, as I've already told you. Then he showed me his driving licence where he looked more like the picture you've just shown me."

"Okay. Would you have any security footage of the day the man came in?"

"No, I'm sorry. We only keep it for a month, then it's automatically deleted. It would all be recorded over by now. But he was the man in the photograph, only, like I said, he had a thick beard."

"How established was the beard? Was it clipped short or long?"

Ryan shrugged. "It wasn't long like you see with some bikers. I'd say it was a couple of inches long as though he kept it neatly trimmed."

"Okay, thanks for your help. Can you give me your surname, Ryan?"

"Why? I haven't done anything wrong, have I? He wasn't a criminal, was he?"

"Not that I'm aware of, but it concerns an ongoing inquiry. That's all I'm able to tell you. I'll need your full name for my report."

***

"I'VE MANAGED TO trace where Sonny Day purchased his ticket," Naomi told India when she returned to the station and proceeded to fill her in on what she had discovered at the Flight Plan store.

"I checked with security at the mall, and they no longer have footage for the time frame either, so I wasn't able to locate him entering and exiting."

"I thought they kept recordings for several months."

"They do normally, but apparently, they had their equipment updated, and so all previous footage was wiped."

"Okay. That's a pain. At least we have him on camera at the airport. Did you say he spoke with a Swedish accent?"

"That's what the guy said. Only he clarified his statement by saying he *assumed* it was a Swedish accent and the man didn't speak very good English. He made reference to a couple of words the man spoke when waving his bent bank card around, and I looked them up on a Swedish translation site. He said something like 'nay bra', then corrected himself to say 'no goot'. 'Bra' in Swedish means 'good'. 'No' is spelled n-e-j but pronounced 'nay'. However, if you were to say 'no good' together, it is 'inte bra'. It's almost as though the person who was speaking to Ryan wasn't fluent in the Swedish language."

"That is so weird. Another twist to this strange tale. It doesn't sound like it was Sonny Day. You mentioned the man had a thick beard? Chrys never mentioned a beard. The recent photograph she gave to us of Sonny showed him with what looked like the beginnings of a beard. Could he have grown a *thick* beard in only a few weeks? And where was he staying between the date he disappeared and when he appeared at the travel agency?"

"I was wondering about all that," Naomi said. "Ryan Faulk insisted it was the same man whose photograph I showed him. He said the beard was only a few inches long—and neatly trimmed. Do you think Sonny Day could have been bunging on an act or something? Could he have grown a beard to disguise himself? Or was he wearing a false one?"

"Hmm. Maybe. Chrys Waters told me that they had done a short stint in amateur dramatics last year, but they both decided it wasn't for them."

"Well, that could explain it. His photo had been in the local and national papers a few weeks before. Not that Ryan had a clue who he was."

"No. Sadly, most young people don't read the papers or watch the news anymore. They use their phones to check out what's going on in the celebrity world or amongst their friends on social media. Other matters seem to hold little interest for them. I'll get in touch with Chrys Waters and speak to her about this beard business."

"Okay. I'll type up a report of everything I've learned today for you. Do you want a paper copy as well? I've noticed you always have hard copies of files lying around. Is that for back-up or personal preference?"

"Both. We need to create digital files on all our work, but I prefer paper copies for reading over case notes." India waved her arm at the small pile on Jacko's desk; he also preferred to work with hard files. "I spend enough hours staring at computer screens. I don't want to ruin my eyes. Also, it works as a back-up system because, as you are no doubt aware, our computers go down every so often."

"Right," Naomi said, nodding.

"In your report, I'd like you to include details of all your findings from yesterday. I noticed they're not on the system yet."

"No problem."

***

INDIA RETREATED TO her office and tapped onto Chrys Waters' mobile number. As far as she knew, Chrys had returned to work. She answered after a few rings.

"Detective Hargreaves? Have you got some news?"

"Yes, I'd like to come and see you this evening when you are back from work if that's okay."

"I'm at home. You can come and see me now if you're able to."

"Okay I'll be there within the next hour."

"You're coming to give me bad news, are you? Have you found another body?"

"No, it's nothing like that. I'll see you soon."

***

CHRYS ANSWERED HER door with a hopeful face. "Come in."

India followed Chrys into the living room.

"I'd offer you a drink or something, but I'm dying to know what news you have. Sit down." Chrys indicated one of the single couch chairs that India had sat in the last time she was here.

Chrys lowered herself onto the couch, perched close to the edge, leaning forward. India sat, mimicking Chrys's position before speaking.

"We've discovered where Sonny bought his plane ticket. He paid in cash. Would he have had access to money in another account?"

"No. You *have* the details of Sonny's accounts," Chrys said, her disappointment showing on her face. She relaxed back onto the couch before speaking again. "As you know, we had our own accounts, but we transferred most of our money to the joint account each month. It was the main one we used. You've already ascertained that Sonny hasn't withdrawn any money. It can't have been him who bought the ticket. Was the man captured on camera?"

"He would have been, but unfortunately, the footage has been recorded over. We do have him on camera at the airport, though. He flew out of Sydney on the twenty-seventh of April."

"No, I'm sorry, I don't believe it was Sonny. It can't have been. Can I see the airport footage?"

"It's quite grainy. You can't really see him in fine detail."

"Then it wasn't him," Chrys said, waving her arms dismissively.

"The man who sold him the ticket was quite confident. Sonny showed him his driver's licence and a bank card."

"I thought you said he paid in cash?"

"He did. But he had his bank card with him, claiming he'd closed the account because he was leaving the country permanently."

Chrys moved back further onto the couch, frowning. "But you know the account hasn't been closed."

India's team had been monitoring the account, and Chrys was correct. Apart from a few direct debits going out of it, there had been no other withdrawals.

"How often did Sonny have to shave?"

"What?" Chrys seemed confused by the question.

"Did Sonny shave daily or more than once a day?"

"He shaved every morning. Why?"

"He had a thick moustache and beard by the time he left Sydney."

Chrys burst out laughing. "No way. There's no way Sonny would willingly grow a moustache and beard. That was something else I meant to mention about the photograph I received with the fake letter. He looks like he has a bit of a beard, but that wouldn't have been through his choice. His father and his father's friends all have them. He hates them. They remind him of his hippy upbringing. Never in a million years would he choose to grow one."

He might if he was attempting to disguise himself, India thought.

"He had one in the security footage we caught of him leaving Sydney, which confirms the details given to us by the travel agent."

"Well, it wasn't Sonny then."

India was beginning to wonder just how well Chrys knew Sonny. They'd only been together a few years, and India's work on the force had revealed actions and behaviour which shocked partners, wives and family members about their loved ones. Sonny Day might've had a side to his character that Chrys hadn't seen.

With Chrys being so adamant that Sonny wouldn't grow a beard, India decided not to pursue that aspect. The clues in Sonny's letter were very curious, though. Could Chrys be right?

18

Three weeks earlier

SONNY WOKE TO the sound of Coldplay blaring in his ears again. Chrys had always loved the band, and he liked them well enough but couldn't say he'd ever been a huge fan like Chrys was. Now he'd be happy if he never heard them again.

His eyes were covered as usual, and his wrists and ankles restrained, but when Coldplay or other types of rock or pop music were playing, it usually indicated that someone was going to come into the room and feed him—an alarm of sorts. When this happened, he would be propped upright, his arm and leg restraints adjusted, and be told to open his mouth to receive food. One day it might be a woman's soft, whispered tones demanding his compliance, another day a man who spoke with a weird, gruff accent.

He knew there was a drip going into his arm, which he suspected contained drugs. When he wasn't being subjected to rock or pop music, softer easy listening instrumental music played through his headphones, soothing and lulling him into a relaxed sleep.

He had no idea where he was or how long he'd been here. He kept fading in and out of strange dreams, including erotic ones, where he was seduced by a woman with the most sensual touch. Try as he might, he couldn't help but respond to her—his body betrayed him every time. In the dream, he could never see her, as she kept him blindfolded, but he felt her hands caress him, her hair tickle his body, which sent shivers through him, her tongue and lips lovingly bringing him to attention. Her ample breasts brushed against his body, and he felt her mount and ride him. It was the most erotic thing he'd ever experienced. He mentally apologised to Chrys after these dreams, convinced it was the drugs that caused them. With little else to think about in the limited time he'd be awake, he would attempt to recapture the dream in all its sexual glory. The pleasure distracted him from the reality of the nightmare he was actually experiencing. Because this wasn't right or normal.

A few times, he'd managed to push the headphones aside: once, he heard a woman's voice; other times, he'd heard muted conversation between a man and a woman. There were definitely two of them holding him, but for the life of him, he couldn't imagine why. He attempted to call out one day, but all that came out was a weak squeak.

He tried to remember the last time he'd seen Chrys. It was just before he'd cycled off to work. How long ago was that? The next thing he knew, he'd woken with a splitting head and his face feeling like he'd received a savage beating. Had he been in an accident? He remembered little after that until the strange dreams started. He wondered if he was dead or in a coma. Perhaps he'd been knocked off his bike and was in hospital? That wouldn't explain the blindfold or the restraints though.

At one point he was sure they had taken him on a long boat journey. He felt the rising and falling motion of a boat at sea, which left his stomach feeling peculiar.

Not that he'd travelled on the sea very often. A few times on the Manly ferry, once across to Tasmania, and a couple of trips on a fishing boat.

A slightly different regime had started now. They regularly released him from his restraints and, with his hands newly bound behind his back, guided him to the bathroom where he was expected to release his bowels or bladder with his captors cleaning him up as though he was a very young child. He couldn't always do it to order and was shamefully aware that he had soiled or wet himself a few times. Then he would be rolled around the bed and cleaned up without anyone speaking to him, so he had no idea if it was the man or woman who did this. Every so many trips to the bathroom, he'd be stood under a shower, and someone would wash him—again, without speaking.

His legs had been very weak, and he needed to be supported to stay on his feet, so now, as well as taking him to the toilet, they walked him around what, he could sense, was a large room. He'd counted the steps. Fourteen wobbly steps to the bathroom. Fifteen steps to what he believed was either a window or door from the bathroom, as the light was brighter there. Nineteen steps down the room again until he was turned around and the process was repeated. After several trips, he was put back on his bed. He could feel some strength returning to his legs as this daily pattern continued. He also noticed that the rooms where he was being kept were all on one level.

He could sense the presence of someone in the room this morning. The bedcovers were pulled back, and Sonny immediately felt their loss, the cold seeping into his emaciated body. The headphones were removed, his feet and hands released from their binds. Unusually, this time his hands weren't bound behind him again. Was something different happening? He was sure he could smell bacon. Was it real or was he imagining it, desperate for something tasty to eat?

After a trip to the bathroom where Sonny was told to clean himself up, he was led into a room and pushed down onto a chair, with a shawl placed around his shoulders. The shawl smelled of a woman's perfume. This was new. His heartbeat increased with nervous anticipation. What were they planning to do to him?

His blindfold was removed, and he heard the word, "Eat." The sudden light hurt his eyes. He screwed them up in agony and placed his hands over them before the man passed him some sunglasses and told him to put them on. The glasses made opening his eyes easier. He blinked a few times and looked around.

"Eat," the man repeated.

Looking down, Sonny saw there was a plate of bacon and eggs in front of him. Some buttered bread sat on a small side plate, and there was a steaming mug of what smelled like coffee in front of him. His stomach rumbled, and his dry mouth immediately filled with saliva knowing that this treat would taste heavenly compared to what he'd been fed. Was it a trick? He looked up to see a man wearing a balaclava standing near him. He was holding a length of metal pipe—presumably intended to be used as a weapon. From a quick glance around, Sonny judged this was the room he was exercised in. They appeared to be in a large, open-plan, wooden cabin.

"I said eat."

Sonny didn't need telling again. He tucked into the food, savouring every mouthful, not even caring that the shawl had dropped off his shoulders revealing his nakedness. The bacon didn't taste like bacon he had at home, but he could honestly say it was the best he'd ever eaten.

Once he'd cleared his plates, the man ordered him to get dressed. A set of clothes were laid out across a lounge chair: a pair of underpants, a white T-shirt, black jeans, a black jumper, black socks and a pair of black trainers. They looked like good quality clothes. With his aversion to black, he was tempted to say the clothes weren't to his taste but thought better of it. To be honest, he didn't care what colour the clothes were. The fact that he was being offered them at all made him optimistic.

Dressing with his shaky hands and legs took Sonny some time. Surprisingly, the clothes fitted him well; clothed and fed, he felt much better. Now what? So far, the man had only uttered a few words. Sonny kept quiet, waiting to see what was coming next.

The man shoved the empty plates further along the table and ordered Sonny to sit again. He produced pen and paper and also a typed letter.

"I wan' ya te copy everyting on that," the man said in a slow, halting voice. Sonny couldn't quite catch the accent. It was definitely foreign, but from where?

He read through the typed letter. It was to Chrys, and he was supposed to write to say why he had left her. He shook his head. No, he wasn't doing this. He couldn't do this to Chrys, the woman he planned to marry. *The marriage!* Had the date come and gone? How long was it since he'd last seen her?

Sonny felt the impact of the pipe across his shoulders. He yelled out in pain.

"Tha' was a warning," the man said. "Now write."

With a shaky hand, Sonny picked up the pen and started copying the typed sheet. He had to add something so Chrys would know the letter was all lies. The letter said he was now married and living in Sweden. Sweden? How on earth had he travelled to Sweden? The boat journey he thought they'd taken hadn't seemed that long. Was that a lie as well?

He finished the letter and passed it to the man, who read through it, comparing it to the typed version.

"What's all dis bollocks about the Pilliga?" he asked. "That was nae in the letter you had tae copy."

Sonny opened his mouth to speak, but his vocal cords didn't seem to be working properly. He cleared his throat a few times and tried again. "The letter wasn't personal enough. I had to add something else to make it seem more real, otherwise Chrys wouldn't believe it was from me. It's where I proposed to her," he said in a croaky voice.

"Why would ya do that?"

"Our trip to Pilliga was so special. I wanted Chrys to understand that. She wouldn't believe me capable of just cutting her off. If I'm going to let her down, she has to know we did have something special."

The man nodded, seeming to accept this. He produced a white envelope and told Sonny to address it to Chrys. When that was done, he placed Sonny's letter inside the envelope, then handed him a black jacket and told him to put it on. Sonny cringed at the sight of it but did as he was told.

"Now follow me," the man said. "And doan try any funny business."

The man parted the curtains at the end of the room, revealing a set of sliding doors that led onto a covered terrace. He opened one slider and beckoned Sonny to follow him outside.

Oh, the fresh air! It smelled wonderful, and a cool breeze caressed his cheeks. There was a beautiful lake before them surrounded by mountains. It was breathtaking. Was this Sweden?

"Now stan agin dat wall, and smile for the camera," the man said.

Sonny glanced around, noting that there were similar cabins nearby. Would he be able to overcome this man and run off to one of them for help? No, he couldn't run; his legs weren't strong enough. But he could walk. How to grapple that piece of pipe from the man, though? As Sonny stood against the wall, the man tucked the pipe under his arm and began snapping photos on a small digital camera. Sonny hadn't seen one of those in years.

"Where are we?" he asked.

"Norway," the man said.

"Norway? But the letter said I was in Sweden."

"Ya didna tink we'd let ye say where ya really were, didya?" the man said before muttering as an aside, "Du dum tull."

Sonny was beginning to distinguish the man's gritty spoken words. He sounded Scottish mixed with something like...maybe Scandinavian. Like some of those police shows he and Chrys had watched on SBS back home. So maybe he *was* in Norway. What the bloody hell did this couple want with him, and who the fuck did they think they were? Bringing him to Norway of all places! His anger rose, erupting into a burst of rage, and he charged at the man, the camera flying off to the side and landing on the terrace table.

Caught unaware, the man fell back through the open door, dropping to the floor with Sonny on top of him. Sonny attempted to wrestle the pipe from the man, but while his rage had given him momentary strength, his incarceration had left him weak, and his captor soon got the better of him, reversing their positions.

"No!" a woman's voice called out as the man was about to swing the pipe down onto Sonny's face.

With the pipe suspended above him, Sonny saw a shadow moving over and felt a needle prick his neck.

"Who's been a naughty boy then?" was the last thing he heard before drifting into unconsciousness.

***

WHEN HE WOKE again with a groggy head, he could tell it was business as usual. He was back in the bed, naked, with his arms and legs restrained.

19

"Look, Lachie, we're home," Greer said as she pulled up outside their house. "Everything will be better now. You wait and see. I've had the decorators in to make sure every trace of those tenants is gone. We have a new kitchen and bathroom. Every room has been painted and the floors re-varnished. There's a ramp for your wheelchair to get in and out of the house, and I've even had a stair lift installed for you, so you can go up and down the stairs." She laughed. "I know you'd prefer to sleep upstairs, and I wouldn't be able to carry you up and down those stairs on my own."

Greer parked the car in the driveway and climbed out, walking around to the rear door. She lowered the vehicle ramp and pulled Lachie's wheelchair down onto the front path, noticing that he was dribbling. "Oh, Lachie, poor you. Let's clean you up before the neighbours see you like this. It looks like they're carrying out major refurbishments on one side of us, so there'll be no neighbours there for a while. I hope the building work doesn't disturb you too much."

Greer pulled some tissues out of her bag and dabbed Lachie's chin. She was just about to wheel him up the new ramp to the front door when she was startled by a voice behind her.

"Good morning and welcome home. Greer, isn't it?"

She turned to see her old neighbour, Gordon Haines, standing behind her. He lived on the other side of them. She and Lachie had only bumped into him a few times during their short stay at the house before moving to Australia.

"Yes, good morning, Gordon. Not working today?"

"I'm retired now. My lassie Fiona and her husband have taken over the shop."

"Oh. Well, good for you."

Gordon Haines owned a butcher's shop over on Byres Road. A couple of times, he'd presented them with gifts of beef or lamb joints after closing on Saturday, saying that he wouldn't want to keep them until the following week. Lachie had thought it wonderful when Gordon had given them to him, but Greer had given the joints a good wash before attempting to cook them, as they smelled on the turn to her. They'd survived eating them without incident, so they must have been all right. If Gordon was retired, hopefully, he wouldn't be turning up with any more meat. She didn't want to become too friendly with him or he might think he could while away his retirement hours intruding into their affairs.

"I noticed the wheelchair ramp being put in the other day and saw the company here fitting the stair lift. I hope you don't mind, but I wandered in and had a look around. The builders and decorators have done a good job on your house. I wondered who the stair lift was for when your outgoing tenants said the owners were returning. What's happened to Lachlan?" Gordon nodded towards Lachie's wheelchair.

"He had a serious car accident in Australia. A large semi-trailer with failing brakes rammed into the back of him as they were winding down a mountain road, sending him into the oncoming traffic."

"Semi-trailer? Is that like an articulated lorry?"

"Yes."

"Ah, ouch. I'm sorry to hear that. And it left him with terrible injuries then?"

"Yes, exactly. He spent months in hospital and rehabilitation, but I'm afraid the damage was so severe, he'll never be able to work again. His condition has deteriorated over the past few months, and he can barely speak anymore. Just a word of warning to you—Lachie makes a lot of loud noises some days. I hope he won't disturb you too much. Just ignore anything you hear."

"Oh, aye?"

"Yes. He becomes frustrated at not being able to communicate like he used to. Well, I need to get him settled in now. Nice to see you, Gordon," Greer said, starting to wheel Lachie up to the front door.

"Let me know if you need help with anything," Gordon called out.

"I will, thank you."

Inside the house, Greer parked Lachie in the dining room. "Did you hear that, Lachie? That nosy old bugger has been in here snooping around. We'll have to make sure there's no more of that."

***

GORDON HAINES WATCHED his neighbour drive off in her new car a couple of days following their move back into the house. He'd been surprised when she'd left in the large black vehicle that could accommodate a wheelchair and returned in an Audi. He couldn't see how she could fit a wheelchair in that.

There'd been no sign of her husband Lachlan since their arrival, although, as Greer had mentioned, he'd heard some shouting and thumping coming from one of the back bedrooms when he'd been out in the garden.

Did she keep him cooped up in that bedroom all day? He'd love to have a look in there and see what was going on.

20

I NDIA WOKE FROM a dream where she'd been holding the
body of a woman and calling out her name. Real tears
were sliding down her face.

"Bad dream?" Rob asked, rolling over and taking her
in his arms.

"Yes. I was dreaming about holding Cate Rossi,
thinking she was dead."

"Well, she's not, is she? Not that we've heard anyway.
You read an article about her remarrying many years
back, didn't you? Strange that you should be dreaming
about her now after all these years."

"I know," she said, wiping her eyes. "I've never had a
dream about her before."

They'd both worked on a case which involved Cate
Rossi twelve years ago; indeed, it was through that case
they'd met. While she'd thought about Cate from time to
time, India hadn't had any further contact with her and
certainly never dreamt about her. Strange. However,
all thoughts of Cate vanished from her mind as Rob
began kissing her, and they were soon lost in the throes
of passion.

***

IT WAS WHILE India was sitting at her desk several hours later, looking at the landscape behind Sonny Day in the photograph Chrys had received, that the connection clicked. She knew where she'd seen this scenery before. She was sure of it. The last time she'd met Cate Rossi was just before Christmas in 2002. Cate had chatted about her trip to Scotland with a friend and shared some of the snaps she'd taken on that holiday. A few of them showed a similar image of a lake with a small island in the background. Could that be it? But Scotland? Sonny Day was supposed to be in Sweden. According to custom records, he'd entered the country at the beginning of May and had not left again.

The police in Stockholm had had no success in tracing Day's whereabouts. Their inquiries into the two women who'd been on holiday in Australia had produced no leads. The Swedish police confirmed the women were a couple and claimed to have never met Sonny Day. No marriage records in his name existed. In the end, the police suggested that Sonny was either living under the radar in Sweden or had slipped across a border into Norway, Finland or Denmark without their knowledge. Checks with those authorities also drew a blank. Sonny Day had vanished off the face of the earth.

If India's recollection was correct, Sonny wasn't in Scandinavia at all, but then how could he have travelled to Scotland? She left her office and walked out to the main room that housed the detectives and admin staff on her team. Only Jacko and Dale were there; the additional admin person they'd been allocated had been transferred back to Richmond.

"I need to make some inquiries regarding the background scenery in the Sonny Day photograph that Chrys Waters received," she told Jacko. "If I am right, the photograph was taken in Scotland."

"Scotland? How did you come to that conclusion?"

"I'll come back to you on that. I need to do some digging first. I might be wrong. What I'd like you to do is contact immigration in the UK and find out if Sonny Day entered the country at any time from May this year. We know he entered Sweden, but we have no idea where he went after that. Do you still have that footage of him from Sydney airport?"

"Yes, of course. It's entered in the system, and there's a hard copy in the case file."

"Well, see if the techies can blow up a still shot from it to send to the UK authorities. I know it's a bit grainy, but it might prove useful. Where's Naomi?" she asked, looking around.

"DC Partinger is out questioning staff from the firm that was involved in the smash and grab raid last night," Dale said.

India nodded her thanks to Dale before turning back to Jacko. "You told me earlier you were both going to do that."

"Partinger suggested she take one of her uniform buddies—you know that other female constable based here?—and Sergeant Warren agreed, so I left them to it." Jacko shrugged.

"What are you planning to do today if you're not dealing with the smash and grab raid?"

"Last night, I was reading over some of the statements taken from families in properties near to where we found our unidentified corpse, and I picked up an interesting point. One of the women interviewed said something about all the houses immediately around them were owner-occupied, unlike the houses down on Pitt Town Road, most of which are rentals. I thought I might take a drive out there and look at houses near the junction of King Road. We didn't cover there. Dale's marked a few properties out on the map, and she's trying to find out who pays the rates on them."

"What relevance do you think rental properties would have to our body?"

"The woman also stated that word had got around amongst the neighbours, who have all been there many years, that the derelict property had been sold. She didn't say so, but the inference was that no one who knew about the sale would have buried a body there. I thought that renters might not have heard about the sale because they wouldn't necessarily be part of the local grapevine and would think the derelict property would be a good place to dump a body."

"Okay. It's worth a look. I'm going to follow up on my inquiry, but can you chase up with UK immigration before you go?"

"Righto. No worries."

**

INDIA RETRIEVED HER copy of the old case file that involved Cate Rossi and retreated to her office. Cate's father would be in his sixties now. Did he still work? She dialled the home number first, and when it went to answer phone, she hung up. Next, she dialled his work number.

"May I speak to Howard Brant?" she asked when the operator answered.

"Whom may I say is calling please?"

She hesitated. Should she give just her name or rank?

"Hello?"

"Yes, tell him it's Detective Inspector India Hargreaves."

"One moment, please."

She was placed on hold with the sound of piped music until a few moments later, Howard Brant's voice boomed in her ear.

"What can I do for you, Detective Hargreaves?"

"I don't know if you remember me. I—"

"I know who you are," Brant cut her off.

"I'd like to meet up with Cate and need a contact number for her."

"You're not going to be raking up all that old stuff again, are you? She's married with a husband, children and a different life now."

"No, I'm not. Cate showed me a photograph from when she was on holiday with her friend in Scotland, and I wondered if I could have a look at it. It concerns a case I'm currently working on."

Satisfied that she was not going to be delving into the old case, Howard Brant gave her Cate's contact details: a landline and mobile number. She thanked him and rang off before remembering to ask Brant what Cate's married name was.

She tapped in the mobile number first. A familiar voice answered after a few rings.

"Hello, is that Cate?"

"Yes."

"It's Detective India Hargreaves here. I wondered if there was any chance we might meet up briefly today."

She explained her reasons for wanting to meet, and
Cate suggested she join her for lunch, saying that she
worked from home as she had an eight-month-old baby.
She gave India her address, and they arranged to meet
at twelve-thirty.

21

INDIA PULLED UP outside a large modern property that sat near the water's edge at Five Dock, a suburb she'd never been to before, which consisted of a range of forties, fifties and sixties houses and larger twenty-first-century houses situated on generous plots. It was the kind of area where young people bought a site with an old house, demolished it and built one of the larger, swanky new houses that families preferred these days. Developers had moved in, replacing some of the old stock with blocks of flats which rose a couple of storeys.

At least they aren't skyscrapers like in some parts of Sydney, India thought. The local planners must have a height restriction on domestic buildings. She and Rob lived in an old single-storey weatherboard, where they'd modernised its interior rather than demolishing and rebuilding, like some of their friends. Cate's house, rising two levels, looked impressive, and India wondered if Cate, who was an architect, had designed it.

Cate welcomed her with a brief peck on the cheek and a hug, leading her through to a light-filled, open-plan space that housed the living room, dining room and kitchen.

"You're looking well," India told her. It was true. Cate, a similar age to her, looked beautiful. Unlike her. India hated looking in the mirror these days. She didn't like the face she saw there—a face no longer in the bloom of youth and starting to show its age. Make-up might have helped, but she rarely applied any, except when she and Rob had a special function to attend.

"You're looking well yourself," Cate said. "You don't look a day older than when I last saw you."

India ignored the compliment, knowing it wasn't true.

"Your house is lovely," she said instead, as they walked through into the kitchen. "Did you design it?"

"Partially. It's a mixture of plans Marco had drawn up to build our dream home in Glenwood and alterations I made to suit us." Cate was referring to her first husband, who had died in tragic circumstances.

"Your family?" India pointed to a large colour photograph that hung on the wall, pausing a moment to take it in.

"Yes. My husband Sam, our daughter Katie, who is six, and our son Lewis, who is almost nine months old now but was only six months old when that was taken."

They both stood in silence looking at the photograph. India was mentally calculating that one of the children she'd lost would have been about Katie's age now.

"I lost a baby in between Katie and Lewis, miscarrying at four months," Cate said. "Do you have children yourself?"

"No. I've miscarried a few also. Rob and I are still hopeful that we'll have children."

"I'm sorry to hear that. I know what it feels like."

"Yes," India said, clearing her throat in an attempt to suppress the emotions that were threatening to bring on tears. Cate had not only experienced a miscarriage but her first child had died when he was only a few months old. India knew only too well how devastated Cate had been and, at the time, couldn't imagine how she felt.

After experiencing a few miscarriages, she now had an inkling of what Cate had been through.

"What would you like to drink?" Cate asked. "I've set some filtered water on the table with a light lunch. Or there's various juices I could make."

"Make? Do you mean with a juicing machine or a hand juicer?"

"Either. I have both."

"Wow. Water is fine, thanks. I know your time will be precious with a young one to look after."

"My sister has taken Lewis back to her place, so we won't be disturbed."

"Still, I'm happy with water, thanks."

"Okay. Let's eat, and then we can look at these photographs."

The light lunch consisted of a range of cold meats, cheeses, coleslaw that looked homemade, lettuce, tomatoes and fresh beetroot. There was also a fresh loaf of wholemeal style bread. It was far more sophisticated than India's usual lunch fare, and she tucked in.

"This bread is delicious," she commented after a few mouthfuls. "Is the bakery nearby? I might pick up a loaf on my way back."

"It's an organic spelt loaf, and there is no bakery. I made it myself this morning."

"You made this?" she asked, incredulous. "I would've thought with two young children and your work, making bread was the last thing you'd have time for!"

"I have a bread maker, which simplifies the job. I just put the mix in and leave it to get on with it."

"Mmm. It's delicious. Perhaps I'll have to invest in a bread maker myself."

**

OVER COFFEE, CATE produced the photographs she'd shown India all those years ago. They depicted Cate and her friend Alan at various sites in Scotland. Several photographs in, India spotted what she was looking for.

"These are the ones I wanted to see." They showed Cate and Alan standing on a terrace with a lake behind them, with further individual ones of Cate or Alan alone in the same spot. An island in the centre of the lake was visible in the background.

She pulled out the blown-up copy of the Sonny Day photograph and compared it to Cate's shots.

"I would say this was taken in roughly the same location, wouldn't you?" she asked Cate.

"Looks very much like it to me, although your image is a bit blurred. That looks like Inchmurrin." Cate pointed to the small island.

"Where were your photographs taken?"

"Hmm. If my memory serves me correctly, the name of the place we stayed in was Arden—on the shores of Loch Lomond. I think there were towns called Helensburgh and Alexandria nearby. One was on the coast, the other not far from the base of the loch. I couldn't tell you which was which, though. We rented a two-bedroom cabin there for a few days."

India pulled out her notepad and made a note of it. "Would you mind if I took a shot of your photographs on my phone so that I can prove to my colleagues that I'm not making it up."

"Of course."

While India was doing that, Cate pulled out some further photographs to show her. "This was Alan last year. He came out to visit us. Sadly, they will be the last photos of him I shall ever have. He died back in February this year."

"I'm sorry to hear that."

"He died peacefully while dozing in front of the fire one night when his granddaughter was visiting. He'd just turned eighty-one. Not that old really, but I somehow expected him to live for many more years. We had talked about all of us going over in another year or two to stay with him. We still might go over to the UK sometime— my great-aunt and her husband live near Alan's old place—but we haven't made any plans as yet."

They chatted for a further ten minutes before India reluctantly explained she had to get back to the station. Cate stepped forward to give her a hug as they parted, reminding India of their last farewell back in December 2002.

As she drove away, India realised tears were streaming down her face. She'd been pleased Cate was settled with a new life, but seeing her again reminded her of what both women had lost—the loss of loved ones and babies who had never been born. If Rob and she had a child, it would be blonde like Cate's baby son Lewis. India had been almost white-blonde as a child, which had mellowed to a silvery blonde in her teens. She'd lightened it from a bottle for some years to avoid teasing from friends about having 'grey' hair. Now she'd let it return to its natural colour—an ash blonde with odd grey strands emerging—whereas Rob was more of a honey blonde. He had a few grey strands appearing here and there too, especially around his temples, which gave him a distinguished look.

She'd noticed Cate's son had brown eyes like his father, while any baby India and Rob had was likely to have blue eyes, seeing as hers were blue and Rob's were a greyish-blue. She imagined those blue eyes looking at her from a large portrait similar to the one in Cate's house but hanging on their walls instead. Would it ever happen for them?

22

"How did it go?" Jacko asked India on her return to the station.

"How did what go?" Her mind was still preoccupied with babies.

"The inquiries you planned to make looking into the Sonny Day photo—linking it to Scotland."

"Oh, yes, sorry. I was right. I'll show you."

She pulled out the enlarged image from the Sonny Day photograph and then opened her phone to show the shot of Alan Mathers in a similar location, placing them on Jacko's desk. Naomi joined them to compare the images.

"You're right," Naomi said. "They look like they were taken in the same location. Where is that?"

"A place called Arden on Loch Lomond in Scotland. So, the Sonny Day letter is a pack of lies. He's not in Sweden at all."

"But the letter was posted in Sweden, wasn't it?" Jacko said.

"Yes. It showed a clear postmark from Stockholm. Someone must have travelled there to post it. Naomi, can you see what comes up on a search for cabins to rent in the Arden area? We need to make contact with the owners of the site and see if anyone called Sonny Day rented one."

"Do you want me to pass on what I find or make the call myself?"

"I'd like you to deal with it."

Naomi nodded and returned to her desk to begin the search.

Turning to Jacko, India asked, "Was your trek out to Pitt Town Road successful?"

"It looks like there are a few small weekender houses there, but there were a couple of larger ones as well. I knocked on a few doors, but no one was home. Dale's tracked the ratepayer details on one of the larger houses. I was about to make a call when you came back in."

"What about your inquiries with UK customs? Any sign of Day entering the UK?"

"No. They have no record of him entering the UK."

"So how did he end up in Scotland? First, he flies out to Dubai, spends several days there, doing what, we don't know. Then he flies on to Stockholm and disappears. Now he's in Scotland. How did he travel from Sweden to Scotland without the UK authorities picking him up?"

"Perhaps he has a second passport in a phoney name?" Jacko suggested.

"I can't see Sonny Day having an illegal passport. Everything we've learned about him indicates he is completely straight so wouldn't be involved in something like that."

"You never know," Jacko said.

"Hmm. No, the information Naomi picked up in Penrith all points to someone *using* Day's passport. Chrys Waters was also convinced it couldn't have been him. We have a character who doesn't speak very clear English and doesn't have an Australian accent booking a ticket in Sonny Day's name. Yes, Day might have been putting on an act, but isn't it more likely that someone was pretending to be him? There was all that business of no longer having a bank account when we know he did. The man certainly had Day's ID. I think the travel agent in Penrith identified him incorrectly. But who is he? That's what we need to find out. Our mystery man may have entered Scotland using another passport."

"How are we going to find out?" Jacko asked.

"Maybe the owners of the cabins will provide us with the answer."

***

"I SENT THE Sonny Day photograph over to the owners of the cabins, but they didn't recognise him. They've had numerous renters since their season started back in April, but no one by the name of Day," Naomi related the following morning. "I've just hung up from speaking to a Mrs. Douglas, the owner of the site. Perhaps he was visiting someone there?"

"Hmm. Maybe. I've been talking to the police in Sweden again," India told Jacko and Naomi. "They said only an EU national could pass through the borders of the UK without it being registered. An Australian passport would be registered, like Sonny Day's was when he entered Sweden. So it's likely that Sonny Day entered the UK on a different passport, unless he was smuggled in somehow."

"How could he be smuggled in?"

"They suggested various means, but boat was the most likely. They said it could have been in a vehicle on a ferry or on a private boat. I've looked into ferry crossings from Europe and Scandinavia to the UK. God, it's like a minefield with so many crossings.

But interestingly, there is only one direct route from Sweden to the UK. It goes from Gothenburg to a place called Immingham on the Lincolnshire coast. Lincolnshire is in the northeast of England. From there, he could have driven up to Scotland. There are ferries from the same place in Lincolnshire to Norway and Denmark as well. Otherwise, the only ferries from the UK to Europe run to France, Belgium or the Netherlands. There's also a ferry from Bergen in Norway that goes to the Shetland Islands. From the Shetland Islands, he could travel to mainland Scotland. If he travelled on a private boat, he could have landed anywhere on the UK coast."

"But surely he couldn't have got past UK border customs?"

"People are apparently smuggled into the UK on a regular basis. The question is, why would he need to be?"

23

Eric Andersson stepped off the Bergen Ferry at Lerwick in the Shetland Islands, relieved to be home. It was more than three years since he'd last walked on this soil, and he was looking forward to surprising his mother with his visit.

His mother had inherited her parents' home just outside Lerwick over a decade ago. At the time, she'd been living in Glasgow, so Erik's older sister Thea and her husband Ross—her childhood sweetheart—took on the house. Then, four years ago, when Thea and Erik's father died, their mother returned to Lerwick and opened the house as a bed and breakfast. Thea, Ross and their children had moved into Ross's croft, although Erik knew Thea helped run the bed and breakfast business, which was open from April until October.

As he trekked out of Lerwick, Erik hoped his mother would have room to put him up. August was traditionally a busy month, and he didn't fancy staying with his sister. They'd never got on, and the croft cottage was tiny.

When he arrived at the house, he walked around the side to enter the kitchen at the back.

"Hello, Midder," he called, stepping through the kitchen door.

"Ah, Erik lad, you surprised me there. What brings you here? I didna know you were back from Australia."

Erik felt deflated at his mother's casual greeting after all this time. She was no doubt annoyed he'd not been in touch more regularly since he'd departed for Australia. He walked over to give her a kiss and a hug, which she accepted with indifference and without kissing or hugging him in return.

"I bin back a few weeks now," he told her. "Travellin' around, catchin' up wi' friends. I joos' came from Bergen."

"What friends would you have in Bergen? It's bin more than fifteen year since we lived there."

"Some ol' schoolfriends."

"You didna like Australia?"

"I liked it well enough. It was too hot though, ye ken. I missed our Scottish weather."

"But you complained 'bout it all the time you were here!"

"Yeah, I ken. The summers out there were too hot and the winters cold, but they dinna heat their houses. It was freezin'. I suffered nearly all year long. Too hot, too cold. Anyway, I'm back now. Any tay on the go, and can ya put me up for a bit?"

"You're not runnin' from the law now, are you?"

"No. How can you ask me that? I joos' want to spend some time wi' me family."

"You can have that peerie room off the kitchen here," she said, pointing. "I sleep in there sometimes if we have a lot of bookings. The bed is all made up ready."

"Takk, mamma."

"You're not in Norway now, lad."

"Sorry. *Thank you, Mother*," he said with exaggeration.

***

"WHAT DOES ERIK want? Thea asked her mother the next morning after he'd left to walk into Lerwick.

"I dinna ken, lass. He says he just wants to spend some time wi' his family."

"I doubt it. He always has an agenda. Has he asked you for money?"

"No. He offered *me* some. Not a lot, you ken, just a few hundred pounds, from his savings. Insisted that I take it—says he owes me."

"It's true, he does. I hope you took it."

"I did," she said, nodding.

"How long is he staying?"

"I canna tell ya. He's offered to do a few jobs fer me around the place, ya ken?"

"Let's hope it's not for too long or he's likely to get into some sort of trouble. He's just like Dad. Trouble follows him around."

***

ERIK SAT AT the bar contemplating his next move after he left Shetland. He would have liked to stay, but there was no work for him here. He'd been asking around all morning. Apart from doing a few jobs for his mother, there was nothing else he could do. He'd considered starting up a business as a handyman—there were lots of little building jobs he could do—but his mother had told him there were enough handymen available on the island. It wouldn't be wise for him to stay, as he knew only too well that he'd drink away the money he still had in his pocket.

He hadn't lied to his mother; he *had* looked up some old schoolfriends in Bergen. They were married with families. One of them ran the family engineering works and had offered him a job cleaning up the workshop of an evening, but that wasn't for him. He'd been envious of his old schoolfriends with their steady jobs and happy families—especially Lars. The lucky bugger had walked into the family business without having to worry about looking for work. As an only child, Lars would inherit the business and was set for life. Luck like that had never come Erik's way. His father hadn't been up to much, and Erik was worried he was turning out to be very like him. The drink was his downfall. He was aware of that. Why did he find it so hard to give it up? He'd managed for those few days in the Middle East on his way home. Why couldn't he do it here? Erik sighed and ordered another whisky.

His drinking had started soon after the family had moved to Glasgow. First, it was boozy parties with his new schoolfriends, trying to impress and show that he could keep up with the best of them. His first jobs on building sites meant a drink in the pub after knocking off work each night. It became a habit, one that he found difficult to break, especially when he was living on his own. Pubs offered warmth and the possibility of comradeship. It was impossible for him to walk past one when he knew there'd be some pals—or 'mates' as the Aussies would say—in there he could chat with. His problem was that he took things too far, drank so much he could barely walk. He needed a woman at home to temper his intake.

He'd phoned his ex-partner Lisa last night, and she seemed pleased to hear from him. She wasn't seeing anyone at the moment and said she'd love to meet up with him. He'd told her he was staying in Shetland with his family for a while and would contact her if he came to Glasgow. He was sure Lisa would let him crash at her place, now her two daughters had left home. That was one option open to him.

Another option was Mrs. McEvoy. Although he'd completed all the jobs he'd been given, Erik was sure they weren't finished yet. He'd managed to pick up her home address without her realising, and that was where he thought he might head to next. Maybe in another few days.

24

GORDON HAINES WAITED until he saw his neighbour drive off. She was all dressed up this morning, so he would've bet that she wasn't just popping down to the shops. She must have had an appointment for something, maybe a job interview, but he couldn't see how she could go off to work all day and leave her husband at home alone. He'd still seen no sign of Lachlan since the day they'd arrived, and weeks had passed now. He just knew something wasn't right. Today, he was determined to look into the rear bedroom window—the room where he thought Lachlan slept. He intended to take his long ladder in, and if she happened to arrive home while he was there in the middle of doing it, he'd say he was cleaning her gutters. He'd mentioned the gutters to her last week and offered to clean them for her, but she'd thanked him and declined. A good thing as well. He wasn't too keen on climbing tall ladders. But needs must.

Gordon unhooked his extension ladder from the side wall where he kept it and carried it further up the garden. With a smaller ladder he'd set leaning against the wall, he climbed up, lifted the extension ladder over the wall, lowered it into next door's garden, and then climbed down. So far so good.

He carried the ladder across to the back of the house, taking it up onto the terrace. There were some large pots standing where he wanted to position the ladder, and so, after resting it against the terrace, he dragged the pots out of the way. He could see that the curtains of the room were closed with a small gap in the centre.

Leaning the ladder carefully against the wall, he positioned it across the middle of the windows so he should be able to see in through the gap in the curtains. He unclipped the extensions and locked them in place. Making sure it was anchored securely to the ground, he began to climb. A coughing fit caught him halfway up; he paused to take out his handkerchief, cleared his throat and wiped his nose. Returning the handkerchief to his pocket, he resumed climbing.

At the window, he stopped and peered in. The room was in darkness, and he wasn't able to make out much. He'd wait a minute until his eyes adjusted.

He was just about to check it again when he felt the ladder begin to move. Looking down, he could see a man standing below him with his hands on the ladder. The man looked like Lachlan, which he thought very strange because he didn't think Lachlan was able to walk. Perhaps he'd misunderstood. Greer had said he'd been in an accident, but she didn't say how disabled he was. Gordon had seen the wheelchair and the stair lift being installed and made an assumption about Lachlan not being able to walk. Maybe he could hobble around.

"Is that you, Lachlan?" he asked.

"Aye," the man said before pulling the ladder away from the wall and knocking it sideways.

Gordon screamed as he fell, clinging to the ladder in the hope the terrace railings would halt the fall. The ladder hit the railings, somersaulted over them and smashed him against the brick boundary wall before it bounced off and dropped into the garden, flinging him aside like a rag doll.

Before he lost consciousness, Gordon managed to turn his head and look back up to the terrace where the ladder had been leaning against the wall. He expected to see Lachlan or someone who would come to his rescue, but there was no one there. He hadn't imagined him, had he?

***

GREER WAS STANDING in the living room next to Lachie's wheelchair, having not long arrived home, when there was a pounding on her front door. She didn't answer it immediately, as there were some precautionary measures to be taken first. The pounding continued, and she heard a woman's voice shouting.

When she was ready, she walked out to answer it and found a very distressed woman standing there.

"I'm sorry—" Greer started to say before the woman cut her off.

"I'm Fiona, Gordon's daughter. My father is lying in your garden. What is he doing there? Didn't you realise he had been injured?"

"What on earth are you talking about?"

"My father is *lying* in your garden!" Fiona shouted. "I've rung for an ambulance."

Greer stared dumbfounded for a moment, unable to take in what this woman—Fiona—was saying. Gordon was lying in her garden? Finally, the woman's words registered.

"Oh my God. He must have been cleaning the gutters. He offered to do it last week, and I said no. The silly man! Sorry, come through." Greer stepped aside and gestured.

They moved swiftly through the house, out of the back door and down to the garden. There, just as Fiona had said, lay Gordon. Greer and Fiona ran over to him, Fiona kneeling and calling, "Dad, Dad!"

Greer knelt on his other side and felt his neck for a pulse. There was nothing.

"I'm afraid he's gone," she told Fiona.

"What do you mean, *gone*?"

"He's dead."

"He can't be! You've made a mistake. Can you go and meet the paramedics? I can hear the siren now!"

That was the last thing Greer wanted to deal with. Paramedics. Next it would be the police. Lachie was going to become agitated by it all. Best if she gave him a sedative.

She returned to the house in time to meet the paramedics running up the front steps. "He's in the garden with his daughter," she said. "I'll leave you to it. I need to see to my husband."

***

MUCH TO GREER's irritation, the police sergeant arrived as the pathologist was removing his scene-of-crime suit in the hallway. From the kitchen window, she'd been able to watch all the activity in the garden. Two police officers were still out there. The paramedics had radioed back to base to tell them the man they had attended was deceased, but it required a medical practitioner to confirm this, and so the pathologist had been called in. Two hours had passed since Gordon's hysterical daughter had arrived at her door, and she could see this stretching long into the evening. She couldn't have that; Lachie had been neglected all day as it was.

It had been like Piccadilly Circus with all the comings and goings of different people. As well as the police officers, there were two scene examiner technicians outside who worked for the Scottish Police Authority.

Without speaking to her, the sergeant walked out into the garden after conferring with the pathologist. He returned a short time later looking at his notes. "I'm sorry," he said, "I don't appear to have your name."

She watched, distracted, as the scene examiner technicians walked through with the extension ladder. Why were they taking that?

"Ma'am?"

"Sorry. Doctor Greer Hamilton."

"A medical doctor?"

"Yes," Greer confirmed.

"I have a few questions for you, Doctor Hamilton."

"Yes, I'm sure. Can we go through to the kitchen? I don't want to disturb my husband too much."

The sergeant followed Greer into the kitchen diner, and she gestured for him to sit at the table. He said he would prefer to stand; Greer sat, as her legs were a little wobbly.

"As a medical practitioner, you will be aware that Mr. Haines's death falls into the category of a police reportable death."

Greer nodded.

"Standard operating procedures in this instance will be that I shall be gathering information to pass on to a police inspector at the Scottish Fatalities Investigation Unit. He will compile a report to be sent to the Crown Office Procurator Fiscal Service."

"Yes. I am aware of the procedures," Greer said.

"It will then be determined whether any further action is required. Now, the deceased, Mr. Gordon Haines, your neighbour—had you arranged for him to come in this morning to do some work for you?"

"Certainly not. Last week, he mentioned my rear gutters needed clearing out and offered to see to it, but I wouldn't consider it. I told him I would find a company to come in to do the whole guttering."

"So why do you think he was on your terrace climbing up his long ladder?"

"I have no idea. How do you know that's what he was doing? When his daughter and I found him, he was lying in our garden with an extended ladder open, yes, but I wasn't here this morning, so I couldn't tell you if he had attempted to climb the ladder. Couldn't he have fallen as he climbed over the fence or something?"

"Not according to the pathologist. He believes Mr. Haines fell from a great height, and we found marks where the ladder base was standing against your wall. He also appears to have moved some large tubs of plants."

"I see. Well, I don't know what the silly man was doing. Perhaps he wanted it to be a surprise. I gained the impression that he was bored with his retirement. He didn't have enough to do. He kept saying to let him know if I needed help with anything."

"And did you ask him for help at all?"

Greer paused. The odd lie wasn't going to hurt anyone. Besides, Gordon was dead and couldn't refute it anyway. "He sat in with my husband to keep him company a couple of times when I had to go out for some shopping, but I didn't ask him. He offered."

"And he didn't offer to come in to sit with your husband this morning when you went out?"

"No. I hadn't seen him. I thought I'd only be out for an hour or so."

"Could I ask where you went this morning?"

"I had a job interview at the Gartnavel General Hospital."

"Wouldn't having a job be bit difficult with your husband as he is?" The sergeant pointed to Lachie, who was parked in his wheelchair near the front window.

"I haven't worked for months now and need to get back to it to bring some much-needed money into the household. I planned to hire a carer to come in and attend to my husband's needs a few times a day once I started work."

"What time did you leave the house this morning?"

"It was about nine-thirty. My appointment was at ten."

"And what time did you return?"

"About eleven-fifty. I'd only been home for a minute when Gordon's daughter pounded on the door. She'd spotted her father lying in our garden. I had no idea he was out there."

"Mr. Haines must have entered your property shortly after you left this morning, as the pathologist believes he'd been lying there for some time."

"As I say, I couldn't tell you. I wasn't here."

"We'll need a contact name at the hospital, someone who can verify you attended the appointment."

Greer sighed. She collected her handbag from the living room, saying, "Sorry, Lachie, I will be with you in a minute."

She retrieved a letter from her bag with the appointment time and passed it to the sergeant, who made a note of the details.

At that moment, two other suited men entered the house carrying a stretcher. The body collectors, Greer surmised. At least they would be removing that thing from her garden.

"Now, if that's everything, I'm sorry, but I do need to attend to my husband," Greer said, standing and moving towards the living room. "He's missed his lunch. We both have."

"Just one last question," the sergeant said, following her. "Did you see anyone on the building site next door this morning?"

"No. The builders haven't been there for a few days now. It's been blissfully quiet. Of course, someone might have turned up there after I left this morning."

"Well, thank you, Doctor Hamilton, and we're sorry to have bothered you, but as you can appreciate, with a sudden death like this, we need to gather all the facts. I think it's unlikely, as it seems as though it was an unfortunate accident, but we may need to contact you again."

"Yes, yes, I understand."

Greer watched as the morticians passed through the house with the loaded stretcher, followed by the police officers. One of them diverted into the lounge entrance and whispered something to the sergeant. Lachie was jerking around in his chair and making noises.

"Oh, Lachie, I'm sorry. The police will be leaving in a minute, and I will fix us something nice to eat."

"Does he understand what's happening?" the sergeant asked.

"I'm sure he does. He just isn't able to communicate very well. I'll see you out," she said, walking them to the door.

Once they were gone, Greer closed the shutters in the living room and pulled out her phone. She tapped in Miguel's number on the direct line he'd given her. It went straight to messages. Should she leave one? Deciding things had now become more urgent, she spoke into the phone. "Hi, Miguel. Greer here. There's been a bit of a development. We need to move things forward if you can."

After disconnecting, Greer pushed Lachie over to the stairs, pulled him up from the chair, strapped him into the stair lift and sent it up. Once upstairs, she transferred Lachie into his spare chair and wheeled him into the bedroom, closing the door behind her.

"Just what the hell do you think you were doing?" she shouted. "Now look what you have done!"

25

F IONA KINLEY HAD been very distressed when the
police had spoken to her the previous afternoon.
She'd spent the night and this morning crying, then
decided to come over to her parents' house to feel closer
to them.

Now, sitting with a cup of tea looking out the front
living room window, she thought back to the discussions
she'd had with the police.

They'd told her that her father had offered to clean the
neighbour's gutters, but Doctor Hamilton had turned his
offer down. Surely that was a lie? He didn't even clean
his own gutters—he got a man he knew to do them—
so why would he offer to clean *their* gutters?

Doctor Hamilton, the police told her, had left the
house earlier in the morning and had no idea that her
father had entered her property. That, she could well
believe. She'd seen Doctor Hamilton's car pull into the
driveway as she was entering her father's house. Her
father hadn't answered when she called out to him.
She'd noticed the back door was open and had gone into
the garden, assuming he was there, to find he'd propped
one of his ladders against the shared garden wall. She'd
called out to him a few more times before she'd climbed
the ladder and seen him lying in next door's garden.
But why had he really gone in there? She didn't believe
it was to clean the gutters.

She remembered him going on about the woman's husband a few weeks back, saying he hadn't seen him and was worried something strange was going on. Fiona hadn't taken much notice, but she had asked her father to explain what he meant. He said he thought something had happened to the husband. Perhaps he'd gone in there to have a snoop? But then the policeman told her last night that her father had gone in to sit with the husband a couple of times when Doctor Hamilton had to go out. If that was the case, he would have known the husband was fine.

He'd not mentioned sitting with the husband, and Fiona was sure he would have, as every time she saw him, he gave her detailed accounts of how he filled his days. Why wouldn't he have mentioned a visit next door? It made no sense. Unless he hadn't wanted to admit he'd been wrong. Her father was one of those people who always had to be right. *If* he had been next door, it could only have happened in the last couple of weeks since he first mentioned his concerns. And if he'd been in on other days, why would he feel there was a need to snoop yesterday?

Fiona had seen the husband yesterday when she'd entered the house and again later when she was led out by the paramedics. She'd been in shock at the time and not really taken anything in. But, thinking back on it this morning, she remembered the husband was sitting in his wheelchair, head bent forward and dribbling down the front of his clothes. The poor sod. And that poor woman having to look after someone in his condition. At least she was a doctor and probably knew how to best care for him.

Should she contact the police and tell them of her father's concerns? Should she tell them that he never cleaned his own gutters and would never have cleaned the neighbour's? It would be so shameful to admit her father might have been sticking his nose into someone else's business. She could just imagine the headline in the local paper: *Man falls to death while attempting to spy on neighbours*.

There was nothing suspicious about his death. The doctor who had formally pronounced it had said he believed it was a tragic accident. Dad had been out there on his own. The silly bugger. *No*, Fiona decided. She didn't want to sully her father's name. It was best to leave it alone.

26

Wilberforce, NSW

DETECTIVE SERGEANT JACKO pulled up outside the house, relieved to see there were lights on and a car parked in the driveway. It was the third time he'd been to the property trying to speak to the occupants. The local council had given him the ratepayer's name: Reuben Fletcher. There had been no telephone listing for him in the directory, and this was the last property Jacko had to tick off his list. He left the car, walked along the path and up onto the porch, where an outside light illuminated the whole front garden. Seeing no bell, he knocked heavily on the metal fly-screen door.

"Who is it?" a woman's voice called from inside.

"My name is Detective Sergeant Jacko, from the Windsor Police. I'd like to ask you a few questions."

The door swung open, and a harassed-looking young woman with a toddler clinging to her legs stepped up to the screen door.

"Can you show me your identification, please? I'm on my own here." She added, "Although my husband is due back any time."

Jacko had his ID ready to show and pushed it up against the screen door.

"How can I help you?" she asked, not inviting him in.

"Are you Mrs. Fletcher?"

"No. There's no one by that name living here."

"I obtained the name Fletcher from Hawkesbury City Council as the ratepayer at this address."

"Oh, that might be our landlord. I don't know his name. We don't pay the rates. We're just renters. The agent could tell you."

"How long have you lived here?"

"We moved in over the weekend of the third and fourth of May this year."

"Would you know the name of the previous tenants?"

"No. Oh, hang on a minute. There was some junk mail with the name McEvoy on it. The agents could tell you more."

"Who are the letting agents?"

"A company called McPherson in Windsor."

"I know them. Okay, I'll contact them. Thanks for your time."

"Is this anything to do with the body you found up the road a few months ago?"

"Why do you ask that?"

"Just curious. I heard someone in the grocery shop in Wilberforce mentioning it a while back, saying the police were knocking on doors speaking to people who lived in the area."

"Okay. Thanks again for your time," Jacko repeated, deliberately not answering her question. He turned and walked back to his car.

***

"McPHERSON'S REAL ESTATE have confirmed that a Scottish couple called McEvoy rented the property in Pitt Town Road for a little under three years," Jacko told India. "They gave notice in March, saying they were returning home, and vacated the property on the twenty-eighth of April. I checked with customs, and the McEvoy couple flew out of Sydney on the same day. Here's the interesting thing. He's a doctor. A Doctor Kenrick McEvoy. Bit of a coincidence, wouldn't you say? Seeing as we're now looking at Day being in Scotland rather than Sweden?"

"I don't believe in coincidences," India said. "Sonny Day supposedly flew out of Sydney the day before them, going to Sweden. And now he's in Scotland. Have you discovered where their flight terminated and who they flew with?"

"Yes. They flew out with Etihad Airways, and their final destination was Edinburgh, with a change of planes in Abu Dhabi and Manchester. There are no direct flights into Edinburgh. I looked up the online telephone directory in Edinburgh for people called McEvoy, and there's lots of them but no one with his initials. Do you think it's worthwhile getting onto the police and passport control in Edinburgh to see if they can trace them?"

"Yes. It's worth a shot," India said, nodding. "I'll leave that to you then. Good work."

***

JACKO HAD NO luck with the UK border control. The McEvoys' entry into Edinburgh hadn't been registered, but their arrival in Manchester had been—where they cleared customs. They'd then taken an internal flight to Edinburgh. Contact with Police Scotland (as he learned they were called) in Edinburgh had proved interesting. They'd had a pathologist attached to their service with the same name, Doctor Kenrick McEvoy—the man he was looking for. McEvoy had worked for them for a year back in 2010–2011, until he left to move to Australia. Police Scotland had no idea of his current whereabouts. The last known address registered for him had proved to be a rental in the city. Jacko sighed as he completed his report and emailed it to the boss. *One step forward, two steps back* sprang to mind.

27

Scotland
August 2014

Fiona Kinley, Gordon Haines's daughter, had recently moved into her father's house with her husband Fergus. They'd spent their entire married life living on the two floors above the butcher's shop in Byres Road, where she had lived as a young child. Over those twenty years, she and Fergus had regularly considered buying their own house, but with prices so high in their preferred areas, they decided instead to invest their savings in a holiday villa on the Costa Del Sol, where they'd escaped to frequently while her father still ran the shop. With the loss of her father, their daughter away at university in Stirling and their son living in Edinburgh, she and Fergus were now free to consider other options about their future.

As his only child, Fiona had inherited her father's large house on Crown Road. He'd done little to modernise the property, not from lack of money to do so, but because he hadn't wanted to lose the memories of Fiona's mother and so chose to keep the house exactly as it had been when she'd died ten years previously. Fiona and Fergus planned to completely modernise the house.

The improvements were being done in stages so she could project-manage them while still working part time in the shop and living in a semi-habitable house. She'd had builders in drilling and hammering away most days and had imagined she could still hear them long after they'd left—until she realised the noises were not in her imagination at all but were coming from next door. Dull sounds of drilling and banging. They seemed to be doing some work as well, although Fiona had not seen any builders' vehicles or workers entering the house.

Fiona had seen a young man coming and going at different times, and Doctor Hamilton seemed to have a job, as some days she left the house and was gone for many hours. Surely the doctor wouldn't leave her husband alone all day in his condition? Was the man Fiona had seen a nurse?

Her father's death had been ruled an accident, but it still bugged her. Why had he felt the need to investigate his neighbours? She wondered if she should do a little sleuthing herself, just to satisfy her curiosity about what exactly was going on next door.

After watching Doctor Hamilton leave one morning, she waited a suitable time, then walked next door and knocked. The last time she'd been there was the day her father died. There was no immediate answer, and she continued to knock. Eventually, the door was opened by a young man wearing what looked like a carer's uniform. So that answered that question. He was here to look after the husband. He said nothing, waiting for her to speak.

"Good morning, I'm Fiona Kinley, daughter of Doctor Hamilton's neighbour who died here recently. My husband and I have moved in next door. I've called for a couple of reasons. I wanted to let Doctor Hamilton know we'd moved in and also to warn her there will be building work going on over the next few months, but I hear you're doing building work as well."

"We've bin makin' a few adjustments for Lachlan, that's all. No major buildin' work," the man said.

"Oh. Okay. Only I thought I heard a lot of drilling and banging."

"I think you'll find it was comin' from the house on t'other side. They still haven't finished. They seem to stop and start the work. Doctor Hamilton said it had bin goin' on for months."

"Yes, my father mentioned it. Well, that explains it then. Would you tell Doctor Hamilton that unfortunately there will also be a lot of noise coming from our house?"

"I will. Now if that's all, I need to get back t'me patient."

"Sorry to have disturbed you," Fiona said, glancing down at the man's trousers and shoes to see they were covered in some kind of white dust. Without looking at him further, she turned and walked back to her house. If she wasn't mistaken, the dust on his trousers and shoes looked very much like the dust she'd seen on her builders after they'd filled the joints on sheets of plasterboard. *Curious.* Exactly what type of adjustments was this man making in the house?

28

Erik Andersson cursed himself. He was such a loser! His predictable foolish behaviour had gotten him into serious trouble this time. Why on earth had he tried to pick up with this woman again? He should have known better. Why hadn't he taken that job Lars had offered him in Norway? Pride, that's why. He'd wanted something better and thought he'd have an easy life following the path he'd chosen. He wished now he'd stayed in Shetland. Anything would be better than this. Lying helpless and unable to move.

If he was totally honest, he'd never had any luck with women. They always led to his downfall. When he was sixteen and had only been living in Glasgow for a few months, he'd knocked up one of the girls at school. She was never a girlfriend, just some drunk lassie he'd shagged at a party. Her brothers had given him a good beating when they discovered who had fathered the child.

Somewhere out there he had a son. He'd heard from some of the girl's mates it was a boy, but he'd never seen him. The family had packed their daughter off to relatives somewhere, and she never returned to school. Not that he'd had any particular interest in her or the child, but he would have liked to have seen him at least once. He would be about fourteen now, and Erik hoped his son wouldn't make the same mistakes he'd made in life.

He'd only had one true love: Rhoda. He'd met her when he was still a young buck, just twenty-one. Rhoda was stunning, and he congratulated himself every day on having such a beautiful woman to come home to. They'd moved into a tiny flat together after three months of seeing each other. Almost four years, they'd lasted, until Rhoda met a lawyer while out with her friends one night. She started seeing him on the sly and eight weeks later announced she was moving in with this man, stressing that he could fulfil all her dreams, unlike Erik, an unskilled and—at that time—unemployed labourer.

He'd met Lisa on the rebound, soon realising it was a mistake. After that, he'd decided to take off to the other side of the world, to Australia. Another factor that had spurred him to make that decision was the knowledge of how close he'd come to being arrested for drug dealing. Desperate to make some money to splash around and impress women, he'd been drawn into that murky world. He was only dealing a bit of dope, which he didn't consider a serious drug, but the police took a different view. He'd just left the apartment of his supplier when the police raided the premises. It was a close call, and he was worried that Jimmy, his supplier, might pass his name on.

After shifting his final stash with his regulars, he'd taken off to London, worked hard on building sites there, and then applied for a work visa in Australia. Australia had been another mistake. For more than three years, he'd slogged away—again, mainly on building sites— but the money he'd earned slipped through his fingers so swiftly he was often in debt. Australian women didn't take to him; they acted like he was speaking a foreign language, but he thought his luck had changed when he met Mrs. McEvoy.

Now he was in this hopeless situation, unable to move, and he knew he had some serious injuries. His head was pounding, making it difficult for him to think clearly. Why had he drunk so much tonight? It was his own fault. She'd warned him about it. He could hear her footsteps approaching and felt his heart thumping out increasingly rapid beats. He suspected he wouldn't like what he was about to hear.

***

SONNY ROUSED TO hear the woman's voice whispering in his ear.

"It looks like you've done your job, young man. I don't think I'll be needing you for much longer."

What did she mean by that? Was she going to let him go? His hopes were dashed in her next sentence.

"But maybe we'll hang on to you for a bit longer—just in case."

Was this nightmare ever going to end? He knew they'd moved him from the cabin. For some time, he'd been in a room where he could tell he was in a more built-up area. When they removed the headphones from his ears, he could hear the occasional siren in the distance or what sounded like building work.

The woman usually communicated with him in whispers, but there were times when she spoke in her normal voice. There was something familiar about it, but he couldn't connect it to any of his memories.

At one point, he'd been sitting near the front window of a substantial house without his blindfolds, restraints or headphones. His vision was not clear, but he appeared to be looking out onto a suburban street. He'd heard the sound of people coming and going, people talking in rooms nearby, and was sure he'd seen a couple of policemen entering the house. What was happening? He'd tried to call attention to himself, hoping one of these people would come to his aid, but nothing happened. He couldn't speak or move. He thought he must have been in some kind of accident, except the next time he woke, he *was* able to move, so they must have given him some kind of drug that paralysed him.

The woman kept coming up to him and calling him 'lucky'. Lucky was the last thing he was. Unlucky was more like it. Why him? Why had they chosen him for whatever they were up to? Neither the woman nor the man had given him any explanation as to what they wanted with him, why they were keeping him imprisoned like this or where they'd taken him this time. Since his brief steps into the sunlight at the cabin, he'd not been outdoors again. Not that he could recall anyway. They seemed to be keeping him heavily sedated, and he couldn't do a damn thing about it. How long had it been since that last morning he and Chrys had been messing about with their Spanish? It must have been weeks. Months even. He'd completely lost track of time. He didn't have a good feeling about how this nightmare would end.

29

KEVIN ROSSITER, ACTING manager of Fillmore's Funeral Service, looked over the paperwork presented by the widow standing in front of him. It all seemed in order. The widow. My God, what a woman! If circumstances were different... His left eye kept wandering involuntarily to her right breast after her jacket had flapped open to reveal its majestic proportions. She'd walked in wearing a low-cut black dress and a black jacket. He'd been busy noticing her cleavage when the jacket had moved allowing him to see the shape of this one breast in all its glory. Had she done that deliberately?

The wandering eye was something Kevin had been born with, and his parents had never taken the trouble to have it seen to. It was six months into his work at Fillmore's before Mr. Fillmore noticed it. "Your left eye is looking in a different direction to the right one!" he'd declared in astonishment.

"I'm sorry, Mr. Fillmore, it won't happen again. It sometimes happens when I become nervous."

Of course, it had happened on countless occasions, but luckily, the boss had not always noticed it. Kevin had been working there for seven years and now had the role of acting manager in the Fillmores' absence. Mr. Fillmore's elderly mother had died suddenly the previous week, and he and his wife had travelled to Dundee to make arrangements for the funeral and to clear out the elder Mrs. Fillmore's house. Kevin had persuaded Mr. Fillmore that he was more than capable of managing the business in his absence.

"Just don't let that eye of yours wander," Fillmore had said as he climbed into the taxi that was to take them to the airport. He'd meant it literally.

Now the eye was doing exactly that. Kevin raised the clipboard he was holding. The only way he could cope was to block out the view entirely or this woman would be his undoing. At five foot seven, Kevin found he was constantly attracted to women who towered over him — like this one. If he wasn't careful, he would develop an embarrassing bulge. He looked down at his feet and waited a beat until he felt his left eye shift back into place.

He cleared his throat, raised his head and said, "I'm sorry for your loss, Mrs. McEvoy." The clipboard was doing a good job of protecting him. He just had to hold it steady. His left eye was behaving itself. So far.

She nodded in acknowledgement of the sentiments he'd expressed. "He'd been suffering for some time, so perhaps it was a blessing to go this way — peacefully in his sleep."

"But so young…"

"Yes, I know."

"What kind of service will you be having?"

"My husband didn't want a service of any kind. He used to be a pathologist and worked for Police Scotland. He didn't hold any truck with religious nonsense."

"I see. So, what is it you would like from us?"

"We plan to hold a large party to celebrate his life. That's what my husband wanted. I want him to be cremated as soon as possible — without a service — and then I can organise the party. He wants his ashes scattered up in the Highlands, where he is originally from."

"So, what type of casket will you be wanting?"

"He said a pine box will do, seeing as he's going to be cremated. No point in wasting money on a fancy coffin, is there? Or making him look wonderful for friends and family to view. He wanted us to spend the money on a boozy party instead."

"We do have some pine caskets that are in the cheaper range. Would you like to have a look?"

"Yes, of course."

Kevin led the woman into the showroom. He understood why she wanted a pine 'box'—not that they had any of those, but his employers always stressed the importance of selling bereaved family members the most expensive coffin possible. "That's where the extra profit is, Kevin," Mr. Fillmore had told him many times. They could offer cardboard boxes to those whose finances were stretched or those who had expressed a wish to be cremated in a cardboard box to save their relatives unnecessary expense. Those weren't on display or advertised and were only mentioned if the customer raised it themselves or it was obvious they couldn't afford anything else, but even they weren't cheap. This widow, though—she looked like she could afford something fancy.

"This one looks quite simple," she said, walking around one of their plainest pine coffins. "It will do."

Kevin sighed. He knew Mr. Fillmore wouldn't be happy to learn he'd sold a coffin in their cheapest price range while he was away. But that was it. Mr. Fillmore was away, and he was in charge. You couldn't push customers into spending thousands on something they didn't want—or need. Besides, he had persuaded other customers this week to choose some of their more expensive stock.

"Are you sure you wouldn't prefer something a little more...decorative?" Kevin suggested, making one last attempt to increase the sale value.

"Quite sure, thank you. Now, can we settle up on this and make arrangements for the cremation? And how soon could you collect his body?"

"Would this afternoon suit you?"

30

Fergus Kinley was leaving at eight in the morning when he spotted two men carrying what looked like a body out of the house next door. He rushed back in and called to his wife.

"Fiona, come and look at this. It looks like a body is being removed from next door."

"What?"

Fiona had just finished dressing and was still dragging on her cardigan as she hurried out the front door. Fergus was right. Two men placed the 'body' into a black van. A body van. That was what they had sent for her father.

She looked across and saw Doctor Hamilton, clad all in black, standing on the front steps, dabbing her eyes with a handkerchief. Not another death? It must be the husband. Fiona didn't think she'd seen that carer for a few days. Clearly, he wasn't needed now. Fiona walked down the stairs and along to the Hamilton residence.

"Doctor Hamilton? What's happened?" she called out.

The doctor waved Fiona up the steps and seemed keen to take her inside the house. That was a first. Since the night of her father's death eight weeks ago, she'd never been invited into the house. Doctor Hamilton hadn't attended her father's funeral or spoken to her. She merely gave Fiona a curt nod if they saw each other outside their respective houses.

"It's my husband. He died early yesterday. Poor Lachie never recovered from his injuries."

"I'm so sorry to hear that. Dad told me he'd been hit by an articulated lorry or something. Is that right?"

"Yes. Thank you for your condolences. I must check to see they don't need me for anything else," Doctor Hamilton said, moving back outside.

Fiona thought the doctor was behaving strangely, but then death could do that to you. Her father almost had a breakdown when her mother died, and she'd been pretty cut up about her father's death, although it had only affected her mental capacity for the first twenty-four hours. Distraught and tearful, then numb with grief. Following that, she'd been angry with her father for being such a fool.

"Everything is fine," Doctor Hamilton said, returning to the house looking relieved.

"Are they going to do an autopsy on your husband like they did with my father?"

"No. His death has been signed off. He died of a heart attack. Poor Lachie."

"I thought that was the police 'body' van that just took him away."

"It was a private ambulance. A firm the funeral company uses. And the police. They aren't police vehicles."

"Oh. Okay. I noticed your carer hadn't been around for a few days," she said.

Doctor Hamilton raised an eyebrow and looked at her warily. Oh God, it sounded like she spent every waking moment spying from her front window.

"Well, I was off duty this weekend, so I didn't need him. And when Lachie passed, I phoned the carer to tell him what had happened. He won't be coming around again."

"No, I don't suppose you'll be needing him anymore," Fiona said without thinking. "I'm sorry, that didn't come out right."

The doctor nodded. "You're right, though. I won't be needing him again, and Lachie is at peace now."

"Is there anything I can do for you?" Fiona asked, hoping the woman would say no. She wanted to get out of this house, as she was feeling distinctly uncomfortable.

"No, I'm fine, but thank you all the same for your kind offer."

"Well, I'd better get back. The builders will be arriving any moment now." Fiona resisted the urge to run to the door. "Once again, I'm sorry for your loss." She turned and walked out with a calmness she wasn't feeling; it wasn't until she closed the door of her own house that she realised she was holding her breath.

31

At Fillmore's Funeral Service, Kevin Rossiter examined the hands of the late Doctor McEvoy. They were quite callused and rough. He picked up one hand and sniffed it. Hand cream. The man, or possibly the widow, had applied cream to his hands shortly before his death, leaving them with a smoother feel, but there was no hiding the fact that these hands had done some rough work in their lifetime. Surely, he would have worn gloves in his line of work? What on earth could a sick man be doing to cause his hands to be like that? Kevin shrugged. It wasn't his place to be nosing into people's business.

Kevin considered himself an artist. He worked on dead bodies, making them beautiful again for their relatives. Mr. Fillmore had trained him, but he found he had a natural flair for the work. He especially liked working on challenging cases where the deceased had been disfigured in some way as a result of an accident. His skills weren't required in this instance. The doctor was going to the crematorium dressed in his smart suit and no make-up. Kevin always thought it was a shame that such beautiful, expensive clothes were destroyed by the flames. It was different with a burial. You wanted them to look their best. He preferred burials personally, carrying the image of the loved one he'd prepared going into the ground in all their finery, ready for the afterlife or whatever came next.

He completed his tasks, sealed the doctor's coffin and rang the crematorium. When the ashes were ready, he planned to collect them and deliver them in person to the widow. He couldn't resist the idea of one last encounter with her. If luck was on his side, she might invite him to the big party.

***

KEVIN PULLED UP outside Mrs. McEvoy's house. It was an impressive, detached property in a tree-lined street. The McEvoys had clearly not been short of money. He'd left a message with the widow, telling her that he would be dropping off the ashes this evening. When she'd come into the showroom the previous week, she'd told him she would collect them, but it was the least he could do. Besides, she might call in at a busy time when he wouldn't have the opportunity to speak to her for long. In fact, he might miss her altogether if he was busy with another customer and Karen—their admin girl—handed the widow the urn. This way, he would get to spend as much time with her as he needed. The funeral parlour was closed now, and he was in no hurry.

He knocked on the door and waited, praying that his eye would behave itself today.

"Good evening, Mrs. McEvoy," he said when she answered.

"Hello, Mr. Rossiter. I received your message. It was very kind of you to drop the urn by, but you needn't have gone to all this trouble. I did attempt to call you back, but the young woman I spoke to said you had already left. I could have picked it up tomorrow."

She reached out as though to take the urn from him. *No!* He wanted her to invite him into the house. He clung to it and stepped forward, making it clear that he assumed she would be inviting him in.

Her good manners prevailed, and she stood aside, allowing him to step through the doorway.

"You have a lovely house, Mrs. McEvoy," he said, turning towards what looked like a living room. He spotted an empty wheelchair parked near the front window.

"Thank you."

"So, when is the big day?"

"I beg your pardon?" Mrs. McEvoy gave him a somewhat haughty look, coupled with, if he was not mistaken, confusion and anger.

"The party? The big wake party you're planning?"

"Oh. I'm sorry." Relief flooded her face. "When I hear people say 'the big day', I automatically think of weddings, and I couldn't understand why you were asking that. I certainly have no plans to marry again."

What a shame that is, Kevin thought. He was sure once the widow had done her grieving, some lucky man would turn her head again. Although he would love to share his life with someone so beautiful, Kevin was realistic enough to know he didn't stand a chance with a woman like her. He realised she was speaking again and looked up to meet her eyes. So far, his wandering eye had held steady. Had he missed something she'd said?

"So no, I haven't organised anything yet. I've warned people but told them I would get back to them with a date. There's no hurry. Can I relieve you of that urn?" she asked, stepping forward with her arms outstretched and a huge smile on her face.

Reluctantly Kevin handed it to her and watched her place it on the mantelpiece beside a photograph of the couple on their wedding day. It must have been taken a good few years before, as they both looked very young and quite different, although Mrs. McEvoy still had the same striking figure.

She hadn't offered him any refreshment, and he didn't want to leave yet. He decided to make some small talk to delay matters.

"Your husband was a pathologist, you said?"

"That's right."

"I noticed his hands indicated he'd done some type of rough work in the past."

The smile faded from her face, and she looked at him with a blank expression before saying, "He was a keen DIY enthusiast. Forever doing work on the house—plastering and painting, you know, that kind of thing. He even built the kitchen in our last house. He hadn't been able to do any of that recently, although he still liked to tinker with bits of wood at the kitchen table while sitting in his wheelchair." She waved her arm at the empty chair behind him. "He was getting so weak in his last few months I had to buy a wheelchair for him."

That would explain it. The rough hands had been preying on Kevin's mind.

"Now if you don't mind, I really need to get on. Once again, thank you for bringing the urn to me. I'll see you out."

Just like that, Kevin was dismissed. With some reluctance, he turned and left, forcing himself to exchange polite farewells. At least he'd managed to see her again. He was sure Mrs. McEvoy would be occupying his night-time fantasies for many weeks to come.

32

INDIA WAITED UNTIL her husband Rob was settled on the couch after dinner before broaching the subject that was on her mind. She plonked herself down beside him and decided to come straight to the point.

"How would you feel if I was to take some long-service leave and head off to Scotland?"

"I see. You want to go over there and follow up on this Sonny Day thing, don't you?"

"No. Well…all right, yes. But primarily, I'd be going over to see my parents, and then I thought maybe I could go and explore some of the famous lochs and take a few days to look into the place where Sonny Day was photographed. Do you fancy coming with me? You're owed quite a bit of long-service leave as well."

"If it was snow-capped mountains we were going to see, I might be tempted, but we could just as easily see snow here in Australia or New Zealand, as we have on our holidays. I don't really have any great desire to visit Scotland, and besides, your parents said it was very cold over there."

India's father, an engineer, had been working in the oil industry in Aberdeen for the past four years. He was close to retirement, and this might be the last opportunity she'd have to go and stay with them, although thinking about it, she suspected her father might stay for another few years if the company were willing to keep him on. His contract was due to expire in December, and her mother had said she was trying to persuade him to retire rather than renew his contract, which was usually for a two-year period.

"According to Dad, Scotland can experience four seasons in one day—including snowfall. But unlike our houses, most properties in the UK are kept warm with central heating. And they might have solid-fuel or oil-fired cookers in their kitchens and wood-burning or coal fires in their living rooms to boost the central heating. Mum said the houses are so hot they don't sit around in woolly garments like we need to here. But if you wanted to see serious snow, we'd have to visit in the winter months, and the place I need to look at, where Sonny Day was photographed, would be closed then."

"See, I *knew* that was the main reason you wanted to go."

"It's *one* of the reasons. The country is beautiful, and I'd really love to see it. Mum and Dad said if I ever came over, they'd take me around to some of the beauty spots."

"Would the super be happy about you going over there sticking your nose into police business in another country?"

"Our inquiries have led us nowhere. I would tell him that I want to visit my parents and then, while there, suggest I could make some discreet inquiries. If anything came of them, naturally, I'd go and see the local police."

"Naturally. If you went, how long do you think you might be away?"

"I'm owed three months, plus holidays, but I wouldn't anticipate being away anywhere near that long. Maybe five or six weeks? The super would probably be happy to leave Jacko in charge temporarily."

Rob didn't say anything for a minute, and India had no idea what he was thinking. His face gave nothing away.

"If you want to go, then by all means go for it," he said finally, putting an arm around her shoulder and drawing her into him. "I just don't want you to take any risks."

"I promise I won't."

"So, now we've settled that, was there anything you particularly wanted to watch on the television tonight? Or any DVDs?"

"No. Why? Oh, I know! You want to set up one of your games, don't you?"

"I thought I might, if you don't mind." Rob grinned at her.

"Go ahead. I think I might head off for a shower, then have a read in bed."

"Great," said Rob, jumping up from the couch.

She stood and walked over to the doorway where she turned and paused to watch him. He looked like an excited kid—he always did when he was playing with his games. Boys and their toys!

"Have you thought about what you'd like to do when you grow up?" she asked.

***

IT WASN'T UNTIL the beginning of September that India finally flew out of Sydney. She would be staying with her parents for the first few weeks and then heading for the village Cate had told her about. She'd booked a cabin on the site they'd identified for the third week in September. Her previous overseas travels had been limited to the Southern Hemisphere; she had never ventured further than New Zealand and Bali, so she was looking forward to this adventure. She wasn't a keen flyer, though, and the long journey, which was going to take approximately twenty-seven hours, might prove something of a trial. She'd managed to persuade her doctor to prescribe some sleeping tablets so she could knock herself out if she needed to—especially on the second leg which, from Singapore to London, would take fourteen hours. She was going to land in the UK at Heathrow in London—at some ungodly hour. From there, she had to take another flight north to Aberdeen.

As she braced herself for the take-off from Sydney, she wondered how she was going to endure this journey cramped in her economy-class seat. Perhaps she might need to take a tablet on this leg of the journey as well.

33

Aberdeen, Scotland

INDIA STUMBLED FROM the aircraft at Aberdeen, her
mind in a haze. She didn't know how all these
Australian celebrities managed to travel on regular
long-haul flights around the world. Although, of course,
they would be travelling first class, not cramped in the
confined economy seats. With aid, she'd managed six
uncomfortable hours of sleep, waking from it to feel no
ill effects from the tablet but suffering from a stiff neck,
despite the neck pillow, and a sore back. After walking
up and down the aisles a few times, she settled down to
watch a couple of films and then devoured the breakfast
they'd put in front of her, requesting a second croissant.
She'd swallowed her tablet with water after the main
meal following their departure from Singapore and
hadn't heard a thing until the man sitting next to her had
nudged her awake asking if she would mind moving so
that he could get past her to visit the toilet. She realised
then that she'd missed the snack meal and when she
made enquiries was told there was nothing left. They'd
offered her a chocolate muffin as a consolation prize.

She knew her father had arranged time off work so
that he and her mother could show her some sights,
but she hoped they wouldn't want to subject her to any
sightseeing today. Her brain wasn't up to taking on

anything taxing, and she didn't think she'd be able to keep her eyes open until tonight—their time. What she needed was a hot shower, a good meal and a long sleep.

***

"YOUR HOUSE IS very sweet," she told her parents after looking around the quaint cottage they'd purchased three years prior. Her exploration took a matter of seconds; the house was so small. She had never understood why they'd opted to buy a place when their stay in the country was limited. They owned their own house back in Windsor and a small holiday rental up on the central coast of New South Wales. Why bother?

"The accommodation the company provided was just horrible," her mother said. "I couldn't stand living there. It was a soulless concrete block, where you heard your neighbours' every move."

"Yes, you've told me that before. But couldn't you have rented a house more to your liking somewhere else?"

"We *were* looking around to do that, but when I saw these little single-storey cottages, I just fell in love with them—and the area. It's one of the oldest areas in Aberdeen. It's almost impossible to find one to rent, but you can buy them from time to time. When I saw the for-sale sign board, I told your father we just had to have it."

India looked at her father, who rolled his eyes. "It's smaller than the flat we had," he said, shrugging.

"But *so* much nicer, isn't it, David?"

"Yes, it's very cosy," he agreed.

India had been shown to a single bedroom, which her mother said she normally used as her wardrobe and dressing room. The bathroom stood between her room and her parents' room, and when she popped her head around the door, she could see why her mother would need to use the second bedroom. It was very tight.

Space wasn't exactly abundant in the kitchen, living and dining area either. The kitchen was arranged in a horseshoe shape and opened into the cramped dining and living area. Her mother had the kitchen jam-packed with everything she needed. The whole ambience of the place was lovely, and they'd furnished it comfortably.

"Imagine," her mother said. "Families with hordes of children lived in these little houses."

"Fishermen, I assume, as we're so close to the docks."

"Yes. I was talking to one of my neighbours whose family has lived around here for generations. She was telling me that some of the kids in her family slept up in a boarded roof loft area, which they accessed via a ladder from the living room. Walls have been knocked out in ours and any loft areas removed. I like it as it is—with the high ceilings, it gives the rooms a feeling of greater spaciousness."

"Hmm."

"Now, Margaret," her father interjected, "India doesn't want to sit here and listen to you going on about the cottage."

"Sorry, darling. I imagine you'd like a nice hot shower, wouldn't you?"

"Yes, thanks," India said, rising from the comfortable couch before she lapsed into a deep sleep right where she was.

"You go and have your shower while I prepare our lunch. I've made your favourite—braised steak with loads of carrots. I only have to put the potatoes and peas on."

***

THE NEXT DAY, the family set off on their trip. India's father announced they were heading ultimately for the Cairngorms National Park. On the journey to the 'Braemar Gathering'—whatever that was—where they were to spend the day, her father stopped briefly at Balmoral to point out Queen Elizabeth's Scottish residence. It wasn't open to the public, so they weren't able to enter.

"Have you ever visited it?" India asked them both.

"Yes, we went a couple of years ago," her mother said. "The grounds are beautiful, and there's a wonderful café, but you don't get to see much of the castle. They close at the end of July because the Queen is in residence in August and September. They open on odd days in the winter."

"What is this 'Braemar Gathering' you're talking about, Dad?"

"It's one of the Highland Games that are held up here."

"Games—as in sporting events?"

"Yes, and other things. We planned to come this year and would have driven home afterwards, but we're heading back to Ballater tonight, then pushing on to Aviemore tomorrow."

The names were meaningless to India, but her father handed her a UK road atlas, so she planned to follow their route on that.

"Presumably, the town Braemar in Victoria is named after this town we're going to?"

"That's right. Many of the places in Australia are named after towns or villages here—or well-known British dignitaries. It's the same in America and Canada."

"There's also a Braemar in New South Wales," her mother added. "But there's nothing much there. They used to have a railway station, though. We holidayed in the area often when I was a child and used to catch the train from Braemar to go to Mittagong or Bowral."

India smiled and continued studying the map. Her parents had driven through the area a few times in India's childhood, and her mother repeated the same story every time they passed along the road into Mittagong, where she always wanted to stop for coffee and talk about what it was like when she was India's age. India and her brother always rolled their eyes.

***

INDIA WAS IMPRESSED with the Highland Games at Braemar. She'd never seen anything like it before—she found it particularly interesting that there were so many men wearing kilts. Rob would never have been caught dead wearing one, and she suspected most Australian men would have the same attitude, although she had seen photographs in newspapers of Scottish events held in the Southern Highlands in New South Wales where men wore kilts—no doubt descendants of Scottish immigrants. There were Scottish named places in the Upper Hunter Valley as well, where events took place.

She watched the huge tug-of-war, the hammer and stone throwing, Highland dancing and pipers until they headed off before the traffic became too heavy. An evening meal had been booked at their B & B in Ballater, so they didn't have to venture out again that night. She hoped it was something she would be able to eat.

The following three nights, they stayed in a comfortable hotel in Aviemore and from there had action-packed days travelling on the Cairngorm funicular railway, the steam railway and endless walks including through the Rothiemurchar Estate, where they saw the last surviving remnants of the Caledonian Forest. They'd eaten their fill at countless cafés and restaurants, her father insisting on paying for everything. With the quantity of food they were eating, India thought she might need to buy some new clothes. Her trousers were feeling quite tight around her middle, and she'd only brought one skirt which would accommodate an expanding waistline. Thankfully, she'd packed a couple of pairs of her Black Pepper jeans, which had elasticated waists.

India was relieved when they returned to Aberdeen where she hoped she could have a few days' rest before her mother dragged her off to Edinburgh.

"It's only a couple of hours away on the train," her mother said. "We could go and see Edinburgh Castle, Holyrood Palace and do some shopping. We could even stay overnight if you'd like to."

It sounded exhausting to India, but perhaps she'd have an opportunity to track down the elusive McEvoy couple while she was in Edinburgh.

34

WITH THE HIRE car she'd booked and equipped with a newly purchased road map—the car had no satnav—India said goodbye to her parents, promising to return soon. She hadn't told them about her potential investigation, instead saying she was meeting up with an old friend and going to explore other parts of Scotland. There'd been a few awkward moments when her mother asked her the name of this friend.

"Oh, you wouldn't know her," India had said.

Her mother continued pushing for a name, and in the end, she'd blurted out, "Chris," thinking of Chrys Waters back in Windsor. She was, after all, partly doing this for Chrys. If she had said the name of any of her real friends, her mother would have wanted to engage in a long, drawn-out conversation about them and question why they were in Scotland. India hated lying to her parents but knew if she told them the truth, they would attempt to talk her out of pursuing inquiries. They'd always been disappointed when, after leaving university, she'd joined the police.

The differences of opinion and difficulties over her choices stretched back to when India was in her final year of her Higher School Certificate and told them she wanted to study Criminology at university. There'd been arguments and attempted bribes—*"Why not take a year off and go travelling? We'll fund you."*—in the hope that, if she had time to think about it, she would reconsider. Towards the end of her degree, her parents suggested she study for a Master's then a PhD and become a university lecturer in criminology. After announcing she planned to join the police, she'd assuaged their concerns by saying she might return to study after a few years' practical experience on the frontline, but that had never been her intention. She *had* considered it when her old mentor, Joe Paramo, died but then changed her mind after meeting Rob. Now she couldn't ever imagine leaving the force. It was a job she loved, and she was looking forward to carrying out some investigations on this side of the world.

***

INDIA MADE GOOD time on her journey across Scotland, arriving in Arden in the early afternoon and settling into her cabin—or lodge as they called it. She was disappointed to discover that the owners, Mr. and Mrs. Douglas, were away for a few days attending a family gathering up in the Highlands. She'd hoped she could question them.

The cabin she was appointed had two bedrooms, but after positioning herself on the terrace and comparing the location with the photograph of Sonny Day, she knew it was not the same one. She would have to walk around all the cabins to locate it.

She'd been told when she checked in that if she needed provisions for the cabin there was a farm shop up the road—she'd noticed the sign to it on the way in—or she'd have to go into Balloch, Alexandria or across to the coast at Helensburgh. As fate would have it, she chose to drive to Helensburgh.

While sipping a much-needed cup of tea and devouring a scone with jam and clotted cream, India watched as a woman, dripping wet from a heavy downpour, stepped into the café and pushed back the hood of her coat. She looked remarkably like Chrys Waters. In fact, India realised, the woman *was* Chrys Waters.

"Chrys?" she called out, pausing as she was about to take a mouthful of scone.

Puzzled, the woman turned and looked around the café, clearly unsure whether she was being addressed or whether there was someone else in there with the same name.

"Over here," India called out, placing her scone back on the plate and waving at Chrys for extra measure.

They looked at each other with mouths open in astonishment. The woman at the counter pulled Chrys out of her shock by asking her what she would like. After placing her order, Chrys walked across to India's table, taking a seat opposite.

"What are you doing here?" India asked her, still in shock. Had Chrys discovered something all their investigations had failed to uncover? Or was it a coincidence? But she didn't believe in coincidences.

"I could ask you the same thing," Chrys replied.

"I've been visiting my parents in Aberdeen and decided to take some time out to for sightseeing while over here," she said cautiously. "Why are you here?"

"I did some investigations of my own after we last spoke. I couldn't carry on with my life as though nothing had happened."

"I can understand that. So, what did you do?"

"I handed in my notice and took off for Canberra in the first instance."

"Yes, I heard you'd left your job. I tried calling you at home and was told you'd moved by the people you'd let the house to. I then tried your work, and they said you'd resigned. Whereabouts unknown. I left a couple of messages on your mobile phone. I was worried about you, Chrys. Why Canberra?"

"I wanted to visit the Swedish Embassy to see if any of the staff there could recognise the place where Sonny's photograph was taken. I saw you'd called me. Both times, I was driving when your calls came in, so I couldn't answer. I did ring into the station and spoke to someone called Dale, but she said you were out. She told me you were still carrying out investigations, but there was no news. I'm sorry I didn't call you back personally, but I saw no reason to after speaking to Dale."

"Fair enough. Were they able to help you at the Swedish Embassy?"

"Yes—and no. I visited them several times after making loads of copies of the photograph of Sonny that I'd received in the mail. I asked them to distribute them amongst all the staff to see if anyone recognised the place. On my last visit, they told me that although there were several staff members who knew Stockholm very well, none knew the location and even said they didn't believe the photograph had been taken in Stockholm. One woman had passed a message back saying she thought the scenery looked more like one of the lochs in Scotland or one of the lakes in the Lake District in England. That was a shock, I can tell you."

"Mmm. I can imagine. When we sent the photograph to the police in Stockholm, we had a similar response. No one recognised the place. So, have you come to Scotland to explore all the lochs then?"

"Not really. I did hundreds of online searches looking at images across the Lake District in England and around the lochs in Scotland and found Loch Lomond was a pretty good match. So…I'm starting here."

A waitress interrupted them at that point, placing Chrys's order down in front of her. A pot of tea.

"The scones are very nice," India said. "Have you not ordered something to eat?"

"I'm watching the finances."

"Ah. How long have you been here and where are you staying?"

"I couldn't afford any of those places around the loch. I'm at the Premier Inn here in Helensburgh. It's only thirty-five pounds a night. I caught a train from Glasgow Central—it doesn't take that long. I only arrived a couple of nights ago."

"So how are you getting around if you want to explore the loch?"

"Today's the first day I've done any exploration. I was too jet-lagged from the flight on my first full day here—which was yesterday."

"Tell me about it. My jet lag lasted for days."

"Yeah, I was still feeling a bit off today, but I was determined to get out and about. This morning, I caught a train from Helensburgh back to Alexandria, then a bus up to Duck Bay around the loch. I walked around that area today. I couldn't find the right location, though. So why are you *really* here, Detective Hargreaves? I know you're not just sightseeing." Chrys gave her a penetrating gaze.

"Ah, you've sussed me out. You might remember I told you the scenery in the photograph you received of Sonny looked familiar, but I knew it wasn't a place I'd ever visited, especially as we believed it was in Sweden.

I thought I must have seen it in one of those Swedish crime dramas, and so I sat and watched several with no success. Then one night, I dreamt about a woman from an old case I was involved in, and the next morning, it came to me where I'd seen similar scenery."

"The woman you dreamt about had been here? But how would you know that? Was it something to do with your investigation?"

"No, it was nothing to do with the case. Months after it was over, she came to see me to follow up on something and showed me some snaps of her travels. This was many years ago now. Anyway, I tracked her down and she dug out her photos. She told me they were taken when she'd been renting a cabin at a place called Arden on Loch Lomond in Scotland."

"So I was right."

"I believe so, and I'm staying in one of those cabins. When I rang you, I wanted to tell you we hadn't given up. I hadn't picked up on the Scottish connection at that point." She paused for a second, instinctively wanting to make an offer to Chrys. Was it the right thing to do? She decided it was. Their roles were quite different now. She wasn't a lead investigator working for the police over here. She could also keep a close eye on Chrys, reining in any impulsive actions she might be considering. Members of the public who carried out their own investigations often got themselves into trouble.

"Look, Chrys, there are two bedrooms in my cabin. If you want, you could come and bunk in the other room. It would save you some money. I have a hire car, and so you wouldn't need to spend money travelling around. We could carry out some investigations together. I'm not here officially. Well, I'm on official leave, but I'm doing this in my own time—and at my own expense.

I'm not here as Detective Inspector Hargreaves. I'm just Mrs. India Ellis."

"Ellis?"

"Yes, that's my married name. I use my single name at work."

"Oh. Well, it's very kind of you Mrs. Ellis…"

"Call me India, please."

"It's very kind of you, India, but I don't think it would be right for you to pay for everything. I mean, for the cabin and hire car. I'm using the money we would have spent on our honeymoon to fund this trip, although I'm being very cautious with my spending. I've leased the house, but the money from that only covers the mortgage, the rates and insurance with a small amount over for any repairs that might crop up. I don't have any income at the moment."

"Well, I do. I'm on long-service leave, and my parents paid for everything while I was visiting them. The only thing I've shelled out for is the cost of my flight, accommodation and hire car. I've paid for the cabin for the next three nights. I wanted to be on site so I could sneak around and find the right one. Save yourself some money and come and stay with me. Two heads are better than one, as they say. I'll only pull out my detective credentials if and when the need arises. The cabin is self-catering, and I wasn't planning on having expensive meals out. If it makes you feel any better, you could contribute towards our food costs."

"I've eaten out for all my meals. I don't even pay for breakfast at the hotel—just buy a bun or something. I've restricted myself to one reasonable meal a day. Otherwise, it's been snacks. There are cheap places to eat here in Helensburgh."

"Well, we can self-cater at the cabin. The hotel will probably charge you for tonight as it's now late afternoon. You could either stay there again tonight and I could collect you tomorrow, or you could come back with me to the cabin when I leave Helensburgh. The bed in the second bedroom is made up. There's only one bathroom, I'm afraid. I've come into Helensburgh to stock up on food."

Chrys sipped her tea. India sensed she was thinking over the pros and cons of working together and was perhaps torn by the idea. What would she decide? India felt she needed to elaborate further to convince Chrys.

"To be perfectly honest, Chrys, carrying out investigations on your own is a lonely occupation. I know that only too well from the past. It's much better working in a team, bouncing facts, ideas and theories off each other."

After a further brief hesitation, Chrys looked up and said, "Okay. I'll come back with you tonight. First, I should go and check out of my hotel. Then we can do some shopping. I know a good supermarket nearby."

As they were walking around the supermarket making selections, India realised there was now truth in the lie she had given her parents. She laughed and explained to Chrys what she had told her parents, reassuring her that was not why she'd asked her to join her.

***

CHRYS RUSTLED UP a quick meal of chicken and vegetables in a cream and red wine sauce served over rice for them that evening. Settled on the couch after the meal with the remainder of the red wine, which was not going down too well with India, she broached the subject of Alex Graham.

"How's Alex doing these days? Have you heard anything from him recently?"

"He's fine. He's back at work now, but they had to alter his route. I don't think things will ever be the same for him again."

When Sonny's closest friend Alex Graham had stepped in for Chrys at the last moment at her press appeal, things had gone spectacularly wrong. At the close of his appeal for information about Sonny, a nervous Alex had reeled off his personal mobile number rather than the formal police number listed on the sheet of paper he was holding. The formal police number had been listed on the television screen, and no one, including Alex, had realised the mistake until he started receiving calls. The appeal had been broadcast on the radio and all the television channels. As soon as she'd seen the clip, India, who had done a separate appeal earlier in the day, *had* realised and attempted to phone Chrys, but her phone had been turned off that night. It had been impossible to get through to Alex. She'd contacted the press and asked them to edit the phone number Alex had quoted out of all future broadcasts. But the damage had been done.

Some bright spark, having discovered the error, put up a post on YouTube and it went viral. Calls started coming in from all over the world. The blunder became a news item itself, with Alex catapulted to fame overnight. His carrier had changed his number and directed all calls from his old number to the police instead, but even they could not cope with the calls and cancelled the number altogether, as there was nothing to be learned from them.

"As you know," Chrys said, "Alex's day job was delivering mail and he had been doing the same run for a couple of years in South Windsor. Suddenly women on his round who recognised him from the appeal and subsequent news item about the error would be waiting to greet him each day, sometimes inviting friends to join them. It was as though he became a celebrity overnight and had a fan base following him around. He had to move house because his neighbours recognised him and started knocking on his door."

India knew from her meeting with Alex that he'd been mortified about his error. She also knew that Chrys blamed herself for the disaster.

"It wasn't your fault, Chrys. You know that, don't you?"

"Oh, yeah. I'm over that. I joked with Alex just before I left, saying he could start paying me commission for all the millions of bucks he was going to earn in the future."

Puzzled by this statement, India asked Chrys what she meant.

"Alex has received countless offers for roles in TV dramas, films and reality shows. He's a good-looking, single man. Agents have offered to represent him. All because of that one little cock-up."

"I find that astonishing. Is he considering taking up any of these offers?"

"Not at the moment, but when we last spoke, he admitted he was tempted. He doesn't feel comfortable moving forward on any of the offers while Sonny's fate is unknown."

"I can imagine. He was really upset that the publicity he attracted overshadowed Sonny's disappearance."

"Yeah, he mentioned that. What happened to Alex is unbelievable, isn't it? It just goes to show how the cult of celebrity dominates some people's lives. So, changing the subject, what is our plan of action for tomorrow?"

35

CHRYS AND INDIA walked around the cabins the following morning. There were a couple of different types: some were constructed wholly of timber; some had timber and rendered walls like the one India was renting. They also located the one that was the closest fit with Sonny's photograph. A woman emerged from the cabin after seeing them holding the photo up against the backdrop.

"Excuse me," she said in a broad American accent. "Can I ask what you're doing?"

"Our apologies," India said. "We didn't think anyone was in the cabin. We're guests here as well, and we're trying to identify the cabin where our friend stayed when he was over here earlier in the year."

"Oh, okay. Can I offer you a cup of coffee?"

"Thank you all the same, but we have to be going," Chrys said, quickly pulling on India's arm.

"Yes, sorry to have bothered you," India called back as they walked off.

"So, cabin number four it is. We need to go and see who was registered there," Chrys said.

"The owners are away for a few days, and I'm not sure if that's going to prove to be a good or a bad thing."

***

On their way to reception, India nudged Chrys, pointing to a woman with cleaning materials entering one of the cabins.

"Let's go and have a word with her first," she suggested.

As they approached the cabin, India could hear conversation in another language. The short, blonde woman they had seen was inside with a second dark-haired woman.

"Good morning. Do you speak English?" India asked them, standing at the cabin entrance.

"Yes, a little," the blonde woman said. "We understand what you say."

The two women had stopped what they were doing and stared, both looking quite worried.

"Were you working here back in early May, through to early June this year?" India asked.

"Yes, we here."

"Do you clean the cabins daily?"

"Only if customers want. Some don't."

"It's cabin four I'm inquiring about. We're from Australia, and we're trying to trace someone who was staying there at some point between May and June."

The blonde woman looked at her friend, who nodded.

"What you want to know?"

"Did you see this man?" India pulled out the photograph of Sonny taken on the terrace.

"Yes, we see him. Only few times. When he arrive, he in wheelchair. Then we not see him for many weeks. We see him outside only once. Maybe for photo," she said, pointing at the picture.

"Who was with him?"

"Woman and strange man."

"Why did you think the man was strange?"

"At first, he look normal. Hair on face—what you call it?"

"A beard?"

"Yes. Then he wear funny thing over head to hide face."

India didn't understand what the woman was talking about. "I'm sorry—"

"Like bank robbers, like in movies," the dark-haired woman said.

"Ah, a balaclava," India guessed, turning to Chrys. "Maybe he didn't want someone to see his face."

"Why do you think he covered his face?" Chrys asked the women.

They shrugged.

"Maybe he not want other man to see him," the dark-haired one said.

"Do you mean the man in the wheelchair? The one in this photograph?" India asked.

They nodded.

"Did the woman and the two men arrive together? You said you saw the man in the wheelchair arrive. Were they all in the same car?"

"No, man in wheelchair and woman first. Then other man. Then woman leave, man with beard stays. Woman returns, man with beard leaves."

"So they came and went at different times?"

"Yes."

"Did you see what the woman looked like at close quarters?"

The two women looked at each other in confusion. She needed to find a simpler way to explain. "Did you ever speak to the woman? See her close like you and me?"

"Yes," they both chorused, nodding with understanding.

"What did she look like?"

"Tall. Dark hair." The blonde woman said spiralled her hand around the back of her head. India took that to mean she had long hair which she wore up— or tied back.

"Did you clean the cabin for them?"

"No, they don't want. Woman clean herself. Even bring own sheets."

"She brought her own sheets to the cabin?"

"Yes. Not at first. She give us back first sheets, then use her own." The blonde one was doing the talking again.

"Did you see them leave?"

Nods from both women again.

"In a car?"

"Yes. Big black car. Special for wheelchair in back."

"Did the three of them leave together?"

"No. Man with hair on face already gone."

"Do you know when he left? Was it days or weeks before the other two?"

"Weeks."

"And there were only two people you saw when they left in the big black car?"

"Yes."

"Do you know the name of the people who were staying in the cabin?"

"No. Not know name," the blonde woman said, although both women were shaking their heads. "Mrs. Douglas know name."

Being the owner, of course she would. India didn't think there was much more these women could offer.

"Can you think of anything else?" she asked Chrys, who had turned a deathly white. India hadn't thought. The reference to the man in the photograph being in the wheelchair. Chrys would be concerned for Sonny's health.

"Ask them whether the man in the wheelchair looked all right," she whispered.

They had clearly heard Chrys because the dark-haired one said, "No, he don't look right. Look like very sick."

"Thank you for your time," India said, already steering Chrys towards the door. "You've been very helpful. Sorry to have interrupted your work."

"They said Sonny looked very sick!" Chrys cried when they stopped a bit further down the hill.

"He may not have been sick. He might have been drugged. There's a difference."

"What do these people want with Sonny? Why are they keeping him prisoner?"

"That's what I intend to find out. Come on, Chrys. I know this is upsetting for you, but we need to keep it together if we're to track Sonny and this woman."

"How are we going to do that?"

"By following the evidence," India said, wondering if she had made a wise decision teaming up with Chrys.

***

AT THE RECEPTION, India introduced Chrys, explaining she had joined her in the cabin. The same woman who had checked her in the day before gave her a knowing smirk. Realising the woman was thinking along the wrong lines, she explained, "Chrys and I know each other from Australia. We met up yesterday in Helensburgh where she was staying. I suggested that as I had two bedrooms, she should move in with me rather than continue to pay for a hotel room."

"Oh," the woman said.

"I'm a detective inspector with the police in Australia, and I'm making inquiries linked to a case I'm working on. We're certain that the people we're looking for were staying in cabin number four. I wondered if it would be possible to find out who was staying there over the May and June period this year." India produced her police identification, but the woman didn't even look at it.

"I'm afraid that won't be possible," she said. "We value our guests' privacy, and that is confidential information which I am unable to give. You would need to contact Police Scotland, and they would have to obtain the owner's permission or a warrant before any names could be released."

"Okay, we'll do that then. Thank you anyway."

"Damn," India said when they were outside again and out of earshot. "I thought she might say that. Looks like we'll have to go to the police."

"We could hang around and wait for the woman to leave the reception. Then we could have a look at the register," Chrys suggested.

"We could, and that would be a last resort, but I think involving the police might be more beneficial. Let's try that first. I don't want to land us in any trouble. I spotted a camera in there. There's a police station in Helensburgh. I checked that out before I came here. We could drive over and see if we can find someone to help us. I brought a copy of everything from Sonny's file with me."

India didn't add that she'd also brought the file on the unidentified male victim who had been found on the building site. There was a tenuous link to Scotland with

Jacko's discovery of a Scottish couple living not far from where he was buried—a couple who were now back in Scotland. She'd need to get across to Edinburgh to follow that up further. She'd decided against making any inquiries when she'd travelled there with her mother.

"Good thinking. Sounds like a plan."

36

At Helensburgh Police Station, they eventually met up with a Detective Sergeant McTavish, who had a strong Scottish accent but was very easy to understand, unlike some of the people India had encountered on the trip with her parents. He took them into an interview room, and India filled him on all the details of Sonny's disappearance to date, with Chrys adding things here and there—particularly stressing that Sonny's letter contained a hidden message.

"It sounds like a mighty strange situation, right enough. And you've narrowed it down to this photograph being taken outside cabin number four?"

"That's right. We need to know the names of all the people who were renting the cabin from late April until possibly early June. The letter was posted on the fourth of June, but we don't know when it was written. We *do* know the photograph was taken in Scotland, not Sweden."

"Okay. I'll come with you to gather the records if the owners will allow it. I'll need to make contact with them. If they won't agree, I'll need to get a warrant, and that might not be an easy thing to do. If you wait here, I'll go and make some phone calls."

***

"Good morning, lass." Detective Sergeant McTavish greeted the woman on reception back at the cabin site in Arden. "Has Mrs. Douglas been in touch with you?" He'd followed India and Chrys back in his own vehicle. After making some calls, he'd managed to get through to the owners and told India and Chrys to meet him outside the reception area.

"Yes, Mrs. Douglas has telephoned. I have the records here if you would like to see them now."

"Well, that's what we're here for."

The woman blushed and stepped back to allow room for India and DS McTavish to squeeze in behind the small desk. Chrys remained on the other side of the counter.

Cabin number four, they discovered, was booked for the entire period they were interested in by one couple.

"What are the names registered there?" Chrys asked.

"Doctor and Mrs. McEvoy," DS McTavish said.

"McEvoy? Isn't—"

"Yes," India said, cutting her off. She'd told Chrys last night that she would need to go to Edinburgh once they'd done as much as they could trying to trace Sonny. She'd explained that she wasn't able to give her the full details, largely because she didn't want to cause Chrys additional worry, but she had mentioned the name McEvoy. Now the name had cropped up in connection with Sonny, and the home address listed was for the house in Pitt Town Road, Wilberforce, NSW—the last known address for the couple. *The cases are connected*, India realised with some excitement. She hadn't mentioned the unidentified body to DS McTavish. Now she had good reason to.

"Why don't we go up to our cabin, Detective Sergeant McTavish, where we can have a cup of coffee? I have another file I'd like you to see."

***

DS McTAVISH AND Chrys listened as India outlined the case of the unidentified body and the discovery that renters named McEvoy had lived not far from the burial site. She told them that the McEvoy couple had departed for Scotland the day after Sonny supposedly travelled to Sweden, with both having stopovers in different parts of the Middle East. She showed the photographs of the dead victim to DS McTavish but would not allow Chrys to see them.

"Grim," he said, shaking his head. "The man died of natural causes and yet they mutilated his body afterwards and buried it? Why would they do that?"

"I don't know."

"They *mutilated* a body?" Chrys asked. "*How* did they mutilate it?"

"Just a few things they did after the man was already dead."

"Is this the man whose body you found that you thought might have been Sonny?"

"Yes."

"You didn't say how he'd died or that he'd been mutilated," Chrys accused.

"Once we knew it wasn't Sonny, it wasn't appropriate to tell you how he died or what was done to him. It was nothing to do with you or Sonny."

"But it *might* be to do with Sonny. This couple might be the ones who have Sonny. He—"

DS McTavish cut in, addressing India. "What connection do you think this doctor and his wife might have to your missing man?"

"I'm not sure."

"You must be formulating a theory?"

"That's all it is at present."

"So what is your thinking?"

"Doctor McEvoy *might* be the masked man who the cleaners spotted. He might have been the one who travelled to Sweden. From what the cleaners said, Sonny Day was the man in the wheelchair. What they want him for, I have no idea. Perhaps for the same reason they wanted the victim in Australia. *If* he was their victim. Now don't be too upset, Chrys, but I think they might be carrying out experiments on the men they've taken."

"What kind of experiments?" Chrys asked, horrified.

"I don't know. Possibly drug related. Doctor McEvoy worked as a pathologist in the UK, but we couldn't find any trace of him doing that in Sydney. The problem we came up against was that when we checked him out at the tax office, the records showed he ceased working twenty-three months into their three-year stay in Australia. He doesn't appear to have worked for the last thirteen months they lived there."

"What about Mrs. McEvoy?"

"There were no records of her working."

"So how did they live?"

"I couldn't tell you that. All I can say is Doctor McEvoy didn't lodge tax returns after the second year. Perhaps they had savings they lived off."

India didn't think there was any point in elaborating on her thoughts because that's all they were. Were the McEvoys responsible for inflicting the old injuries they'd found on the man buried in Wilberforce causing him to have a massive stroke? She didn't know. He may have been held captive by them for some time. There was evidence of traumatic injuries to his body which were not recent. Nor had the injuries been treated in any hospital in the Sydney area. She could only surmise those injuries were either sustained in a completely different location or the McEvoys had inflicted them on the victim. God knew what they were doing. It was a startling thought, though, and they needed to find Sonny before he too ended up like their Sydney victim.

"If the doctor didn't work as a pathologist in Australia, was he working as a general practitioner?" DS McTavish asked India.

"No. He worked in a scientific research laboratory," she answered in almost a whisper, as though by speaking quietly this news would have no impact on Chrys. No such luck.

"Oh my God," Chrys exclaimed. "We need to find Sonny before they kill him!"

37

DS McTavish was waiting for Chrys and India when they walked into the station the following morning.

"Tea or coffee?" he offered.

"None for me, thanks," India said. She was feeling a little queasy this morning.

"Me neither," Chrys said.

"Well, ladies, after you." The DS led them through to an interview room and, once they were settled, launched into his findings.

"I spent some time following up on inquiries yesterday afternoon. The McEvoy couple booked and paid for their accommodation online from Australia, the payment made with an Australian bank account. However, they extended their stay beyond their original booking and paid for it with a British credit card. I've chased that up and found it registered to an address in Glasgow. It wasn't a new card and has been registered at that address for almost four years, with a new card issued in July this year."

"So they must have lived at the Glasgow address before travelling to Australia," India said.

"Yes. I found the sale of a property to a Doctor K. McEvoy in November 2010—a little over four months before they left for Australia. He was working in Edinburgh up to that point—presumably commuting daily."

"What's the 'K' stand for?" Chrys asked.

"Kenrick," both India and McTavish said in unison.

"And his wife?" India asked. "Did you gather any information on her?"

"No. I'm afraid I have no information on her. She seems a rather elusive character. The card I mentioned earlier, which was in the husband's name, was recently cancelled."

"Can we go and question them at the address you have?" Chrys asked.

"*We* can't. I'm afraid I won't be able to join you. I will be remaining here and will interview the cleaners formally. They are from Poland. I'm passing everything you've told me on to a Detective Inspector Angus Rendle. You can meet up with him in Glasgow, and he'll take over things from there. These are his details." The DS passed India a slip of paper. "I've organised for you to meet up with him tomorrow at eleven a.m. That's the earliest he could make. In the meantime, he's asked me to email him copies of everything you have in your files. Did you bring them in as I asked?"

"Yes, they're here. I can't let you have them, but you're welcome to make copies from them."

"That's what I intend to do. It will take some time — do you want to wait here or come back?"

India looked at Chrys. "What would you like to do?" She didn't fancy sitting here for the next few hours and hoped Chrys wouldn't want to either.

"We could go for a walk along the waterfront and then have something to eat," Chrys suggested. "It's not raining today."

***

"INDIA, HOW ABOUT we head off to Glasgow tonight?" Chrys suggested after they left McTavish.

"You want to stake out the McEvoys' house, don't you? We're not in an American film here, Chrys. We need to play this by the book, or we could put some noses out of joint. Besides, we don't have the address in Glasgow. I doubt DS McTavish will give it to us."

"But Sonny might be lying in their house somewhere— in grave danger."

"I know that's a possibility."

"Well then, we need to *act* before it's too late."

India could tell Chrys was very worked up. Her voice had risen as she spoke, and she was breathing like someone who had just completed a jog. India couldn't help but agree with everything Chrys had said, but as an officer of the law visiting from overseas, she had to tread warily.

"I'm finding the breeze off the water a little chilly," she said to change the subject. "Why don't we go and find somewhere to keep warm, have a bite to eat and talk it through? We can look up some accommodation in Glasgow and see what deals are on offer. I've got roaming internet on my phone."

"Okay," Chrys agreed reluctantly.

***

INDIA FOUND A guest house with reasonable rates fairly close to the city centre. Parking was available and breakfast included in the cost. There were either twin rooms with an en-suite available or single rooms with shared bathrooms that were 'not far from the room'.

"I don't know about you, but I don't fancy the idea of having to walk out into a corridor to find a bathroom in the middle of the night," India said.

"Me neither."

"It's either something like this guest house or we have to pay about £100 each per night—and that's sharing a room as well. The guest house is only £56 a night for *both* of us, with its own bathroom and breakfast included."

"A twin room in the guest house it is then. If you don't mind sharing. Can you book that and then we could go there this afternoon?"

"What's the point? We don't know where this couple live in Glasgow. I've paid for another night in the cabin, and I doubt they'll refund me at such short notice."

"We could try to see if you could get a refund. Mrs. Douglas came back this morning, don't forget. See if you can appeal to her good nature."

"Shall we head back to the police station and see if DS McTavish has finished with the files?" India suggested, wanting to divert Chrys's thinking.

"Do you want anything else to eat or drink?"

"No, thanks. I'm off my food a bit today. I've been wanting to eat really plain things, but I couldn't even manage this toasted ham and cheese. It might have been better without the cheese—it's a bit strong for me."

"Yes, mine was a bit strong as well. I believe it's what they call extra mature here, seeing as the mature one we bought the other day wasn't nearly as strong as this."

"Hmm. They can keep it. Let's go then."

38

Much to India's surprise, DS McTavish gave her the address in Glasgow, making her promise that they wouldn't attempt to speak to the McEvoys without the presence of DI Rendle.

Chrys persuaded her to leave that afternoon, and once India had explained their reasons for vacating the cabin a day early, stating it was due to police business, Mrs. Douglas gave her a fifty per cent refund on the cancellation.

Their booking at the B & B made, they set off for Glasgow late in the afternoon. After checking into their room at the guest house, which Chrys pronounced "wasn't too bad," they set off to find the McEvoys' house, armed with a small map they'd been given as they checked in.

India slowed as they passed the house, a large, detached property in a pretty, tree-lined street.

"Posh, eh?" Chrys commented. "Aren't you going to pull over?"

"And do what?"

"Observe the comings and goings. We might get to see what Doctor McEvoy or his wife look like."

"I said we weren't going to stake out the house all night. I'll turn around, drive back and park nearby. In a street like this, we'd stick out like a sore thumb. We can't stay too long."

"Okay," Chrys conceded.

India pulled up a few houses down from the McEvoys', parking on the opposite side of the road. There was a black Audi parked in the driveway. It was not a car which could accommodate a wheelchair so they must have changed vehicles at some point. What that meant, India didn't want to think about, but Chrys noticed it immediately.

"They haven't got a car that would fit a wheelchair anymore. Do you think that means they've killed Sonny already?" she asked, her voice trembling.

"It could mean a number of things, Chrys. Maybe Sonny is walking now. The Polish women saw him walking at the cabins."

"But they said he left in a wheelchair."

"Yes, months ago. Anything could have happened in the intervening time."

"Exactly. Why can't we go and look around the property?"

"We wouldn't be able to see anything anyway. They have the shutters closed on those front windows, and if we start creeping around, one of the neighbours will notice us."

"We could try to get in around the back."

"No," she said firmly. "I gave my word to DS McTavish. We'll just sit here for a while and then leave. We have to wait until we see this DI Rendle tomorrow."

"It's so frustrating, knowing Sonny might be in there."

"I know. If we were back in Australia, I could obtain a warrant and we could search the place, but we're guests here and my hands are tied."

***

DI RENDLE LOOKED to be in his early fifties. His greyish hair was overdue a cut, and with his crumpled appearance and abrupt manner, India thought he'd been around the block more than a few times. He didn't seem happy about being drawn into this case.

"Have you got a search warrant organised for the McEvoy house?" Chrys asked Rendle after the women briefed him. India frowned at her, signalling for her to be quiet. By rights, Chrys shouldn't even have been there, but Rendle had been willing to meet them both today, even if he had kept them waiting for almost an hour, using the excuse that he'd been going through things with DS McTavish. McTavish had completed the interviews with the two Polish women, and Rendle filled them in on the outcome of those interviews.

"With some doubts being cast on matters from what the cleaners have now disclosed, there's insufficient probable cause for a search warrant at this point," Rendle said. "The witnesses couldn't be one hundred per cent sure it was your missing man. We need to carry out informal questioning of the McEvoy couple in the first instance."

"What more do you need? They were seen with Sonny months back!" Chrys argued.

"Precisely. Months back. Not now. And that's not absolutely clear. We'll see what they have to say, shall we? If you're ready, we can leave now."

"But—"

"Chrys!" India warned.

***

A TALL, STRIKING, dark-haired woman eventually answered the door after DI Rendle had been knocking for some time. There was no bell on the door, just an old-fashioned large brass knocker, which India could hear booming inside the house. The woman must have heard it—the whole neighbourhood would have heard it—so why had it taken so long to answer?

"Hello, how can I help you?"

"Mrs. McEvoy?"

"Yes," the woman said with a slight incline of her head. Her face held no expression, so India couldn't gauge what she was thinking.

"I'm Detective Inspector Rendle from Police Scotland. We'd like to ask you a few questions. May we come in?"

She noticed Rendle hadn't introduced her or Chrys. Was that a deliberate strategy to not alarm the woman?

"Questions about what? If it's anything to do with Gordon Haines's death, I've already told your sergeant I wasn't at home that day. He should have verified that."

"Gordon Haines?"

"Yes, my next-door neighbour."

"We're not here about Mr. Haines, Mrs. McEvoy."

"Oh, well, you'd better come in then."

Mrs. McEvoy led them through to a kitchen diner and invited them to take a seat without offering them any refreshments. The woman appeared to have no interest in being introduced to India or Chrys.

"Now what is it that you wanted to ask me?"

"Is Doctor McEvoy home? We'd also like to ask him a few questions."

"He's here in a manner of speaking, but I'm afraid you won't be able to ask him any questions. He's in that urn on the mantelpiece. Sadly, my husband died a few weeks ago. Those are his ashes."

That was unexpected. A new twist on events. India glanced at Chrys, who had a horrified look on her face. She would be thinking it was Sonny the woman was talking about. India shook her head to warn Chrys not to say anything. They mustn't jump to conclusions.

"Can I ask how he died?" Rendle asked.

"A heart attack. My husband was seriously injured in a horrific accident last year while we were in Australia. He never really recovered, despite many months of operations and rehabilitation. He was wheelchair-bound."

"Where was he treated for his injuries?" India asked.

Mrs. McEvoy turned her head and looked at her as though seeing her for the first time. "Sorry, who are you?"

"I'm Detective Inspector India Hargreaves from the New South Wales Police."

"Why would someone from Australia be sitting in my kitchen? Is this related to my husband's accident? I thought that was all done and dusted. We had an out-of-court settlement."

She's good, India noted. *Not a flicker of nervousness or sign of a guilty conscience.*

"Can you tell me where your husband's accident occurred and where he was treated?"

"The accident happened in Queensland. He was on his way to start a new job on the outskirts of Brisbane, coming down the mountains through Cunningham's Gap. I don't know if you are familiar with it?"

India nodded. She had driven through there a few times. That was why there was no record of the doctor working after he left the scientific research company in Sydney. He'd been unable to work. And, if Doctor McEvoy was so badly incapacitated, then that was her theory out the window.

"An articulated lorry lost control, knocked into the back of Lachlan's car and sent him into oncoming traffic," Mrs. McEvoy continued. "When they got him down the mountain, he was airlifted to a hospital in Brisbane."

"You'd been planning on moving to Brisbane?" she asked.

"Yes, we had. My husband was intending to make a start up there. We hadn't found anywhere to live yet. It all happened so fast. I would have joined him the following month. Due to the accident, we never moved there."

"He remained in Queensland for all his treatment?"

"Yes. I flew back and forth as often as I could. Someone had to keep the money coming in. I had to work."

"You were working in Sydney then?" This was news to India. The tax office had no records of her working.

"Of course I was working."

"Can I ask—"

"Sorry to interrupt, but we're getting off track here somewhat," DI Rendle said. "We're here to ask about a young man called Sonny Day."

"Sonny Day? Is that a real name?" Mrs. McEvoy said, smiling.

"You were staying in a cabin up in Arden from the end of April until early July this year. Is that correct?" Rendle asked her.

"Yes, that's right. I stayed there with Lachie—my husband. This house still had tenants living here, and we had to wait until their notice was up before we could move back. I had to have adjustments made to the house as well before we could occupy it—a stair lift for Lachie and a shower that could accommodate his disabilities with a hoist and special chair."

Rendle nodded. "I noticed the stair lift as we were coming in."

"I suppose I should have that removed now. I just haven't had time to think about it."

"Back to Sonny Day. He was seen in the cabin you rented in Arden."

Mrs. McEvoy opened her mouth, expressing shocked surprise. She was *really* good.

"That's ridiculous," she said after a pause. "I don't know where you got that from. I don't know anyone called Sonny Day. Only Lachlan and I stayed at the cabin."

"You didn't have anyone else there with you?"

"No. Just us. A young man came in to be with Lachlan a couple of times when I needed to go shopping and didn't want to take my husband with me—but only a couple of times."

"What was this young man's name?"

"It was Eric. I'm not sure if I ever knew his surname."

"And where did you meet this Eric?"

"I met him one day while I was shopping in Alexandria. I was struggling with Lachlan's chair, and he kindly came over to assist me. To thank him, I treated him to a coffee, and he said if I ever needed help, he would be very happy to assist. He gave me his number, and I called on him a few times, paying him in cash."

"Do you still have this Eric's number?"

"Yes, I do. I never seem to get around to deleting names in my contacts. Hang on, I'll get it for you."

She stood and walked over to the kitchen counter, unplugging the phone which was charging there. Pressing the screen a few times, she passed it to DI Rendle.

"That's his number."

Rendle immediately tapped the number into his phone and listened. "It's just ringing out," he said.

Mrs. McEvoy nodded. "Yes. I've attempted to phone him a couple of times in the past few weeks without success."

"Well, thank you for your help," Rendle said, standing. 'I think we've taken up enough of your time. Just one last thing—you wouldn't happen to have your husband's death certificate, would you?"

"Yes, it's in the drawer here somewhere. One moment."

Frustrated, India watched as Mrs. McEvoy passed the certificate to DI Rendle. There were many more questions she'd like to ask this woman.

Chrys, who had sat at the table without saying a word, had quietly moved into the lounge room which opened off the kitchen diner. India found her standing in front of the mantelpiece where the urn had been placed, staring at a photograph propped against the wall. It was of a young couple on their wedding day.

***

"Is THIS YOUR wedding photograph?" Chrys asked Mrs. McEvoy.

"Yes. That was Lachie and I when we were young."

"Your husband's name was Lachlan?"

"Yes—well, Lachlan was his middle name. His first name was Kenrick, but he never liked it and the idea of being a 'Ken' never appealed to him. He went by the name of Lachlan instead—except on official documentation, of course. His death certificate lists his name as Kenrick Lachlan McEvoy, you might have noticed." She directed that last statement at Rendle, who nodded and handed the certificate back to her.

"Like Lachlan Macquarie," Chrys said. "One of our more famous governors in Australia."

"I'm sorry?"

"Lachlan Macquarie was the British appointed governor of Sydney in the early nineteenth century. He was from Scotland originally and named the local town where we live Windsor and a nearby town Richmond because the area reminded him of those two places, somewhere near London. Many towns in Australia have Macquarie Streets, and we even have towns, buildings, institutions or other places named after him."

"I see. I've never heard of him," Mrs. McEvoy said.

"Would you mind if I used your toilet? I don't think I can wait until we return to the station."

"Yes, certainly. If you turn right out of the living room door and head towards the back, it's the last door on your left."

"Thank you," Chrys said, heading off—thinking it was interesting that Mrs. McEvoy hadn't asked who she was.

She could see that the room on the front left was a more formal living room. She opened the next door and saw it was a dining room furnished with a smart table, matching chairs and a sideboard. The toilet would be the next door, but she wanted to see where the others led to. The first one proved to be a small, under-stair storage cupboard. She closed the door quietly and tried the next one, which was also under the staircase leading up to the next floor. It was locked. She rattled the handle and pulled on it in case the door was stuck, but it didn't budge.

"The toilet is the last on the left, I said," a loud voice boomed down the hallway at her.

"Oh, sorry." Chrys laughed, turning to the door behind her. "I'm always mixing up my left and right."

She scurried into the toilet and sat on its seat in nervous relief. It wasn't just a toilet but also a wet room with a shower. That was a close call. Looking up, she could see the frosted sash window was slightly open. She stood, pushed it up further and peered out. Outside the back door, there was a large terrace with railings. Stairs led down to the backyard—or garden, as she knew it was called here. It was small by most Australian standards, but this house was close to a major city, and she supposed it would be considered a generous size in inner Sydney suburbs. Was there some kind of basement or cellar? Was that what the locked door led to? She'd have loved to get in there and take a look around. For that matter, she'd like to explore all the upstairs rooms. Chance would a fine thing. That crafty woman had come up with plausible answers, which may have fooled the Glaswegian detective, but Mrs. McEvoy hadn't fooled her for a minute.

39

"WHY DID YOU cut me off when I was questioning Mrs. McEvoy about her situation in Australia?" India asked Rendle on the way back to the station.

"We were there primarily to investigate a potential kidnapping situation regarding Sonny Day, not what Mrs. McEvoy did for a living. There was no relevance."

"I disagree. If you'd read the entire file on our unidentified body, you would have seen it was found very close to where the McEvoys lived in New South Wales. You would have also seen that the Australian Tax Office had no records of a Mrs. McEvoy ever having worked. Yet she freely admitted that she worked to bring money into the home. I need to find out what she was doing."

"Relevance to Sonny Day?"

"I believe there may be a connection between the body we found and Sonny's disappearance."

"We have no evidence of that. Your witnesses in Arden did not see Mrs. McEvoy and the man you believe to be Sonny Day together."

"They did," Chrys called through from the back of the car. "They identified Mrs. McEvoy arriving and leaving with Sonny."

"They identified *a* man arriving with Mrs. McEvoy. She says she was there with her husband. When DS McTavish questioned your Polish women more

221

thoroughly, it turns out they were some distance away from Mrs. McEvoy when she arrived and departed with her husband. They were also some distance away when they saw this Eric person wearing a balaclava and taking photos of Mr. Day. They weren't sure the man being photographed was the same man they saw with Mrs. McEvoy. This Eric character could have brought Mr. Day to the cabin with him on the day the photographs were taken. After all, the man they saw was abled-bodied, and from what we have learned, it doesn't sound like Doctor McEvoy was."

"This is bullshit," Chrys said. "She has Sonny there in her house. I'm sure of it. And by not doing anything, we're putting his life in danger."

"Chrys!" India warned her.

"Miss Waters," Rendle said crisply, "I have many years' experience of working as a detective in this city. I can assure you I have seen everything possible there is to see. That woman is no murderer or kidnapper. It's this Eric we need to chase down. Now we have his phone number we might get somewhere."

Rendle's condescending tone made India want to slap his face.

"So what do you plan to do next?" she asked him. "Are you saying you don't believe there's a case to justify a search warrant for the McEvoy residence?"

"Correct. There is no justification for it. I intend to try and track down this Eric person."

India looked back at Chrys, who she could see was absolutely furious with Rendle, and shook her head, hoping Chrys would heed the warning to remain quiet. They needed to handle this tetchy chauvinistic detective with care otherwise they would get nowhere. While

India and Chrys had been in the living room examining the wedding photograph next to Chrys, Rendle and Mrs. McEvoy had been back in the kitchen chatting amicably. She was very beguiling, and Rendle had fallen for it.

"You don't think Eric had something to do with the man you're looking for, do you?" Mrs. McEvoy had asked, reinforcing Rendle's thinking. Well, of course Eric was something to do with it. He was in cahoots with her!

India believed the *thorough* questioning of the Polish women had caused them to backtrack, intimidated and afraid of saying the wrong thing. They'd certainly seemed quite positive about who they had seen and with whom when she and Chrys had spoken to them.

"What about the neighbour's death? Are you going to look into that?" India asked, and she could tell from the blank look on Rendle's face that the idea hadn't occurred to him.

"I suppose I should chase it up," he said after a pause.

***

"Did you see anything interesting when you went to the 'toilet'?" India asked Chrys, making inverted commas in the air when she said 'toilet'.

After allowing India to send an updated email to Jacko back in Windsor, Rendle had parked them in an interview room, and they were waiting for him to come back with information he was following up on Eric's phone and the neighbour's death.

"There was a locked door. I think it might lead to a basement or cellar. When I looked out of the toilet window, I could see the ground sloped away. The back door leads onto a large terrace, and then there are steps down into the backyard. On the other side of the house from where we were, there was another living room and behind that a formal dining room. No sign of anyone else there. It's upstairs or that cellar I'd be interested in looking at."

"Me too."

"So you didn't buy into the rubbish Mrs. McEvoy told Rendle?" Chrys asked.

"Not in the least. I think she's in it up to her neck. I could have killed Rendle when he cut off my questions."

"Yeah, that's why I had to get up and move away. Otherwise, I was going to say something I shouldn't. I wanted to scream at her and ask what she'd done with Sonny."

"I can imagine. Your little excursion to the toilet distracted her long enough for me to take a snapshot of her wedding photo. While I was on the computer here, I sent the photo through to Jacko."

"I'm surprised Rendle let you do that, seeing that he thinks Mrs. McEvoy is so wonderful."

"I didn't tell him what I was sending. One of his friendly DCs gave me the attachments I needed for my phone while Rendle disappeared into his office. He didn't see me take the shot either. His eyes were on *her* the whole time."

Chrys laughed. "Good one. What use do you think that photograph will be to your detective back in Windsor?"

"Our unidentified body had sustained some serious injuries at some point. They weren't recent. Although Mrs. McEvoy didn't give a full account of her husband's injuries, the little she described could well tally with old injuries we saw on the unidentified body. Now we know the accident happened in Queensland, Jacko can investigate it. They might have some of McEvoy's DNA stored somewhere. I'd like to compare it to the DNA from the unidentified remains."

"You think the body you found might be her husband?"

"I don't know, but I've also asked Jacko to have McEvoy's face aged to see if it matches our victim. I thought his face looked like a younger version of our dead man."

"If he was her husband, whose ashes are sitting on her mantelpiece?"

"Good question."

"You think it might be Sonny, don't you?"

"It's a possibility, Chrys, but I'm more inclined to think it might be the man called Eric who Rendle is trying to chase down. If Eric was Mrs. McEvoy's accomplice in Sonny's kidnapping, then she might have wanted to get rid of him."

"I thought about it being Sonny at first. That's also one of the reasons I went in to look at the urn. But it didn't *feel* right. I don't think it's him. I'm clinging to the hope that Sonny is still alive somewhere—probably in her house. So if Rendle isn't going to let us search her house, what are we going to do?"

"Let's wait and see what he comes up with now he's got this Eric's phone number. I think we'll find it's a dead end, though."

Chrys screwed her face up as though thinking hard. "You know, there was something very familiar about that woman's face, but I can't for the life of me figure out where I've come across her before."

"Well, she lived in Wilberforce and probably shopped in Windsor sometimes. Perhaps you've seen her in a supermarket, a café or on the street somewhere. Can't say I've ever seen her before. I'd have noticed her height."

"Hmm. Maybe, but I can't visualise her anywhere in Windsor, and I've been racking my brain trying to picture her in different settings. I think it was somewhere else. I just wish I could remember."

***

"The phone number Mrs. McEvoy gave me is an unregistered pay-as-you-go," DI Rendle told India and Chrys. "We've requested the records—they might give us a lead. The phone is definitely switched off."

"Have you been able to locate where it was last used?" India asked.

"We're waiting on that information. We might know something tomorrow."

"What about Mrs. McEvoy's neighbour who died? What did you find out?"

"I looked up Gordon Haines's death on our system. It was an unfortunate accident. It seems Mr. Haines was attempting to clean the gutters at the rear of his neighbour's house when he fell to his death."

"There was nothing suspicious about it?"

"It was fully investigated and ruled an accident. Now, if there's nothing else, I need to get on. Why don't you give me a ring tomorrow morning and I'll let you know if I have any news over the phone."

In other words, he was dismissing them. India decided there was no point in arguing with the man, but she wanted to know more about the neighbour's death.

"Okay, I'll do that. Come on, Chrys, let's go."

***

"WHERE ARE WE headed now?" Chrys asked, almost running to keep pace with India. "Why are you in such a hurry?"

"I spotted an internet café down the road. I think we should go there and see if there is anything online about the neighbour's death. My phone needs charging, and I didn't want to waste precious battery looking it up back there. Rendle has kept us hanging around so much today that we've achieved very little. I'm hoping we might learn something from it."

"Okay, now you're talking."

She looked at Chrys with amusement. "I think you've been watching too many films."

***

THE TWO WOMEN huddled around the computer reading the online reports of retired butcher Gordon Haines's death. It was confirmed as a tragic accident: the man had fallen to his death while helping a neighbour.

"It says here that he ran a family butcher's business up in Byres Road," Chrys said. "That's not far from the McEvoy house. We drove up there last night—why don't we go back up there now and see if we can find his daughter who's mentioned here? See if she has anything interesting to tell us."

India looked at her watch. It was four twenty-five. Would the butcher's shop still be open by the time they got there?

"I'm not sure we'd make it. We have to collect the car from the police station first, but we'll give it a shot."

***

IT WAS JUST after five by the time the two women arrived at Haines Family Butcher's. India could see a woman and a man clearing up. She knocked on the door, but the woman pointed at the sign indicating they were closed. India pulled out her identification and held it up, hoping they would respond.

The woman opened the door a fraction asking what they wanted.

"Are you Fiona Kinley?"

"That's right."

"We've been to your neighbour's house today with a detective inspector from Police Scotland making some inquiries, and while there, we learned about your father's death. I wonder if we might have a quick word with you."

40

Fiona and Fergus Kinley led India and Chrys to a compact room at the back of the shop, where there was a small table with a couple of chairs.

"I'm sorry we can't offer you anywhere more comfortable," Fiona said. "We used to live above the shop, and I could have taken you up there, but we've moved into my father's house now and let the upstairs."

Fergus muttered something about getting on with things and left them to it.

"We're fine here," India said.

"I'm intrigued as to what you want to ask me. You mentioned you were at Doctor Hamilton's house today with Police Scotland, but I assume from your accent you're not part of Police Scotland."

"Doctor Hamilton?"

"Yes. You said you were at my neighbour's house today. She's my neighbour."

"To clarify we have the right neighbour, I'm talking about the woman who lives in the property where your father died."

"Yes. That's where Doctor Hamilton lives, and it was on her property that my father died."

"Ah," India said, realisation dawning. Mrs. McEvoy must use her maiden name, much like she did, in her professional work. "I didn't realise she went under the name of Hamilton. We believed we were interviewing a Mrs. McEvoy."

"I don't know the name McEvoy. My father only referred to his neighbours by their first names, Lachlan and Greer, and I know her name is Hamilton. What were you there to question her about if you say you *learned* about my father's death while you were there? You didn't know about him before you went there?"

"No. Mrs. McEvoy initially believed we'd come to question her further about your father's death. That's when we learned of it, after she made reference to him. Police Scotland have been assisting us with inquiries into a missing Australian man. I'm Detective Inspector India Hargreaves from the Australian Police and Chrys here is the fiancée of the missing man."

"I don't think I can help you then. I've never come across any Australian men at Doctor Hamilton's place."

"Have you seen *any* men at her house?"

"Well, there was her husband, of course—I saw him there after they moved back in, the poor sod. Then there was a strange man who said he was her husband's carer. But when I knocked on their door and spoke to him, I saw he had plaster dust over his trousers and shoes."

One of the Polish cleaners had used the expression 'strange man'. India wondered if Fiona Kinley could be referring to the same person.

"Why did you refer to him as strange?"

"I thought he was acting a bit strange when I spoke to him, and he had a funny accent. I couldn't quite pin it down. I wanted to ask him where he was from, but I didn't dare. I felt a bit uneasy, so I left and went home."

"Was there a particular reason you knocked on their door?"

"I'd been hearing noises coming from their house that sounded like building work, and if I'm honest, I was being nosy. My father had told me they'd had builders in before they returned, and he'd been in there. He said they'd refurbished the house from top to bottom, so I couldn't understand why they'd be doing more work."

"Perhaps they were working on the cellar," Chrys piped in. "There *is* a cellar, isn't there?"

"Ah. Yes, there is," Fiona said. "Perhaps that's what he was doing. I never thought of that. But why would the carer be working on the cellar? He claimed the noises I'd heard were coming from the empty property on the other side where building work had been going on for months."

"I'll admit it does seem a bit odd," India agreed. "When did you last see this man?"

"Not long after I spoke to him. I saw him entering the house one day, then I never saw him after that. Doctor Hamilton's husband died soon after, though, and as she said, she didn't need the carer anymore. I thought she cremated her husband with indecent haste. I don't think she held a funeral. When Fillmore's handled my father's funeral, it took several weeks. They delivered Lachlan's ashes back to her within days."

"Fillmore's is a funeral service?"

"That's right. They have their showroom on the other side of the road from here, just a few doors up on the next corner. I know Fillmore's handled the cremation because I saw one of their staff members arrive in a vehicle with their name on the side. He carried an urn into the house."

India made a mental note to call there before they returned to the guest house.

231

"Did you ever see Mrs. McEvoy's—I mean Doctor Hamilton's husband at close quarters?" she asked.

"I saw him the day my father died. That was the only time."

"Can you tell us about the day your father died? That's if you feel up to it," she added.

***

FIONA SIGHED. WHAT good would it do to rake over all this? But perhaps she could be honest with this detective and say what she thought her father was really up to.

"I went around to Dad's to see him that day. I usually called in most days to see him. I couldn't find him anywhere in the house, and he didn't respond to my calls. I saw the back door was open and so thought he must be in the garden. I could tell he was at home because his coat was hanging up in the hall and his keys were lying on the kitchen worktop."

She paused for a second, and the detective nodded at her, as though encouraging her to continue. The next part was going to be hard for her.

"I went out into the garden and called him. He didn't answer. Then I noticed one of his ladders propped up against the boundary wall. I climbed up the ladder and saw him...saw him lying in next door's garden with his long extension ladder nearby." She swallowed back the emotion she could feel rising.

"The press said he'd been cleaning the neighbour's gutters," the detective commented.

"That's nonsense. Dad didn't even clean his own gutters. Why would he clean hers? No, the truth is I believe my father was snooping. He'd mentioned that he was concerned about Doctor Hamilton leaving her husband alone, and he was worried something was wrong. I think he was trying to see in the back window. That's where I think he'd heard weird noises coming from."

"Right. What did you do after you saw him lying there?"

"I raced around to their house, calling for an ambulance on the way. I knew she was home, as she'd pulled into the driveway as I arrived there. She let me in—not straight away, mind you. She took her time. Then we went out to the garden. I noticed her husband sitting in the front room as we went through. She examined Dad and said he was dead. The paramedics arrived shortly after and confirmed the same. Another official was called in to confirm death and issue the certificate. A couple of policemen arrived and some forensic people to look over the scene. I was led through the house, and that's when I saw the husband more closely, sitting in his wheelchair in the window. He was turned at an angle, and I could see he was dribbling."

Fiona watched the two women exchange nods, and then the detective pulled out a photograph.

"Would this be the man you saw sitting in the wheelchair?"

Fiona examined the photograph carefully. It did look a bit like the face she remembered, but…

"It's difficult to say. In this photo, he looks fit and healthy. The man I saw looked dreadful. He was very pale, his head was lolling to one side, and he was dribbling. But he did look a *bit* like this man. Is this Doctor Hamilton's husband before he had his accident?"

"That's my fiancé," the woman called Chrys said, her voice shaking. "His name is Sonny Day. He is *not* her husband. She's just pretending he is."

"I don't understand. Why would Doctor Hamilton pretend your fiancé is her husband?"

A deathly silence descended on the room. Fiona could tell from the frown on the detective's face she was not happy with Chrys's statement. Fiona looked at both women, waiting for an answer to her question.

"We're not sure," the detective said finally. "Can I take you back to your father for a minute? Were you satisfied that he'd died as a result of an accident?"

"Not entirely. The whole thing was very strange in my opinion. I never told the police what I thought Dad was up to. I was too embarrassed to admit my father might have been snooping on his neighbour. It *could* have been an accident. Dad wasn't used to climbing up long ladders. He hadn't done it for years. When I looked up at the house, I could see the curtains were slightly parted on the back window nearest to where he was. I think he might have been trying to see inside. But if he saw anything in there, we'll never know."

41

"WE'RE GOING TO have trouble crossing the road here. It's peak hour now," India said. "We need to go up to the pedestrian crossing further up. Come on." They continued up the hill.

"Why did you glare at me when I told Fiona her neighbour was pretending Sonny was her husband?" Chrys asked.

"In the first place, you were making an allegation — an allegation which you *believe*. We don't have enough proof to confirm your thinking. You heard Fiona. She wasn't positive the man she saw was Sonny. As a member of the police force, I have to be careful about making allegations without solid proof. Especially to members of the public whom it doesn't concern. We don't talk about police investigations in any detail. We ask questions and gather evidence."

"Well, I don't have those restrictions as a member of the public. I'm more than a member of the public, though. Sonny is my fiancé."

"I know, Chrys, but I was also worried that Fiona might involve herself and cause problems. If she suspects the doctor had something to do with her father's death, she might stick her nose in and scare the good doctor off. We want Mrs. McEvoy — or Doctor Hamilton — to believe everything is hunky-dory until we pass all this new information on to Rendle. I'm hoping once I present photographs of Sonny and Doctor McEvoy to this funeral service, we'll have more to tell him."

They paused at the crossing, and India took a tentative step off the pavement. The traffic stopped, allowing them to cross.

"Hmph! As if Rendle's going to do anything about it," Chrys muttered, once she'd caught up with India on the other side of the road.

"He'll have to. If we don't get a positive ID here, then it will be obvious—even to Rendle—that something is amiss. He can then formally interview them. Fiona has agreed to tell him everything she told us this evening."

"Well, you needn't worry about Fiona causing problems. She's given you her word she won't speak to Mrs. McEvoy or Doctor Hamilton or whatever she's called."

"Let's hope she sticks to it. The guest house has wi-fi. I'll link into it and send another email to Jacko tonight, asking him to investigate the doctor back home now we know the name she used professionally. Someone she worked with might recognise her husband's photograph."

"What I don't understand is why the tax office didn't pick up that there was another taxpayer living at the same address as her husband. Why didn't they tell you that?"

"No doubt because the right question wasn't asked. A member of my team probably asked them to look into a couple called McEvoy at the address. We didn't know she used the name Hamilton. I suspect they weren't asked if there was anyone else registered at the same address."

"All the same, you'd think they'd mention it. They must have *seen* it on their records."

"I don't know how their records come up. Anyway, we know now."

They paused outside the funeral parlour, looking in the front doors.

"It's not open. Let's check around the corner—they might have a side door. Someone might still be there."

***

A MIDDLE-AGED MAN answered their knocks. "I'm sorry. We're closed, ladies," he said. "If you wouldn't mind coming back in the morning, we open at nine a.m."

"We're not here as customers," India said, flashing her ID. "I'm Detective Inspector Hargreaves. We're working with Police Scotland making inquiries about a cremation you recently handled."

"In that case, you'd better come in." The man stepped aside for them. He hadn't looked at her identification or queried her accent, which was handy as far as India was concerned. Otherwise, they would have had to return with Rendle, and it was unlikely Rendle would be willing to visit the funeral parlour while he believed Mrs. McEvoy was not involved in anything dodgy.

The man led them through to an office, asking them to take a seat while he walked around to sit at his desk. "My name is Mr. Fillmore, I'm the owner of this establishment. What's the name of the person you're making inquiries about?"

"A Kenrick Lachlan McEvoy."

"Ah, I recognise the name. My assistant manager handled that one while my wife and I were away. I think he's in the showroom. There was nothing untoward about it, was there?"

"We just need him to look at some photographs."

"I see. If you would like to follow me," Mr. Fillmore said, standing.

They followed him through to a spacious area where a range of coffins were on display. A man, who looked to be about forty, was moving the displays around. While they'd been walking, India had opened the photo gallery in her phone and brought up the photograph of Sonny Day.

"Kevin, these young women would like you to take a look at some photographs. It's about the McEvoy cremation."

Kevin looked up, startled. "Is there a problem?"

India stepped towards him, holding up the photograph of Sonny.

"Can you tell me if this is the man you cremated?"

"No, it wasn't him. Definitely not."

She was relieved to hear him say that and heard Chrys, who was standing behind her, sigh heavily. She would be happy with that news.

"What about this man?" India swapped the photograph of Sonny Day for an enlarged image of a young Kenrick McEvoy.

"No, it wasn't him either," Kevin said.

"He would look older than this picture, which was taken some years ago."

"No. He didn't look like either of the men you've shown me. The only resemblance was that he had dark hair. The nose is completely wrong for a start. And Mr. McEvoy had a much higher forehead. Why are you showing me these photographs? Was there something suspicious about the cremation? I can assure you, all the paperwork was in order."

She noticed that the man's left eye suddenly wandered, and he seemed on edge. Was he hiding something?

"Kevin!" Mr. Fillmore shouted at him.

"Sorry, Mr. Fillmore," Kevin said, casting his eyes down to the floor.

"We're making inquiries into a missing person case. Thank you for your time, you've been very helpful," India said, wondering if Fillmore had noticed Kevin's eye as well and if that was why he'd shouted at him. Perhaps it was a nervous quirk of Kevin's. The question was, why was he nervous?

She refrained from saying they might receive a follow-up visit from Police Scotland. Mr. Fillmore was under the impression that was who they were, and she didn't want him to discover it wasn't the case. He seemed the type who'd make a complaint.

"I'll show you out," Mr. Fillmore said, indicating with his arm that they should retrace their steps.

They walked in silence to the door, where India thanked him again.

***

"IT WASN'T SONNY, thank goodness," Chrys said as they walked back to the car, which she'd parked in a street off the main road, further down on the same side as the funeral parlour. "I didn't think it was him, but it's good to have it confirmed. Who was in the other photo you showed him?"

"Doctor Kenrick McEvoy. From their wedding photograph."

"So, not her husband either. You think it was her little helper then? This Eric person?"

"Could be. Now Rendle has another lead to follow up. He can't ignore this one."

"No. Where to next?"

"The guest house so I can send Jacko that email, then I'll try to reach Rendle. I doubt he'll do anything tonight, so I think finding somewhere to eat would be in order. What do you fancy?"

***

CHRYS WOKE UP in a sweat shortly after one a.m. She'd been dreaming about finding Sonny with blood pouring from every part of his body. She shuddered, hoping it wasn't a sign that something awful was about to happen. She needed a pee so dragged herself out of bed, felt around with her feet for her slippers, slipped them on and padded off to the bathroom.

It was while she was sitting on the loo that she realised where she'd seen Doctor Hamilton before. Sonny had been injured at work last year, and he'd been taken into the emergency department at Nepean Hospital. She'd left work early to go down and join him. It was Doctor Hamilton who'd stitched Sonny's wound and chatted to them. They'd also bumped into her shortly after at one of their Spanish lessons in Penrith. Sonny had recognised her, and she'd told him the class wasn't advanced enough for her and she'd be switching to a higher-level class which was held on a different night. They'd never seen her again. So she knew who Sonny was and would have had access to his home address from the hospital records. Had she been stalking him? Did she kidnap Sonny on the day he disappeared? She could have easily knocked Sonny off his bike and injected him before bundling him into her car.

Chrys didn't care what India thought. She had to go round to the McEvoy house tonight. The doctor might have been alarmed by their visit and do something; if Sonny was still in there, she might decide to kill him and dump his body.

After washing her hands, Chrys splashed water onto her face to make sure she was fully alert. She tiptoed into the room, collected the clothes she'd stripped off earlier and returned to the bathroom to dress. The clothes she'd worn today would have to do—she couldn't afford to rummage around in her bag looking for clean ones. It could disturb India, and if she woke up, she'd try to dissuade Chrys from leaving. Once dressed, she picked up her boots and bag and slipped out of the door.

***

CHRYS MANAGED TO pick up a taxi in a street near the guest house and asked the driver to drop her at the corner of the road where the doctor lived. Glasgow cabs had loud diesel engines, and she was worried it would cause a disturbance in the quiet street. She didn't want the doctor looking out of her window if she was woken by the noise of the taxi.

She reached the doctor's house and stopped. There was a light on in the hallway. Was the doctor still up? Moving over to the driveway, Chrys examined the fence and gate behind it that prevented anyone gaining access to the back of the house. She could make out a lock on the gate, so she'd need a key to get through there. It was too high for her to scale without the aid of a ladder. There was nowhere to hide outside the doctor's house, and if she were to crouch down on the other side behind the front wall, she could be spotted by neighbours across the street or passing traffic. Fiona had told them the house on the other side of Doctor Hamilton's was empty and builders had been working on it for months. There was a hedge at the front of the property, and Chrys decided to move in there to keep watch. She also might need to relieve herself, and the hedge would provide good cover. She could be here for hours. If Doctor Hamilton tried to leave the house, she'd hear her and could call the police.

Chrys wished she'd brought a bottle of water with her. She hadn't had a drink since the meal last night, where she'd drunk virtually a whole bottle of wine—India had only poured herself a small glass, which she'd barely touched. Chrys had meant to gulp down a glass of water back at the guest house, but she'd forgotten. She'd also love to have a cigarette, but the glow might be spotted. Since Sonny had disappeared, she'd taken up the habit again, something she thought she'd left behind in her youth. Accepting that having a cigarette wouldn't be sensible, she hunkered down by the boundary wall and waited.

42

INDIA WOKE FEELING refreshed. For a low-budget guest house, the bed was remarkably comfortable. She reached across for her watch to look at the time. It was 7:45 a.m.—later than she normally slept. Her stomach was rumbling, demanding food. Eager to go down to have breakfast as soon as possible, she turned over to see if Chrys was awake and was greeted with her empty, unmade bed. She could see the bathroom door was open, but there was no sound coming from there, so Chrys had either gone down to the dining room already or was outside having a quick cigarette.

When she'd first met Chrys, India hadn't realised she was a smoker, as she'd never seen her smoking. But up at the cabin, she'd ducked outside after meals, and when India had remarked on it, Chrys had confessed it was an old habit she'd recently taken up again—"To deal with all the stress about Sonny."

With no smoking permitted in public buildings, anyone who wanted a cigarette had to go outside. Convinced that was where Chrys would be, India washed and dressed and headed downstairs, expecting to find Chrys in the dining room, but she wasn't there. Retracing her steps to the reception, India asked the woman who had checked them in whether she'd seen Chrys.

"No, I've not seen her at all. Mind you, I've stepped away from reception a few times. She might have gone out without me noticing. Perhaps she went for a walk."

"Yes, perhaps. Thanks anyway."

India returned to the dining room, deciding to go ahead with breakfast. She couldn't hold out any longer. She planned to have the full works today. A nice, large, cooked breakfast as well as a croissant and one of those delicious pastries they had on the buffet.

***

FORTY MINUTES LATER, she was in the bathroom losing much of the breakfast she'd consumed. *That'll teach me to be so greedy*, was her first thought, *unless…unless this is morning sickness!* She'd felt queasy a few times over the past week. Could she be pregnant? When was her last period? She couldn't remember, but it was certainly some weeks before she'd flown out of Sydney. *That must be it!* She'd stopped thinking about babies altogether, being so preoccupied with cases and all that had happened since, including flying to the UK.

It was now nine a.m., and Chrys still hadn't reappeared, nor was she answering her phone. Where could she be? India decided to pop out to find a pharmacy to pick up a pregnancy test. Hopefully, by the time she got back to the guest house, Chrys would also be back from wherever she'd gone.

***

THE TEST WAS positive! India hardly dared believe it and was delighted, of course, but 'wrong time' sprang to mind. If she phoned Rob to give him the news, he might demand she come home sooner. She'd booked a flight to leave the UK in three weeks' time, intending to return to Aberdeen and spend another week or two with her parents first. Deciding to leave it for a few days before phoning Rob, she turned her attention back to finding out where Chrys had disappeared to. She was beginning to worry that Chrys might have gone over to the McEvoy house first thing this morning. Would she have been so stupid? Yes, she probably would. India needed to get over there, pronto.

***

THERE WAS NO sign of Chrys at the McEvoy house. No sign of the doctor's car either, but India saw what looked like drops of blood on the driveway, which worried her. She knocked on the Kinleys' door, hoping for but not expecting an answer, as Fiona and her husband would be at the shop, so she was surprised when the door opened.

"Good morning, Fiona. I'm looking for my friend Chrys. Have you seen her or spoken to her this morning at all?"

"No, I haven't. Not that I spend all my time looking out the window, mind."

"What about Doctor Hamilton? Did you see her leaving the house this morning?"

"No. When Fergus left at eight, her car wasn't there. We've been up since seven, and I didn't hear it leave, so she must have driven off while we were still asleep. I didn't hear a thing."

"Well, thank you for your time anyway. Sorry to have troubled you. I need to make some phone calls."

"You look worried, lass. Why don't you come in and I'll make you a nice cup of tea?"

India hesitated. She *would* like a cup of tea, it might help settle her stomach, and she could phone Rendle from Fiona's house. She'd tried to get hold of him yesterday evening on both his mobile and the station's landline, only to be told he'd left for the day, so she'd left a message asking him to call her, then called his mobile again this morning before she left the guest house. He still wasn't answering. If she was unsuccessful again, she'd have to ask Police Scotland to send someone else to the McEvoy house.

***

RENDLE ANSWERED THE phone on her third attempt.

"Apologies, I wasn't able to take the call earlier. I was in a meeting."

"We've uncovered a lot of new information since we saw you yesterday afternoon, one of the chief points being that it *wasn't* Doctor Hamilton's husband who was cremated. She also employed a carer, who could have been this Eric character. But the main worry I have is Chrys Waters has disappeared. I woke to find her gone this morning. I'm at Fiona Kinley's house—she's Gordon Haines's daughter. Fiona and her husband live in her father's property now, next door to Doctor Hamilton's, and the doctor's car isn't here. I think you need to organise a search warrant for Hamilton's house and get around here as soon as possible. Chrys might be lying in there injured. I found what looked like drops of blood on the driveway. I've been trying to get through to Chrys on her phone, but it just goes to voicemail."

"Did you say Doctor Hamilton?"

"Yes, sorry. That's one of the things we learned last night from Fiona Kinley. Mrs. McEvoy goes by the name of Doctor Hamilton. Both she and her husband were doctors."

There was a moment's silence before Rendle said, *"Right. I'll organise a warrant and be there as soon as I can. You wait at the neighbour's for me. Do not attempt to enter the house."*

43

RENDLE ARRIVED ACCOMPANIED by two team members, whom India recognised from the station, with two separate squad cars following closely behind.

"I still haven't been able to get through to Chrys," she told Rendle, having rushed out to meet him.

Rendle nodded to one of the uniformed officers, who smashed Doctor Hamilton's front door open.

The team moved swiftly through the house, spreading out in all directions, to Rendle's barked orders. India followed them cautiously, and when she walked into the living room, the first thing she noticed was McEvoys' wedding photograph was gone, as was the urn of ashes. She went to find Rendle to tell him. He was in the kitchen searching through the drawers.

"I'm looking for the death certificate she showed me yesterday," he said. "I'm positive it was signed by a Doctor Hamilton."

"That wouldn't surprise me. With a different name on the death certificate, it wouldn't have raised any queries with the funeral parlour. The urn and wedding photos are gone as well. I think our doctor has flown the nest. But what has she done with Chrys—and Sonny for that matter?"

"You still believe she had Day here in the house?"

"I think it's highly likely, and Chrys also believed that. She must have come here in the middle of the night or very early this morning and encountered the doctor."

They were interrupted by one of Rendle's DCs. The one who had helped her yesterday. "Sir, you need to come and see this. It looks as though someone has been occupying a cellar room recently, and there's some kind of pulley system on the stairs."

India and Rendle followed the DC down the cellar steps. The first thing that struck her was the smell of disinfectant and bleach permeating throughout the cellar. She could see what the DC had meant by the pulley system. It appeared to have been partially dismantled, but perhaps it could have been used to pull a disabled person up the cellar stairs. She mentioned this to Rendle, who agreed.

A small room had been partitioned off in the middle of the cellar and contained a chair, a bedside cabinet and the iron frame of a fold-up bed. No mattress or bedding. At the back of the room, another space had been created, containing a plastic shower cubicle, sink and toilet. An extractor fan was running, which India assumed had activated when the light was switched on.

"It looks like it has been thoroughly cleaned up," the DC said.

"Agreed," Rendle said. "Get forensics down here and see what they can find. Where's the nearest dump and recycling centre? Find out and get someone over there to see if we can find the mattress that came off this bed frame. Right, let's see what's upstairs."

They returned to the ground floor, where they were met by a member of Rendle's team on his way down.

"There's no one up there, Sir, but it looks like some clothes are missing from one of the wardrobes. Women's clothes. There's still some in there, but there are also empty hangers. The other one still has men's clothes in it."

"Find out the registration of the house owner's car. It could be registered in the name of McEvoy or Hamilton. It's a black Audi. Put out an all-points bulletin on it. I want it stopped and searched. And alert all airports, docks and train stations—throughout the country. If a Doctor Greer Hamilton or Greer McEvoy attempts to board any, I want her detained."

Rendle turned to India, saying, "I need Miss Waters' phone number. We'll see if we can do a trace on it."

***

By EARLY AFTERNOON, there was still no news on Chrys, Sonny or Doctor Hamilton. India was convinced the doctor was well on her way out of the country by now. But what had she done with Chrys and Sonny?

The forensic team were still working on the McEvoy house, and despite someone's attempt to thoroughly clean up in the cellar, they had found traces of blood on the flagstone floor near the foot of the stairs. Otherwise, nothing else was found that could move the search forward.

India and Rendle were back at the station now. She was sitting in his office, rather than in an interview room or reception this time.

"Do you have any results in from your searches of the recycling centres?"

"The reports aren't back yet. They're still out there looking."

"What about the phone number Doctor Hamilton gave you yesterday for the man Eric?"

"Last located up in the Arden area. The phone only called one number—another pay-as-you-go no longer in use, which I suspect belonged to Doctor Hamilton. I'd say he dumped his and bought another phone. When she gave me his number, it was from a phone sitting on the kitchen worktop, indicating it was her current phone."

"You didn't take the doctor's mobile phone number, did you?"

"No, but I managed to obtain a number for her from the records pertaining to Gordon Haines. A phone number that is no longer in use. I have the team searching to see if she has a registered phone with any of the carriers in the name of Hamilton or McEvoy."

"I doubt you'll find a current one in her name. The funeral home, Fillmore's, might have a number for her."

"I'll get the team to check. I should have taken her number when we saw her. I'm sorry, but I just didn't see that she could be connected in any way. Neither of us knew she was a doctor or went by the name of Hamilton. I know. I know. If I'd let you finish questioning her, we might have found out that information. I apologise."

"Thank you, but she was damned good and very convincing. You wouldn't have been the only one she fooled."

After a rap on the slightly open door, one of Rendle's team stepped in. "We've found the car, Sir. It was parked near Glasgow Central station and had been ticketed. They were about to tow it away. I've organised for it to be taken to forensics."

"Great. Get someone down to Central to look through all the CCTV and see if we can spot her. Have we got access to her bank accounts yet?"

"Not yet. We're still attempting to track down who she banked with. There were no papers found at the house. I think she'd shredded everything. We found a shredding machine in the dining room."

"That blasted woman is too clever by half."

India had to agree. She thought it highly unlikely they'd find any trace of Hamilton on CCTV cameras at the station. A train would be too slow. She no doubt dumped the car there to mislead them. It was more likely she would have flown out of the country. The doctor could be halfway across the world by now.

44

Eleven hours earlier

CHRYS ROUSED, GROANING in pain, and became aware that she was in a dark, confined space. She could feel movement and what sounded like an engine. A car. She must be in the boot of the doctor's car. Was Sonny in here with her? Her hands and feet were bound, limiting movement, but she wriggled back and bumped into something soft. Yes, it was Sonny; she was sure.

She'd been in the middle of relieving her bladder when she'd heard quiet footfalls coming from the house, followed by the click of a car door or boot hatch opening. The footsteps retreated, and Chrys stood to look over the fence. That was when she'd seen the doctor struggling with what looked like a body out to the car, where she hefted it into the open boot. It had to be Sonny! The doctor returned to the house a second time, and Chrys ran around, phone in hand.

There was someone zipped into a sleeping bag, and when she opened it a little, she was shocked to see the pale, grey face of the man she loved. He had a pulse, so she wasn't too late. She'd tapped in 999, but before she could press the call button, she'd heard Doctor Hamilton's voice behind her, and something hard smashed against her head.

What had the doctor said? She'd been speaking in such a quiet tone, it was difficult for Chrys to catch, but it was something like, "You just couldn't leave things alone, could you?"

Her head now felt like it had been split in two, but it obviously wasn't that serious, as she could still think clearly. Where was the doctor taking them? Was there someone else with her or was she acting alone?

Chrys whispered Sonny's name a few times and attempted to nudge him, but he didn't respond. He was still unconscious, probably drugged.

It seemed like hours before the car stopped and she heard footsteps approach. A dull light filled the boot's interior as it popped open.

"Ah, you're awake then. Good. I didn't really fancy carrying you as well as your boyfriend."

The doctor moved out of sight again, and Chrys felt the judder of one of the doors opening, followed by a dragging sound and then a dull thud of something being placed on the ground. From her position, she could see it was a light of some kind. Was the doctor going to release her? If so, would she be strong enough to overpower the woman who was at least twenty centimetres taller than her and probably twice as strong?

It soon became apparent that the doctor had no intention of releasing her. She dragged Chrys out of the boot and ordered her to jump while pulling her off the road into a patch of bushes, where she pushed her down onto the ground. Chrys tucked her head in as she fell, grunting as her left shoulder and arm thumped against the hard earth.

Silhouetted by the light she had placed on the side of the road, the doctor half carried, half dragged Sonny from the car, depositing him on the ground beside Chrys. Then she walked back to the car and returned with a small bag and the light. Setting down both, she unzipped and opened out the sleeping bag Sonny was in and told Chrys to wriggle in next to him.

"I suppose you're going to kill us now. But you have to tell me *why* before you do. You owe me that, at least."

"What are you talking about, you silly young woman? Of course I'm not going to kill you! Why on earth would you think that? Doctors *preserve* life, they don't destroy it. Well, most doctors, anyway. There are exceptions, like Harold Shipman, but you probably wouldn't have heard of him, coming from Australia."

"But you killed your husband in Australia, didn't you? That was him you buried in that property in Wilberforce, wasn't it?"

"It *was* my husband I buried, but I didn't kill him. He died of natural causes. Oh, I admit, I fantasised about killing him countless times after his accident, but I couldn't do it."

"But you slit his throat and mutilated his face! I've seen the pictures." While India had been in the bathroom at the cabin, Chrys had taken a quick look at the file with the gruesome photographs India wouldn't let her see. If this woman was responsible, she was a monster.

"Lachie and I were married for fourteen years. My life with him wasn't always easy. He could be an arrogant control freak and tyrant who made decisions that affected both our lives without consulting me. I often wished something would go wrong for him one day and bring him down a peg or two. Be careful what you wish for—isn't that the saying? It's so true. The Lachie I knew before his accident, despite his shortcomings, was far better than the Lachie I experienced post-accident.

"After extensive treatment, he was left with disabilities that would affect him for the rest of his life—although I always suspected he exaggerated his problems and that he wasn't nearly as disabled as he made out. He became intolerable, with extreme mood swings, whiny complaints and a speech impediment which made it extremely difficult to understand his demands. If I didn't respond to his bidding, he became aggressive and violent. His face was permanently set in a ferocious scowl."

There was a rustle in the nearby bushes. The doctor paused, picked up the light and swung it around, searching for signs of movement. Chrys hoped it wasn't a dangerous animal. Did they have any of those in Scotland?

"It's nothing," the doctor said, waving her arm dismissively. "Where was I? Ah, yes. So, night after night, I'd return from work to be greeted with his aggressive attitude, and I'd have to spend all my time dealing with him. I was lucky if I got any sleep most days. It wears you down after a while." The doctor sniffed, and Chrys realised the woman was close to tears.

"One night, I opened the door to complete silence. I thought he must have fallen asleep, so I crept through to my bedroom—after the accident, Lachie needed his own room. There, I grabbed a few hours' sleep. When I woke up later and went into the kitchen to make our meal, I noticed he hadn't moved, and he was unusually silent. I took a closer look at him and discovered he was dead. I couldn't be sure, but I suspect he died of a massive stroke that killed him instantly. No doubt while he was in the middle of one of his tirades, working himself into a frenzy. I think he spent much of the day doing that."

"Why didn't you call someone? Why slit his throat and mutilate him like that? And why take Sonny? What was that all about?"

"Money, my dear. What else? But I'll tell you about the slit throat and mutilation first. As I said, I had been fantasising for months about killing him, and I *really* wanted to slit his throat. After he was dead, I thought it wouldn't harm him and might give me some satisfaction to do it. It did—a little. I carved a smile into his face because even in death he still had that miserable scowl. I wanted to see him smile like he used to in the past. It was just a bit of fun.

"As for the money—we'd been awarded a very large settlement from the company whose vehicle caused Lachie's injuries. He'd been fully assessed with regard to his injuries and future needs, but up to that point, we hadn't received a penny, and our finances weren't too good. Lachie had left his job and was on his way to start another, so there was no sick pay. We had private health insurance, but that didn't cover all the costs. I also had to fly up and down to Brisbane from Sydney.

"If they'd discovered Lachie was dead, the insurance company would have withdrawn the offer and given me very little. I probably would have had to do battle with them for years. There was to be a home visit before the settlement payment. They had only seen him in the hospital and rehabilitation centre in Queensland prior to Lachie coming home.

"That's where Sonny came in. I don't know if you remember, but I treated him for an injury last year at the Nepean Hospital where I worked. I noticed you two lived not far from me. I used to pass your place on my way to work and regularly spotted him cycling along the road."

So the doctor *had* known where they lived.

"After Lachie died, I realised if I wanted that settlement, I needed to do something. Sonny was a similar height, build and colouring to Lachie. Of course, his face wasn't perfect, there were differences, so I had to do something about that. I caused some damage to Sonny's face, leaving it swollen, and told the insurers' assessors that he'd tipped his wheelchair over. Don't worry, it's all healed now. Don't forget, I'm a doctor, so I was able to treat him.

"It worked and I received the payout. I buried Lachie on a property that had been empty for twenty years. *Twenty years*. I expected it to remain derelict and empty for a further twenty years. I thought that if Lachie's body was ever discovered, there was no way the police would be able to identify him many years on. How was I to know the property would be sold shortly after I buried him? From my online searches, though, I see they have nevertheless had difficulty identifying Lachie."

"Not for much longer," Chrys said. "If you received your money, why not release Sonny then? Why bring him to the UK? What was your plan?"

"Oh, I had to have a husband to bring back with me."

"You must have broken into our house to take Sonny's passport."

"I didn't need to *break* in. I had Sonny's keys."

Of course you did, Chrys thought. That's why she hadn't noticed. "Why all the games with Sweden? Who did you use to travel on Sonny's passport to Sweden?"

"Ah, that was Erik. A fellow half-Scot, half-Norwegian. We met up in the Nepean Hospital in Penrith, and

I offered him some work. After he returned to Sweden and posted Sonny's letter—which we believed would stop you or the police looking for him—that should have been the end of our association. He'd been paid handsomely.

"But, like a bad penny, Erik turned up again at our house in Glasgow, and the stupid fool killed my neighbour. I don't know what Gordon was up to, but Erik spotted him trying to snoop in one of the back bedroom windows. That's where Sonny was. All the idiot had to do was go up there and fully close the curtains so Gordon couldn't see in there and gag Sonny if he was awake— but no. He had to go outside and cause Gordon to fall to his death. His actions jeopardised my whole plan."

"So you killed him, pretended he was your husband and had him cremated?"

"No, no—you have it wrong again, dear. Erik was a drinker. I'd warned him about it, but when I was out at work, he drank large quantities of whisky. After Gordon's death, we had to move Sonny in case the police wanted to look in the room where they knew Gordon had placed the ladder. We moved him temporarily into a different upstairs room while Erik prepared space for Sonny in the cellar. He's been down there ever since. There are steep stone steps down to the cellar, and that fool Erik, while highly inebriated, tripped and somersaulted to the bottom, breaking both his back and neck on the flagstone floor. I found him after arriving home from a trip I'd made. He was still alive—barely—but died a few minutes later. There was no point in calling an ambulance. So yes, he is the man I had cremated. Don't worry—I've sent his ashes along to his family now, telling them what happened to him."

"I don't understand why you were working if you had received this large sum of money. Why would you need to?"

"I needed access to documentation covering deaths, computerised prescription systems and, of course, drugs. I only took on a temporary position in Glasgow and worked part time. But it was necessary. As a doctor, I could prescribe drugs—but a limited amount. I needed more."

"Before this Erik died, were you planning on killing Sonny to pretend *he* was your husband?"

"No, that was never my plan. I was always going to release him and drop him off at a hospital. I kept putting it off until I was ready to leave, but the detective's visit earlier today meant I had to speed things up. And you turning up like you did tonight added another problem for me to deal with. It made things far more complex, which is why we're where we are now. If you hadn't stuck your nose in, things would have been different."

"So if you weren't going to kill Sonny, why would you need access to death certificates?"

"I didn't at first. It was prescriptions and drugs I wanted access to. After Erik died, I needed a death certificate for the funeral service in Lachie's name to simplify matters and then a real one for Erik's family in his name. I considered sending his body back home, but it was too complicated. Cremation was simpler."

Chrys wasn't convinced the doctor was telling the truth. About anything.

"Now, Chrys—it is Chrys, isn't it? Much as I've enjoyed our little conversation, I need to hit the road. Places to go, people to see, you know how it is."

"You're bloody mad if you think you'll get away with this."

"You're quite right. I am probably a little mad. But I do intend to 'get away with this', as you say. I'm going to inject you with something that will knock you out for several hours. Once you've nodded off, I'll release your ties and zip you both up tight. I don't want either of you dying of hypothermia out here. It's quite a chilly night. I'll place your phone in with you. When you wake up, you'll be able to call for help—if you can pick up a signal. Otherwise, I'm sure someone will come along and find you—or you could walk off looking for help."

"You don't have to knock me out, just leave me and go."

"I can't leave you bound up. And I can't undo your ties and leave you with your phone to use as soon as I'm gone. Be fair. I need time to get where I'm going to. I'll leave your bag beside you. Stop worrying, everything will be all right. Now you and Sonny are reunited, you can return to Australia and live happily ever after. I've left his passport and his wallet with enough cash to pay for his airfare home in his jacket. Well not *his* jacket—it was Lachie's. Also, as I've caused him all this inconvenience, the least I can do is compensate the two of you."

As the doctor filled a syringe with liquid and turned Chrys's head to reach her neck, Chrys wondered if these would be her last moments alive. She felt the prick of the needle followed by a warm glow spreading throughout her body, and the pain in her head dissipated. She struggled to remain awake as the doctor cut her ties, but it wasn't long before she faded into a deep, relaxing sleep.

45

SONNY STIRRED AND sensed he was no longer bound to a bed. He was lying on something very hard and could feel the warmth of someone lying next to him. *Chrys's scent*, he thought — a combination of the soap and shampoo she favoured, mixed with her own sweet smell. He must be imagining it. Or dreaming. His eyes were no longer blindfolded, so he opened them but could only see darkness. He willed his hand to move and touched clothing. There was definitely someone lying close to him.

Could it be true? Could this possibly be Chrys? And if so, where were they? He opened his mouth to speak, but nothing came out. His throat was too dry. Normally, he had a tube feeding fluids into him, but that hadn't happened today, nor had he been given much to drink.

They seemed to be cocooned in some tiny, dark place. He couldn't make any sense of it. He was unable to move his left arm; it was pinned between him and whoever he was lying next to. He reached his right arm across his chest, attempting to feel the body next to him. Was this Chrys? He prodded the body, getting no response.

With his right arm bent, he gradually moved it up, brushing against a woollen hat fixed to his head. This was different. Was he thinking back to days spent camping in the bush? Or was it real? There seemed to be some kind of opening behind his head, and he could feel cold air. That couldn't be right. They wouldn't camp on open ground in Australia. Never. It was too dangerous. So where they hell were they? The effort of thinking proved too much for him, and soon he drifted back into sleep.

***

CHRYS WOKE TO a thumping head. In fact, every part of her body seemed to be aching. She had an unpleasant taste in her mouth, her tongue felt it was lined with fur, her throat was parched, and when she attempted to part her lips, they were stuck together. She felt skin rip off as she opened her mouth and tried to gather some saliva. She desperately needed a drink.

Where am I? Realisation dawned, and her first thought was perhaps the doctor had told the truth because Chrys was very much alive, and as far as she knew, so was Sonny. But she had to get help for them both, otherwise they might die out here in what was most likely an isolated place. The doctor was hardly going to dump them in a busy suburban street, was she?

With her left hand, Chrys tapped down her body looking for her bag or phone but could find neither. She tried to sit up but couldn't manage it. She was deep inside the sleeping bag, and she was too weak. She collapsed back calling out a feeble, croaky, "Help," before lapsing once more into unconsciousness.

46

THEA MCFARLANE ANSWERED the door to a young man she recognised—her neighbour's son, who worked for a courier company.

"I have a parcel for Mrs. Andersson," he said. "It has to be signed for."

"Can I do that or does my mother have to?"

"It's okay, you can sign for it, seeing as I know you're Mrs. Andersson's daughter." He grinned.

She scrawled her signature on his digital gadget. He thanked her and handed over the parcel. It was heavier than she'd thought it would be.

"Thanks," she said to his retreating back. Looking down at the parcel, it gave no clue as to where it had come from, and her mother hadn't mentioned she was expecting a delivery.

Thea walked through to the kitchen and dropped the parcel onto the table. "This is for you," she said to her mother, who was at the stove making one of her large pots of soup.

"Me? I hadna ordered anything."

Thea shrugged, feigning indifference. She was curious to know what was in the parcel. Her mother continued stirring the pot on the stove. "Shall I open it for you?"

"Are ya sure 'tis fer me?

"Yes, Mum. It's addressed to Mrs. Andersson at this address."

"Aye, well, open it then."

Thea grabbed a small knife from the drawer and ran it through the tape that sealed the box. She opened it up to find an assortment of items inside. She picked up the first two items, a passport and a wallet, opening both in turn.

"This is Erik's passport and wallet," she said. "Why are we being sent these?"

Her mother stopped what she was doing and hurried over to look.

"Ya dinna think somethen's happened to 'im?" she asked, heaving in a large breath. "I ken there wis something wrong. He promised he'd call again the week after 'is last call. I tol ya!"

"You know what Erik's like," Thea said. "He was no doubt on a drinking binge somewhere and not sober enough to call. There's an envelope here addressed to you. Maybe there's a letter in there that will explain everything."

"Open it, for I cannae."

Thea slit the envelope open to find a certificate and a letter. She could see it was a death certificate but decided not to say anything to her mother straight away.

"I'll read you the letter," she said.

Dear Mrs. Andersson,

In this box, you will find some of Erik's personal possessions and his ashes.

Thea could hear her mother was having difficulty breathing.

"Sit down and use your inhaler. Is it in your pocket?"

Mrs. Andersson, once a heavy smoker, now relied on an inhaler to ease her breathing when she became distressed. She nodded, retrieved her inhaler and drew in two large breaths.

"Carry on," she said after a minute.

> Erik has been working for me for the past few months, living in, helping to look after my disabled husband and also doing some building work. Unfortunately, he liked drinking too much and, after consuming a large quantity of alcohol one night, fell down the cellar steps, breaking his neck and back. I found him when I returned home, but it was too late to do anything to help him.

> Feeling responsible for him, I organised his cremation and death certificate. I hope you don't mind. It would have been expensive and difficult to arrange for his body to be shipped home to Shetland. Erik doesn't appear to have used a bank, as I found a quantity of cash in his room. I have added the last wages I owed him, making a total of £2,500, which you will find in the plastic bag. I am sure Erik would have wanted you to have this and the last of his personal possessions. I gave his clothes to a charity shop.

> I am sorry for your loss and trust you will know the best thing to do with Erik's ashes.

> With very best wishes,
> Greer McEvoy.

"Two and a half thousand pounds. My God." Thea was shocked. "I can't believe Erik saved that much money. It would be a first, I think. Mum?"

Mari Andersson was slumped in her chair, tears pouring down her face. "My Erik is gone."

Thea realised her comment about Erik's money had been insensitive. Of course her mother would be upset to learn her darling son had died. And he *had* been her special boy when he was young, grabbing all the attention and being fussed over, while Thea, as the 'capable' older sister, was expected to just get on with things, with few demonstrative shows of affection. Personally, Thea felt little about Erik's passing. If anything, she thought about the same as when her father died. *Good riddance.* But she did care about her mother, who was now finally free of worry about both the male members of the family.

"I'm sorry, mamma." She walked over and placed her arm around her mother's shoulders. Thea only used 'mamma' when either she or her mother were distressed, reverting to the childhood address she'd used for her when they lived in Norway.

"Ye dinna think somethin's not quite right there?" Mari sobbed. "Should we go to the police?"

"The police? Why would we go to the police? It seems straightforward to me. Erik's death certificate is here. It's signed by a Doctor Hamilton. What's suspicious about it? Or are you worried about the money? If he was working for this woman and he lived in, then he wouldn't have had a lot to spend his money on. I imagine she provided all his food."

"Mebbe."

Thea carefully lifted what she now realised was an urn out of the box and placed it on the table. They both stared at it without speaking until Thea broke the silence.

"What shall we do with Erik's ashes? Throw them off a cliff or something? You know how he loved the sea. No...on second thoughts they would probably blow back in our faces. What about planting a new bush in the garden and burying his ashes at the foot of the bush? Then you would know he was always close by."

Her mother nodded, dabbing her eyes with a hanky. Thea could see the idea appealed to her.

"I'll think on it," Mari said after a pause, then stood and walked over to the stove to stir the pot.

47

BERTHA McCAULEY HAD had enough; she needed a break, and she'd spotted a handy clump of bushes, unusual in this remote valley. She called out to her fellow cyclists, who were some distance ahead of her. Hearing her, one of them signalled to the others, and they turned back to join Bertha, who by this time was sitting by the side of the road gulping water from her flask.

"Sorry, guys, I need a break," she said. "I also need a pee."

"I'm not surprised with the quantity of water you've been guzzling down," her companion Monty said.

"This seemed like a good place to stop." Bertha nodded towards the bushes over to her right. "It's all right for you men. You can just stand at the side of the road with your back to us and let it all hang out. I need cover, and there's some here."

Bertha went over to the clump of bushes. Ensuring the boys could not see her, she pulled down her tracksuit bottoms and lowered herself down into a crouch to release her bursting bladder. A strong gust of wind ripped through the valley, causing the bushes to sway. Bertha glanced around her and almost toppled over when she spotted a lumpy-looking sleeping bag lying a few feet away.

Her mission completed, Bertha stood and rearranged her clothing before taking a cautious step towards the sleeping bag. Could some homeless person be sleeping way out here? There didn't appear to be any other belongings around, so that was unlikely.

"Hey, guys," she yelled, not wanting to tackle this on her own, in case some giant of a man leapt out and attacked her.

"Guys?" she called out again. "Can you come over here for a minute?"

Bertha heard raucous laughter and her name mentioned a few times. *Seriously*? Did they think she was trying to lure them into the bushes to expose herself to them? *Typical bloody men. Hopeless.* She edged closer to the sleeping bag and reached over to unzip it a little. Two grey faces greeted her. She let out a squeal and went running back to the group.

"Has anyone got reception on their phone?" she asked, frantically looking from one person to another.

"What's wrong, Bertha? You look like you've seen a ghost."

"We need to call the police. There are a couple of dead bodies back there in the bushes. They're zipped up in a sleeping bag."

The three men stared at her, disbelief showing on their faces.

"Take a look yourselves! I did call out to you a couple of times, but of course you were too busy making lewd jokes about me having a pee."

Monty lowered his bike to the ground and walked towards the bushes, while the others took out their phones to check for a signal, shaking their heads. Within seconds, Monty returned.

"Bertha's telling the truth. We need to get hold of the police—*now*."

"None of us have a signal," she told him.

"Then I suggest two of you stay here, so the police will know the location when they arrive. I think you should be one of them, Bertha. Evan, you stay with her. John and I can cycle on until we get a signal."

48

INDIA WAS HELPING herself to a cup of coffee when DI Rendle appeared by her side.

"A report has just come in to say a couple of bodies have been found up near Clachan of Campsie. The descriptions fit those of Mr. Day and Miss Waters."

"Oh God, no!" she gasped, dropping her mug onto the counter and spilling coffee everywhere. She looked at the mess, not sure what to do.

"Never mind about that now. I'm heading out there. It would be useful if you came to confirm identities."

"Certainly," she said, gathering herself. "Where is this place?"

"North of Glasgow. It won't take long. A group of cyclists found them and phoned it in. Local police are on their way to secure the area."

"I'll just grab my bag and coat."

"Okay, I'll wait for you in the car park. We'll go in my car if you don't mind. A couple of my team will follow us."

***

"I DON'T SUPPOSE you've had any news on Doctor Hamilton's whereabouts?" India asked Rendle as they raced towards the place he'd mentioned.

"Yes. Sorry. I was about to come and tell you when I got news of this latest development. We located her

271

on a flight from Prestwick Airport flying to Barcelona. She flew out early this morning. She'd driven another car across to Prestwick and left it in the car park there. It turns out she'd purchased the car a few weeks ago, so she'd clearly had this escape planned even before our visit."

"I don't know where Prestwick is. Is that an airport in Glasgow?"

"It's called Glasgow Prestwick, but it's about thirty-two miles from Glasgow over towards the west coast just outside the town of Prestwick."

"Right," India said, not understanding why it was called *Glasgow* Prestwick when it was some distance from the city. "What happens next with her?"

"We're getting onto Europol to see if they can trace her."

"Are Europol the same as Interpol?"

"Similar. They're the combined unit attached to members of the European Union. Look, I'm sorry about your friend. I feel terrible about it. If only I'd—"

"There's no point in going down the *if only* track," she said, cutting him off. She didn't want to hear it. She'd been tormenting herself with it all day. *If only Chrys had woken me. If only I'd woken when she was leaving the room. If only I'd kept her away from this investigation.* It went on endlessly. "It'll drive you crazy. I've stopped beating myself up about it. You need to stop doing it as well. Anyway, we won't know if it's Chrys and Sonny until we get there."

She couldn't bear the idea that the two of them might be dead and didn't really want to think about it.

"Why would you be beating yourself up about anything?"

"Oh, there are endless 'if only I'd done this or that's' I could come up with, but as I say, there's no point. It won't change what's happened. I can't believe after all these months of surviving, Sonny Day might now be dead. And Chrys. What I don't understand is why Hamilton kept Day for so long."

"I've been wondering that as well—if she did, of course. Not too far now. We'll be there soon."

The way he'd been driving, it was a wonder they weren't up in Aberdeen by now. It reminded India of Jacko's driving, and she'd had to close her eyes a few times. She couldn't afford to become too stressed, which was why she'd dropped the 'if only' circuit looping in her head. She was pregnant and determined nothing was going to stop this baby being born. Turning her head away from Rendle so he wouldn't see the tears threatening to spill over, she looked out the window at the Scottish scenery they passed by. She needed to remain professional.

***

WHEN THEY PULLED up at the cordoned-off area, a young, uniformed constable approached them.

DI Rendle identified himself and asked, "How far away are the bodies and has the pathologist arrived yet?"

"Pathologist?" The constable seemed confused. "Don't you mean the crime scene examiners?"

"I mean the pathologist, you dolt. The pathologist has to examine the bodies before the crime scene examiners wade in."

"Oh, sorry, Sir. You mustn't have heard. The cyclists thought they were dead but hadn't touched the victims to check. They've been taken to the Royal Infirmary over in Kirkintilloch. They're not dead. Not yet anyway."

"They're not dead? Oh, thank goodness," India cried out. "Do you know how serious their injuries were?"

"I'm sorry, Ma'am. I only know they were in a bad way."

"Can we go to this Royal Infirmary now?" she asked Rendle.

"I suppose we should. I might be able to question one—or both…with any luck."

Before it's too late, she knew Rendle was thinking. The second car with further team members pulled up behind them, and Rendle went to speak to them. When he returned to the car, he did a U-turn and set off once again.

"I've asked my team to take details from the cyclists who found them plus photos of the scene."

She nodded, pleased he hadn't insisted on seeing the scene himself.

When he reached built-up areas, Rendle put the siren on, and they wove through the traffic to pull up outside the Accident and Emergency department of a large hospital.

"They might be down here or maybe moved onto a ward. Let's go and see," Rendle said, climbing out of the car.

India followed him to the front desk. In answer to his inquiries, they learned that both patients had been moved to Intensive Care. That didn't sound great; it meant that their condition was serious, and they still didn't know if the man and woman who had been found were Sonny and Chrys. They were about to find out though.

***

"IT'S DEFINITELY THEM," India confirmed to Rendle after looking in briefly on Chrys and Sonny, who were either still unconscious or heavily sedated, with tubes and breathing equipment attached to them. Chrys's head was also bandaged so she must have sustained a head injury. It was startling to see them like this. Sonny looked quite different, his face so grey and thin. India checked with the Intensive Care receptionist that the hospital had Sonny and Chrys's full details. She confirmed that their passports had been amongst their possessions so, yes, they had their details. Judging by the smirk on her face and comments made, the receptionist found their names amusing. India turned and walked quickly away before her rising anger at the woman's attitude erupted.

"Can we find out exactly what's wrong with them?" India asked after re-joining Rendle, who had been busy organising a twenty-four-hour guard outside Chrys's and Sonny's rooms.

"I've asked for someone to come and talk to us. I need to know how long it will be before they regain consciousness so I can question them."

That'd be right. The first thing most investigators wanted to do was question victims, even if they weren't really up to it. India had been guilty of it herself a few times. Family members often accused them of being insensitive, but if a serious crime was still being investigated, early information was vital in solving it.

"As we know who the likely perpetrator of these crimes is, do you need to question them with any urgency?" India asked Rendle.

"Maybe. Maybe not. I've told Europol Doctor Hamilton is wanted for kidnapping and murder, but I need these facts confirmed."

India nodded. Rendle's reasoning seemed fair enough.

A woman wearing doctor's garb approached them. "Inspector Rendle?" she asked. When Rendle nodded, the doctor continued. "You wanted to know the condition of the couple who were brought in?"

"That's right."

"I'm the doctor in charge of their treatment. Both patients are suffering from dehydration. I understand they were initially believed to be dead. That would be due to the grey appearance of their skin. In addition, Mr. Day is suffering from early stage hypothermia with an abnormal metabolic rate. He's severely malnourished and was pumped full of medications. Indications are that he's been subjected to these for some time. These symptoms, combined with exposure to low temperatures and inadequate clothing or covering, led to the hypothermia. His body is covered in pressure sores. He has severe bruising and swelling on his wrists and ankles from prolonged restraint. Miss Waters also appears to have been restrained, although damage to her skin is minimal. However, Miss Waters also received a heavy blow to the back of her head. There are no skull fractures, but there was swelling and bleeding."

"When do you think—"

"Are you expecting them to make a full recovery?" India asked, cutting Rendle off. She knew what he was going to ask and was more concerned about Sonny and Chrys's chances of survival.

"They're both in a stable condition at present. I *would* expect them to make a full recovery. Mr. Day's recovery will take considerably longer, as his body has been subjected to greater trauma."

"Thank you," she said, relieved to hear both Chrys and Sonny would survive.

"So how soon before they may be conscious and in a fit state to be interviewed?" Rendle asked.

"Miss Waters perhaps later this evening—if she regains consciousness. I couldn't tell you about Mr. Day. I think you need to leave him alone for another few days—at least. Now, unless there's anything else, I need to get on."

"No, that's all. Thank you," Rendle said, nodding at the doctor, who turned and walked away. "Right, I think I'll head back up to the find site while there's still some light. I assume you'd prefer to remain here—I'll come back and see if we can talk to Miss Waters later." Without waiting for India's response, Rendle walked off with a slight movement of his arm that she took to be a wave.

49

INDIA SPENT THE rest of the afternoon and early evening sitting beside Chrys's bed. When her stomach had started rumbling, reminding her that she hadn't eaten since losing her breakfast that morning, she popped down to the canteen for a cheese sandwich and a cup of tea. She also bought a chocolate muffin and a bottle of water to take back to Intensive Care. She looked in on Sonny, shuddering at his appearance. She didn't understand that woman. Why had Doctor Hamilton kept him imprisoned for so long? And if she wanted him alive, why not care for him adequately? He'd looked healthy enough in the photograph taken up at the cabin—a far cry from the emaciated grey skeleton lying in front of her. Was it Doctor Hamilton's intention to slowly starve him to death?

The medical staff had removed Chrys's breathing tube, and she was now breathing independently. A nurse had told India that Chrys would be transferred to a general ward the following morning.

The same nurse had brought in Chrys's belongings in hospital plastic bags. One contained her small handbag and phone; the other, the clothes she'd been wearing. India placed the clothing bag to one side and Chrys's handbag in the small locker beside the bed. It wouldn't be sensible to leave the handbag and phone in full view.

She thought Rendle's team might want the clothing for forensic testing.

At six thirty, Chrys stirred. India stood and pressed the call button next to her bed. A minute later, a nurse and the same doctor she'd spoken to earlier came into the room.

"Chrys seems to be coming around. I thought you might want to examine her."

"Good evening, Chrystal," the nurse said, leaning over her. "How are you feeling now?"

Chrys opened her eyes, blinked a few times and turned her head, looking around the room.

"It's *Chrys*, not Chrystal. Ow."

"Try not to move too much," the doctor said. "Lift the bed up," she instructed the nurse. "If she's in a sitting position, she'll be able to move her head with greater ease."

The nurse mechanically raised the bed, and Chrys asked for a glass of water. The nurse poured her a glass from the jug on the bedside cabinet and passed it to Chrys.

"My throat feels bloody awful," she complained after taking a few sips.

"That's because we had you intubated when you were first admitted, and you were quite dehydrated," the doctor said.

"My head doesn't feel great either."

"You have a nasty wound," the nurse said. "Try to avoid touching your head in any way."

As soon as the nurse mentioned that, Chrys lifted her right arm as though to touch the bandage, but the nurse stopped her. Chrys gave the nurse a dirty look for her trouble.

"Hello, Chrys," India said, moving closer to the bed.

"So you found us in time then. How's Sonny?"

"He's doing fine, but he'll take a lot longer than you to recover."

"He *is* going to get better though, right?" Chrys asked the doctor and nurse for confirmation.

"We expect him to recover...in time," the doctor added without committing herself too much.

Chrys sank back into the pillow, the relief clear on her face.

The doctor's words seemed to finally penetrate Chrys's brain. "Hang on, what do you mean, 'in time'? How bad is he?"

"Mr. Day needs complete rest and time to heal," the doctor said.

"But—"

"I think we can leave these two alone now," the doctor said, cutting Chrys off and addressing the nurse. "I'll check back on you later, Miss Waters."

Chrys nodded, and the two medical staff left.

"So tell me the truth, India, how bad is Sonny?"

"He's still unconscious. I don't know much more than that. But the doctor told me earlier that she expected you both to make a full recovery. Sonny's recovery will take longer, that's all."

"Okay." Chrys lay back again, wincing with pain.

"Rendle wants to take your statement, and I should really wait until he gets back, but tell me what happened. Why did you go to the doctor's house alone?" India tried to make it not sound like an accusation.

"When I got up for a pee in the middle of the night, I suddenly remembered where I knew that woman from."

"You mean Doctor Hamilton?"

"Yeah. She treated Sonny in the Nepean Hospital Emergency Department last year after an accident at work. We also saw her a few months later at our Spanish class in Penrith. Just the once."

So that was the connection.

"Okay, but why go rushing off to the house alone? Why didn't you wake me?"

"Would you have been prepared to go there in the middle of the night? You didn't want to stake out the place when we arrived in Glasgow. I didn't think you'd be willing to go there this time either, but I was worried our earlier visit would cause her to panic and take action. I reckon the doctor recognised me. That's why she didn't ask who I was when we went to her house. I intended to call for help if I saw her doing anything suspicious. And it's a good thing I did go there as well."

"So what happened?"

"I saw her carrying something which could have been a body out of the house and put it in the boot of her car. I went to check after she went back inside, saw it was Sonny and tapped 999 into my phone."

"No calls for help came from the house. Rendle checked."

"No. She must've knocked me out before I could press the call button. The next thing I remember was waking up in the boot of her car."

Chrys related everything that had happened from when the doctor stopped the car—her story of her husband's accident, his dying, why she needed Sonny, how her accomplice had killed Gordon Haines and what had happened to Eric.

"She told me she sent Eric's ashes back to his family. I don't know if that's true. She didn't tell me what his full name was or where the family lived."

"No, I don't suppose she would. Her story sounds feasible. If that was her husband she buried, she was right. He did die of a massive stroke."

"Right. Well, she lied about leaving my phone so I could call for help when the drugs wore off. I only remember waking the once, and I couldn't find it."

"Your phone and your bag were found with you. I'm not sure where exactly, but they were brought in with you. I've put them in your bedside locker."

"Oh. Well, I couldn't find it."

"Did she go into any detail of how she managed to get Sonny into her custody?"

"No, and I forgot to ask her. She said she knew where we lived and used to see Sonny cycling to the station. Didn't you think she'd knocked him off his bike?"

"It's the most likely explanation. The front wheel was damaged. She could have swerved into him, knocking him off. If he wasn't wearing a helmet, he could have been knocked unconscious, and then she could have injected him. It would have been so fast, he wouldn't have known what happened."

"I wonder if he knows now. Do you think she would have told him why she took him?"

"I don't know. The insurance money and her explanation about needing Sonny to travel with her to the UK kind of stacks up. The thing I'm so curious about is that was months back. Why would she keep him for so long? Did she give you any kind of explanation for that?"

"No. She only said what I told you and claimed she always planned to drop him off at a hospital. She blamed my turning up for having to change her plans—as well as our visit to her house. She said she'd had to speed things up then. Have they caught her?"

"Not yet. She dumped her car at Glasgow Central station, causing a lot of time to be wasted looking for evidence of her catching a train somewhere. I knew she wouldn't have done that. But Rendle had all exits out of the country covered and managed to track her down on a flight to Barcelona early this morning. She'd used another car she owned to drive the thirty-two miles to an airport on the west coast. She'd already left the country by the time we started the search."

"Couldn't they have had the plane turned around or pick her up at Barcelona?"

"It was too late by the time they received the information. Her plane had landed long before, and she would have already cleared customs. If I'd realised sooner, we *might* have been able to catch her at Barcelona. I doubt it, though. She caught an early flight, which departed before I woke up. There was a delay of several hours before I got hold of Rendle this morning. I thought you'd just gone off for a walk or something. Then, when you didn't return, I drove over to the doctor's house, saw her car wasn't there and knocked on Fiona's door to ask whether she'd seen you. So time was wasted, as I then had to get hold of Rendle." She didn't mention her other distraction this morning; discovering she was pregnant.

"Sorry. I should have sent you a text when I arrived at her house, and you would have picked it up first thing. So, she's disappeared into Spain somewhere. Maybe that was always her plan. She *was* learning Spanish."

"I couldn't say."

"I want to see Sonny. Will they let me go to his room? If not, can you sneak me in there?"

"I wouldn't be able to do that, Chrys. Both of you have had police guards on your doors—in case."

"What? They think the doctor might turn up and attempt to finish us off?"

"It's a precautionary measure. Rendle agreed for me to stay, but no one else, apart from medical staff, is allowed to enter your rooms. He needs to take statements from you both first."

"No one else would be visiting us anyway. Anyone who would is in Australia."

"I know, but the press could turn up if they got wind of the story. When Rendle comes back, I'll ask him whether you can see Sonny. He'll probably want to take your statement first, though."

"Okay." Chrys sighed. "But could you see if they could fix me something to eat? I'm famished."

***

RENDLE AND ONE of his DCs returned to the hospital shortly after Chrys had finished her meal. She put forward her request to visit Sonny, but as India had suspected, he wanted to take her statement first. She'd cleared Chrys's visit to Sonny with the doctor, who had since gone off duty and promised to pass the information on to the next duty doctor.

India took advantage of Rendle's presence to nip out of the hospital to get herself something to eat. She found a Chinese restaurant a short walk away and ordered a beef dish. She was always wary of eating chicken and usually stuck to beef or bean curd dishes, but this basic restaurant didn't serve bean curd, so beef it was.

She was inclined to rush the meal, wanting to return to the hospital as soon as she could, but remembering she was pregnant, she ate at a sensible pace. The last thing she wanted was an upset stomach. There'd be plenty of upset stomachs of a morning if her previous pregnancies were anything to go by.

She hadn't been in touch with anyone from home since leaving the station with Rendle to view the 'bodies', and while sipping some weak green tea after her meal, she tapped out a message to Jacko, informing him Sonny and Chrys had been found and were recovering in hospital. She added that the doctor had escaped to Barcelona and asked him to look into her work record at the Nepean Hospital in Penrith. She decided to tackle a call to Rob early tomorrow morning when he would, in principle anyway, be at home. Of course, he might be taking advantage of her absence and going out every night, but she didn't think so. Rob was a good cook and liked decent food. He was more likely to spend his evenings at home playing with his toys.

50

ONNY WAS SURE he could hear Chrys's voice. He willed his eyes to open but without success; he was unable to move any part of his body. He had definitely *felt* and *smelled* Chrys the last time he'd been awake— at least, he thought it was her, so what was going on? Had the woman injected him again? Was he dreaming? Hallucinating?

Being with Chrys again was what Sonny wanted more than anything in the world. To escape this hideous nightmare that his life had become. What would he tell her? Many nights when he'd woken, hungry, thirsty, blindfolded, restrained and lying in his own waste, he'd thought it might be better if he simply died. How could he bear the shame of telling Chrys what his days had been like as the victim of these lunatics? Victims were people he read about in the newspaper. It didn't apply to him, and yet he'd become exactly that. How could he explain it to Chrys and his mates back home? He'd be a laughing stock. Those kinds of things didn't happen to men. He could just imagine his mates asking, 'How did you *let* that happen?'

Sonny still had no idea how he came to be their victim. His captors had never spoken of it or explained why they took him, despite him asking many times. There were days when he thought they'd abandoned him and left him to die wherever he was. Then someone would eventually appear, give him something to eat and guide him to a shower or the toilet without speaking a word.

He'd gained the impression that the man hadn't been around for a while. He'd felt softer skin brushing against him, so he was sure it was the woman. She wasn't whispering to him these days. She barely spoke except to say 'open your mouth' on rare occasions. Otherwise, the visit was conducted in total silence. He sensed that something had changed, but he didn't know what. Had he angered them in some way? Had the man and woman had a falling-out and she was so angry she couldn't be bothered with him anymore? If that were the case, why didn't they let him go? Or were they going to kill him?

***

CHRYS WAS SITTING beside Sonny's bed chatting to him when India returned to the hospital. Rendle was gone, and it looked like the guard detail had been reduced to only one officer outside Sonny's door. Unless Chrys's guard was on a break. Now Rendle had taken her statement, there was no real need for her to have a guard anymore.

Chrys noticed her and waved her into Sonny's room. The duty officer, recognising her, allowed her through.

"Sonny's eyes keep flickering," Chrys told her when she joined her at his bedside. "The doctors reckon he's dreaming. I think he's close to waking up. What do you think?"

"I don't know, Chrys. I've never seen anyone suffering from the same condition as Sonny."

"But you've seen unconscious patients just before they wake up and you question them. Right?"

"A few, but circumstances were entirely different."

"They said I can only have five more minutes with him, then they want me to go and have a bath and return to my room for the night. They won't let me have a shower. A *bath*! I haven't had a bath since I was a kid."

"You can't have a shower with your head injury, Chrys, even if you were to cover it. They're only looking after your best interests."

"I suppose. But I want to stay with Sonny."

"I'm afraid that won't be possible," a nurse entering the room said. "I've come to take you for your bath now, Miss Waters."

Walking over to the wheelchair Chrys was sitting in, the nurse promptly turned her around and began wheeling her out. Chrys was pulling stupid faces that the nurse was unable to see, while India struggled to keep hers straight.

"You'll have to leave now," the nurse said to her as she passed. "Visiting hours are over."

"I'm not exactly a *visitor*," India said.

"I know, but the police have finished their business for the night. There's no need for you to be here. Miss Waters does not need tucking up in bed. I'll have to ask you to leave."

India considered arguing as she followed them out of the room, but the nurse had a point. The only reason to remain at the hospital was to keep Chrys company, and they weren't going to allow that. It was probably better for her to return to the B & B and have an early night. It had been a long and stressful day.

"I'll come in early tomorrow morning," she called after Chrys, receiving a waving arm for a reply.

51

INDIA DIDN'T WAIT until the morning to phone Rob. She phoned him as soon as she arrived back at the guest house and caught him as he'd arrived at work. She filled him in on events over the past few days and then dropped her news.

"That's so wonderful darling," he said. *"So I assume you'll be coming home earlier than planned?"*

She'd known that would be his response. He would no doubt suggest she avoid going out to investigate any cases after she arrived home as well, saying she should direct events from the safety of the station. If he had his way, she wouldn't be working at all but would be at home with her feet up being mollycoddled for the remainder of her pregnancy.

"Maybe. I need to make sure everything's fine with Chrys and Sonny before I can leave Glasgow, then I promised Mum and Dad I'd spend a bit more time with them. My ticket's booked to fly out of Aberdeen anyway."

"You could alter your flight," he said. *"Your mother might want to come home with you when you give her the news."*

"I doubt it, Rob. Once the baby is born, she might come back to Sydney for a while. As I told you, I gained the impression Dad would like to renew his contract and stay on for another few years."

She refrained from saying her mother would probably wait and see if she carried the baby to full term, knowing about the miscarriages she'd experienced in her previous pregnancies.

"Well, see what you can do. We need to celebrate—although no alcohol for you. I can't wait to see you again. I don't know why, but I find myself missing you."

"Ha-ha. I'm surprised to hear you say that, considering you've had free reign to play all your games. I bet you've had them permanently spread out across the living room while I've been gone."

"You know me too well. But I have a good feeling about this one, India. He's going to make it."

He?

"It might be a girl."

"Might be, but I think it's a boy. You know I don't mind what gender the baby is."

"I know. Me either." Boy, girl, she didn't mind as long as she could carry the baby to full term.

"Well, darling, I'm sorry to cut you short, but I have to go to a meeting now. We'll talk again. Soon."

"Okay. Love you."

"Love you too."

Rob and she had never been in the habit of saying 'love you'. She'd never heard her parents express the term to each other or India and her brother either. It lost its meaning if it was repeated too often, so she and Rob only said it to each other if they were away from home— or on other rare occasions. Since her parents had been working abroad, they might end phone conversations with 'lots of love to you, darling' or something similar. Hearing them speak to her like this still seemed out of character, although she welcomed it and found herself returning the sentiment. She wondered what she'd be like with her own child.

***

INDIA ROSE EARLY the following morning, had breakfast and packed a set of clean clothes for Chrys. As she'd suspected would be the case, Rendle had taken the clothes Chrys had been wearing the night of her attack for forensic testing. She doubted Chrys would be released so quickly, but it would be useful for her to have clean clothes to wear once she was. The only thing that was missing was a jacket. Chrys had only brought a thin raincoat and one thick jacket with her. Rendle had taken her thick jacket, and there was no telling how long Police Scotland would want to keep it. Perhaps she should offer to buy Chrys a new one? She decided to see what Rendle said first.

It was on the drive to the hospital that India's stomach started to heave.

"No, no, not now!" she shouted as though her stomach could hear and would conveniently obey. She was on a busy dual carriageway, and it wasn't safe to stop. Rather than do so, she tipped the shoes and slippers she'd packed for Chrys out of the carrier bag, which sat on the passenger seat beside her—in case she needed it. But her stomach seemed to have settled down, so perhaps she'd make it to the hospital. She didn't have far to go now.

It wasn't to be. The heaves started again, and she had no choice other than to slow, pull into the kerb as much as she could and put the hazard lights on while simultaneously bringing the bag up to her mouth in the nick of time. A large proportion of her breakfast shot into the bag, making her feel wretched.

She knew it was too good to be true that she'd escaped a vomiting bout this morning. She'd had a light breakfast as early as she could to ensure the tiresome event would be over and done with before she left for the hospital. In the past, her morning sickness occurred within minutes of finishing breakfast. This morning, she'd felt fine with no indications of stomach unease. It was the same last night. The Chinese meal had gone down well with no sign of queasiness, which she put down to the absence of wine that normally accompanied her meals. She was convinced that was what had made her feel queasy over the past week. There'd be no more glasses of wine now.

Once her stomach settled, she tied the bag and placed it in the foot well of the passenger side. She'd have to dispose of it at the hospital. She'd been aware of other drivers honking their horns at her, as, although she'd pulled over a bit, there was no hard shoulder, and she was still blocking the traffic. Knowing there would be a long line of cars held up behind her, she switched the hazard lights off and drove on. While she was packing Chrys's toothpaste and toothbrush this morning, she'd decided to take her own too and had put them in her handbag—in case of an emergency situation like this. She'd need to clean her teeth before going up to Intensive Care.

***

INDIA HADN'T EVEN walked through the door of the room when Chrys shouted, "Sonny regained consciousness, but they won't let me be with him. It's so unfair!"

"That's great news, Chrys. About Sonny coming around, I mean. So they haven't let you in to see him?"

"Only for a few minutes—with that copper standing guard over me. Can you believe it? All the time I was eating breakfast this morning, he was awake. They sauntered in and casually told me. I demanded that I be taken to him immediately, but they said I couldn't see him yet. It wasn't until I climbed out of bed and set off in my bare feet that they finally agreed to take me and fetched the wheelchair. I have to say, I was pleased they did, as my legs are still a little wobbly. Then, when we got to Sonny's room, that copper said I couldn't go in and that Rendle needed to see him first."

"I know that must be frustrating for you, Chrys, but it is standard practice."

"Bugger their standard practice. I wanted to see Sonny. I promised I wouldn't talk about *the case* with him, and so his guard let me in for a few minutes."

"How is he?"

"Not great. He broke down crying when I bent over and gave him a kiss and as much of a hug as I could. It was awful, the two of us blubbering like babies. Then he said he was sorry. I asked him what for, and he said he was sorry he hadn't managed to get away from them. He said, 'I tried, but…' Then the copper asked Sonny to stop talking and pulled me out, saying I had to leave and could see him later. How long before I can see him, do you think?"

"I don't know, Chrys. The interview with him could take some time, and depending how strong Sonny is feeling, it might have to be done in stages. Rendle agreed I could sit in on it, so I'm going to pop along to see if he's here. Do you know what ward you're being moved to this morning?"

"Yeah. 'D' ward up on the second floor. Rendle's asked me not to speak to anyone from the press if they come sniffing around."

"I think that would be sensible. Look, I've brought your bag of toiletries, a set of clean clothes, shoes and slippers. Sorry I don't have a bag for the shoes and slippers. I had to use it for an unexpected vomiting bout on the drive in this morning."

Chrys looked concerned for a moment, and then her face broke out into a wide grin. "You're pregnant, aren't you?"

"Yes. I am, as it happens. I only discovered I was yesterday morning, which caused another delay in me getting over to the McEvoy house. I was sick after breakfast, which made me wonder, so I rushed out to buy a pregnancy test."

"Well, congratulations. I know it's something you really wanted. Does that mean you'll be going home now?" Chrys's face took on that worried expression again.

"No," India said, shaking her head. "I plan to leave on the flight I'm booked on in a few weeks. That's if everything is okay here."

"I'm pleased you'll be around a bit longer, but don't worry about us. Sonny will be right as rain in no time."

India wasn't so sure about that. Sonny had to rest and rebuild his strength. He'd need some counselling sessions too. Anyone who'd been through what he had would need them.

"Right. I'm going to find Rendle. I'll see you later."

52

THE DUTY DOCTOR agreed that Sonny could be interviewed for as long as he felt up to it. If he showed any signs of weariness or distress, the interview was to cease. Rendle kept his word and allowed India to sit in and even agreed that she could ask Sonny questions about the events in Australia that led to his kidnapping.

Rendle introduced them both, explaining she was from the police in Windsor, New South Wales, and that they had a series of questions they wished to ask him, which they would be recording.

"The nurse told me Chrys couldn't spend any time with me until you'd interviewed me," he said and then coughed a few times. India offered him a glass of water, which he sipped slowly. His voice was quite hoarse, and he wheezed as he spoke. The doctor hadn't mentioned a chest infection, so perhaps this was a new development. No doubt the cellar environment Sonny had been kept in hadn't helped.

"Can you tell me what you remember about the day you went missing?" she asked as her opening question.

The curtains on the window in Sonny's room were open, but the light was switched off to make things easier for him. He looked as though he was about to play a game of tennis, as he was wearing a type of sun visor to protect his eyes from the strong light, and India couldn't see his eyes properly. This was not going to be easy, but the doctor had explained that Sonny's eyes were very weak, and light bothered him because he'd been blindfolded for so long. It was going to take some time for his eyes to adjust, and the doctors didn't know if his sight would fully recover—for psychological rather than medical reasons.

"The last thing I remember is cycling off to the station," he said. "Then it's a complete blank. I don't know what happened. Do *you* know what happened to me?"

She exchanged a look with Rendle, who nodded.

"We think you might have been knocked off your bike. I don't know if you remember, you weren't wearing a helmet that day."

"That's right, I wasn't."

"What's the next thing you do remember?" India asked.

"I woke up to find my head throbbing, I was blindfolded, and my hands and feet were bound. I remember someone coming into the room and injecting me with something. They didn't say a word. That was the beginning of my nightmare."

"What happened after that?"

"The next time I woke up, I could tell my face was badly injured. Whether they did it or I injured myself trying to escape, I have no idea."

Doctor Hamilton had told Chrys that she'd injured Sonny's face to disguise him for the insurance inspector's visit linked to the settlement payout. That must be what he was referring to.

"Things followed a pattern after that. Someone would come and feed me, clean me up and then leave again. I think they were injecting me with drugs constantly, as I kept hallucinating."

"What were you hallucinating about?"

"I kept imagining a woman making passionate love to me. It was all in my head, though. I dreamed about Chrys as well."

Sonny started coughing again, so she paused to give him time to recover. She wondered if the woman Sonny mentioned *was* a hallucination. Perhaps the doctor had been having sex with him. Why would she, though, when all she needed him for was to make sure she received the money? With the injuries her husband had received, perhaps she hadn't had sex for a long time and took advantage of Sonny being handily available.

"You said 'they', Sonny. Was there more than one person with you?"

"There was a man and a woman. I heard muffled arguing a few times. Some days, just the man seemed to be there, sometimes the woman on her own."

"Did they ever speak to you?"

"Not much in those early days. They only said things like 'open your mouth' or 'chew' or 'swallow'. Sometimes the woman would whisper things in my ear, and she kept saying I was lucky. I certainly didn't feel lucky. It was like torture. I kept asking them what they were doing, why they'd taken me, but they never answered. After what seemed like weeks, they took me on a boat somewhere."

"Are you sure it was a boat? Could it have been a plane?"

"I've never flown, so I couldn't tell you, but it felt similar to experiences I've had on ocean-going boats in the past. Besides, I was lying on what felt like a comfortable bed some of the time, so I don't think it could have been a plane. I wasn't fully conscious—again, I think I'd been heavily drugged."

Rendle turned aside and whispered in her ear that Sonny must be talking about the flight to Edinburgh. He said he'd take over the questions.

"Mr. Day, we believe you're talking about your journey to Scotland. Can you tell me what you remember once you arrived here?"

"Scotland? No, the man told me we were in Norway. I saw it myself—it was the only time they let me outside without a blindfold. They put some sunglasses on me because my eyes weren't used to the light. It certainly looked like a Scandinavian country."

They exchanged glances again. Had they taken him to another country first?

"What could you see when you were outside?" Rendle asked.

"I was sitting outside some kind of cabin. I could see other cabins, a lake—or fjord, I think they call them— in the distance. There was an island in the middle of it."

Arden. It had to be Arden he was talking about. Up at Loch Lomond. They'd certainly tried their best to confuse him.

"The man took a photograph of me that day and made me write a letter to Chrys saying I was in Sweden and was married. I put something in the letter so Chrys would know it wasn't true."

"Yes, Chrys picked up on that and brought the letter in to us," India told him.

Sonny nodded.

"I tried to escape that day. I felt a lot stronger than I had been. They'd been exercising me regularly around the cabin. The man was holding a length of pipe, and when I tried to get it off him, we fell to the ground. Then the woman appeared from nowhere and injected me."

Sonny broke down sobbing at that point. India suggested they take a break and come back later. They left Sonny's room and headed off to the canteen.

"They certainly did a number on that poor bugger," Rendle said after they'd been sitting in silence for some minutes.

"Yes. They did. Is there any chance you could arrange counselling sessions for him? He's going to need them."

"I'll speak to the doctor. I suspect she'll say it's a bit premature. He needs to become stronger in his physical body first. Then they could start on the mind."

"When he said the woman kept saying he was lucky, I wonder if he misheard her—she was whispering, after all. Do you think she might have been saying 'Lachie'? When we were talking to her, she sometimes referred to her husband as Lachie."

"Hmm. Yes, she could have been."

"What did you think of the doctor's disclosure to Chrys about this Eric character causing Gordon Haines's death? Are you going to reopen the inquiry into his death?"

"There's little I can do about that without speaking to Doctor Hamilton and gathering more information. It would be only her word on the matter anyway. We do know she wasn't involved. Well, she wasn't present anyway. At the time of his death, she was being interviewed in a hospital. I think I'll let that one lie for the time being."

As they approached Sonny's room on their return from the canteen, the doctor took them to one side and asked them to leave further questioning until the following morning. They had given Sonny something to calm him down and said he wouldn't be up to answering questions. India thought that was probably a good thing. He'd only been conscious a few hours. He needed time to sort things out in his head.

***

IT WAS ANOTHER two days before questioning could resume with Sonny. He *had* developed a chest infection, and the doctor insisted he needed time to recover. They'd given him a large dose of intravenous antibiotics and he would be on smaller doses for another seven days. The doctor would have preferred them to leave Sonny for another week, but Rendle stressed the importance of gathering information without delay.

India understood Rendle's position, but really, there was no urgency. They knew Doctor Hamilton was in Europe somewhere and hadn't been located yet. The man called Eric they were almost certain had been Doctor Hamilton's accomplice throughout Sonny's kidnap. From the interviews with Chrys, it was also fairly conclusive that Eric had been the man Doctor Hamilton had cremated. But they would only discover his full identity if the doctor was caught. Searches Rendle's team had made through criminal records had failed to locate an Eric who could fit the bill. There were several Erics in the system, but not one who fitted the description the Polish cleaners and Fiona Kinley had given them. Fiona had seen him at close quarters and described a tall slim, clean-shaven man, possibly in his late twenties, with dark hair. She had helped Police Scotland compile a composite sketch of him. In a separate sketch the police made of the same man with the addition of a beard, he looked very much like the man who'd been captured on camera at Sydney Airport leaving on Sonny's passport. India had produced a still shot from the airport for them to compare. Kevin Rossiter at Fillmore's Funeral Service had confirmed the beardless sketch looked like the man he'd cremated.

Rendle was confident Europol would locate the doctor and return her to Scotland. He wanted the case against her watertight so he could make formal charges.

Chrys was due to be discharged that afternoon and was going to return to the guest house later. She'd been down to see Sonny a few times each day but was unable to enter his room and had to content herself with calling out through the door to reassure him she was nearby.

A few days later, Rendle and India visited Sonny to begin the second round of questioning.

"How are you feeling today?" she asked him.

"A bit better, thank you." He immediately coughed, and India wondered how far they would get.

"Good morning, Sonny," Rendle said. She'd taken him to task about calling him Mr. Day and suggested he adopt a more informal approach. He hadn't answered her, just grunted, so she was pleased to hear he'd taken her advice.

"I'd like to ask you some questions about the man you fought with. Can you describe him for us?"

"I didn't see exactly what he looked like. He wore one of those balaclava things the few times my blindfold was removed. He was about my height and had blueish-green eyes."

"Anything else you noticed about him."

"He had a strange accent, sounding a bit Scottish at times, but other times foreign. He used some strange words as well when he was either talking to me or when I heard him talking to the woman."

"Can you remember any of the words he used?"

Sonny was silent for a moment before saying, "I caught the word 'spist' and something like 'brer'. I can't pronounce them like he did, and I couldn't make sense of what he was saying. He also said 'peerie' and 'dastreen'. They are the only words I can remember. I'm sorry."

"No, you're doing fine, Sonny, this is very helpful." Rendle made notes, as did India. She couldn't make sense of any of it, but perhaps Rendle could.

"I've just remembered, he also swore at me the day he took the photograph. Or called me a name. I couldn't really tell which."

"Can you remember what he said?"

"It was something like 'de dum'…no. 'Du dum…' I'm sorry, I can't remember the rest. There was a third word he said, like it was a phrase—I thought it sound a bit like he was saying I was a dumb something or other."

"And the woman? What can you recall about her?"

"I only saw her a few times. She had me in a wheelchair sitting in a room of a house one day. Everything was a bit hazy, I couldn't see too well, but I think it was her I saw. She was tall. She had dark hair that she wore pinned up."

Sonny had just given an approximate description of Doctor Hamilton.

"I saw some uniformed policemen that day and tried to call out to them for help. I don't know what she'd done to me, though. I couldn't move, couldn't speak properly and just made unintelligible noises and dribbled. It was so frustrating and humiliating. They were right there, and I couldn't do anything. I think she'd given me something that caused paralysis."

Rendle nodded knowingly, and India could imagine him hauling someone over the coals about this. From what Fiona had told them, Sonny had to be talking about the day Gordon Haines died. If they had looked into matters further at the time, Hamilton could have been caught red-handed with Sonny in her custody.

"Do you remember whether the man was there that day?"

"Yes, he was. I heard the woman shout at him after everyone had gone. There seemed to be quite a few people coming and going that day. She took me back upstairs after they'd all gone. I think that's where they were keeping me."

"Do you remember what she shouted at him?"

"Something like, 'Now look what you've done.' I don't remember much else, as I was fading into unconsciousness. She'd given me another injection. Things changed after that as well."

Sonny's statement had definitely put a new perspective on Gordon Haines's death. Was she admonishing Eric because he'd caused it? It sounded like it, and it tallied with what Hamilton had told Chrys.

"How do you mean, things changed?" Rendle asked.

"I could hear a lot of hammering, and I'm sure they moved me. Although I was wearing a blindfold, the place I was in after that seemed darker, felt colder and smelled different. Before, they walked me eleven paces to the bathroom. Now, it was only about four paces. The man seemed to leave not long after I was moved, and I'm sure the woman kept forgetting about me. Sometimes it seemed like days before she'd come and give me food or clean me up."

Sonny's emaciated and damaged body certainly had the appearance of serious neglect. While he was still unconscious, India had watched nurses turn him and apply cream to the bedsores on his back, legs and buttocks. Had Doctor Hamilton really forgotten him, or had she been away somewhere organising her escape plan?

There was little else Sonny was able to tell them. The next thing he remembered was imagining he was lying next to Chrys. She told him that he hadn't imagined it— they had been lying together—and explained what had happened. Rendle concluded the interview and left to make some calls.

"Can I...can I see Chrys now?" Sonny asked after Rendle left. India detected a note of hesitancy in his voice.

"Would you like to?"

"More than anything. But...I feel so ashamed about everything that happened to me. As though it was my fault somehow. I'd like to know why she picked me. I kept asking myself, 'Why me?'"

"You have nothing to be ashamed of, Sonny. You happened to fit Doctor Hamilton's agenda. There was nothing you could do against the drugs she plied you with. I think it's time I explained why you were taken."

She filled Sonny in on the explanation Doctor Hamilton had given to Chrys—the reason why she'd picked Sonny, where she knew him from.

"So she was that lovely doctor who treated me in the Emergency Department after my accident?"

"Yes."

"Ah. I had no idea. I knew there was something familiar about her voice when I heard her talking normally, but I didn't recognise her and couldn't place her at all."

"No, why would you imagine that a doctor who'd treated you once in Emergency would be kidnapping you eight months later?"

"Thanks for telling me. It makes a bit more sense now. Why didn't she release me sooner then, if she just wanted to use me to get her hands on the money? Why take me out of Australia at all?"

"She told Chrys she needed a living husband to return to Scotland with, otherwise she'd have to explain his death."

"Right. But why keep me all this time? It's been more than five months, you said, nearly six. Almost five months since she took me out of Australia. I knew it was a hellish long time, but I had no idea it was that long."

"We don't know why she kept you so long, Sonny. When we catch her, that might come to light. But I do know Chrys has been dying to talk with you properly. I'll go up and tell her she can see you now."

53

Rendle asked India to come down to the station the following morning. She dropped Chrys at the hospital and headed off to her meeting.

Once she was ushered into Rendle's office, she could tell he had important news. He looked like the cat who'd got all the cream.

"You've found her?"

"No, there's been no news on her. But we've identified our man Eric. It's Erik with a 'k' not a 'c' like we assumed. Erik Andersson."

The name immediately conjured up images of home. Her grandfather used to manage an electrical store called Eric Anderson's down in Penrith. They apparently had stores all over New South Wales. Did they still exist? She couldn't remember seeing one in recent years. Her parents still had a sixties vinyl stereogram player that came from Eric Anderson's. It looked more like a sideboard and sat in the back enclosed veranda of their house. India's mother had inherited it from her father, and it held fond memories of her childhood.

She looked up and saw Rendle was watching her expectantly. "Sorry. I was distracted by the name for a moment. How did you manage to identify him?"

Rendle tapped his nose. "Basic detection," he said. "Those words Mr. Day gave us. Two of them I recognised as Shetland expressions. The other two I believe may have been Norwegian. I phoned through to the station and got one of the boys to get onto the local sergeant in Shetland. We sent him the composite sketch of our man. He recognised him. Erik's mother had bumped into the sergeant in town the previous day and told him she'd received notification that Erik had died. He paid her a visit yesterday afternoon. The mother related how she had received a parcel containing Erik's ashes and letter from a Mrs. McEvoy, together with a death certificate and some of Erik's personal possessions, including his passport. Guess who signed the death certificate?"

"Our elusive Doctor Hamilton?"

"Correct."

"Good work, Detective Rendle. Those words were meaningless to me."

"Well, they would be, wouldn't they? Coming from 'down under', as they say." Rendle made inverted commas in the air as he said 'down under'. She couldn't help smiling at his corniness.

"You wouldn't have come across them before," he added.

"No, I wouldn't. So, what the doctor told Chrys was true. She did send Erik's ashes back to his family. What we don't know, though, is whether he died as she described to Chrys, or whether she murdered him."

"No, but our man in Shetland said Andersson had a reputation as a serious drinker. The letter Doctor Hamilton wrote to his mother mentioned that he'd died from a fall down the cellar steps where he broke his back and neck—after consuming alcohol."

"You said the crime scene examiners found blood there, so she might have been telling the truth."

"Yes, maybe. We don't have his body to compare the DNA to, but it wasn't a match for Mr. Day, so I suspect it was Andersson's. I've asked the police in Shetland to collect a DNA sample from his mother—it will give us a familial link. Erik was half-Shetland, half-Norwegian. His father was from Norway, and the family lived in Norway for some years when he was younger. He also lived in Glasgow and spent about three years in Australia."

"Presumably he and the doctor met up in Australia. I'll pass his name and information on to my DS, see if he can find a connection. I think the hospital would be the best place to start."

***

Records showed that Erik Andersson had been treated by Doctor Greer Hamilton at the Nepean Hospital in Penrith towards the end of March. Jacko tracked down this information and emailed it across to India. So the mystery of their connection was also resolved. Jacko also spoke to one of the doctor's ex-colleagues and confirmed that the sketch they had created from their unidentified body looked like Doctor Hamilton's husband Lachlan. Jacko had had no success in obtaining any DNA from the hospital which had treated Kenrick McEvoy in Brisbane, but from everything they had learned, it was pretty conclusive he was their mystery body.

Now all they had to do was find Doctor Hamilton. There was still no news on her. She'd been tracked to a large hotel in Barcelona, but there was no record of her staying there. CCTV showed her walking through the hotel lobby and entering a lift, but she wasn't sighted on any of the cameras on any of the hotel floors. The camera in the lift had been broken. There was no record of her leaving the hotel. Where she had gone to next remained a mystery.

***

SONNY HAD AGREED to counselling sessions and was seeing someone regularly at the hospital. Ten days on, he was still nowhere near fit enough to be released, although he had been moved to a general ward with three other patients in his room and was receiving physiotherapy every day to strengthen his limbs. Being able to talk to other people around him seemed to help.

"He's getting stronger every day," Chrys told India over a meal that night.

"That's great. Look, Chrys, I've decided to head off to Aberdeen tomorrow. There's no need for me to be here anymore. My flight back to Australia is next week, and I'd like to spend some more time with my parents before I go."

"No worries. You go. I know you've only stayed here in Glasgow to keep me company. I'll be fine."

"What about our room? Do you have enough money to pay for it? Sonny might not be discharged for another few weeks."

"Don't worry, India. DI Rendle has returned the money Doctor Hamilton left with Sonny. She left him a couple of thousand pounds. That will cover everything. They think he might be fit enough to fly in another week. You never know, we might arrive back in Aus the same time as you."

***

INDIA'S PLANNED RETURN to Aberdeen was delayed after she received a call from Rendle later that night, asking her to meet him at the hospital the following morning.

"What's wrong," she asked as they were walking towards Sonny's room.

"You'll hear soon enough," he said with undisguised anger.

They found Sonny and Chrys sitting in a small lounge area in the ward. Rendle asked the other two patients who were there to leave.

"I also need you to leave, Miss Waters. We have some questions for Mr. Day. On second thoughts, it might be better if you stayed."

Rendle was back to using formal names, which India thought was ominous.

"What's going on?" Chrys asked. India shrugged and shook her head.

"Right, young man, when were you going to tell us about the money?"

"What money?" Sonny asked.

"The money Doctor Hamilton paid out to you."

"You know about the money, Inspector Rendle," Chrys butted in. "You returned it to me yourself."

"I'm not talking about that money. I'm talking about the two hundred and fifty thousand pounds she sent to your joint bank account in Australia. Was this the amount you agreed on when you embarked on this little charade with her?"

India saw Sonny's and Chrys's jaws drop open in surprise. She knew hers was doing the same.

"I'm sorry, DI Rendle," she said. "Could you enlighten us on what you're talking about? I think this information has come as a shock to both Chrys and Sonny." *And me.*

"Fiona Kinley phoned us yesterday afternoon. She saw men entering the McEvoy house and called to check it was us, not someone breaking in. We sent a car around there urgently, and it turned out it was the new owners of the property. The doctor arranged for the sale of the house more than a month ago. The property had been transferred into her name while they were still living in Australia.

"She sold it under market value to some property company, who have now taken possession. From them, we were able to obtain the name of her solicitor, and he has informed us that after repaying the outstanding mortgage, deducting his fees and taxes, Mrs. McEvoy left instructions for the balance to be split in two—a sum to be donated to Cancer Research and the second and larger sum to go into your joint bank account. The money was sent through to your account in Australia. Two hundred and fifty thousand pounds."

"What?" Sonny exclaimed. "Tell me you're kidding."

"I am not kidding," Rendle said. "I think you have some explaining to do, don't you? According to the solicitor, Doctor Hamilton told him she owed you this money."

Sonny shook his head. It was obvious to India he knew nothing about the money, yet Rendle was suggesting Sonny had gone through all this for a large payout.

"I know *nothing* about this. You seriously think I'd suffer through everything I have done to make some *money*? Chrys and I were about to be married and head off on our honeymoon. Why would I?"

"For the money, of course. Did you know anything about this, Miss Waters?"

"No. Of course not! I'm as flabbergasted as Sonny. When the doctor told me she was leaving some money to cover his expenses, I assumed she was referring to the money you found on Sonny. She didn't mention anything else. Ah, no, hang on—she did say the least she could do was compensate us for all the trouble. Perhaps that's what she meant. I thought she was just talking about the cost of the airfare home and other expenses, but I already told you that."

"It doesn't paint a good picture for you two," Rendle said.

"How much did Doctor Hamilton sell the house for?" India asked.

"Four hundred and twenty-five thousand pounds. It was worth closer to six hundred and fifty. It's a desirable area—some nearby properties have fetched up to a million pounds."

India whistled. She knew the McEvoys' house was in a smart area but had had no idea of the value. She'd wondered what the doctor's intentions had been when Rendle mentioned the couple had bought the house before travelling to Australia. She thought it strange that she'd just abandon it and take off.

"There was almost ninety thousand outstanding on the mortgage," Rendle added.

"Leaving a hefty sum over," India said. "Doctor Hamilton may not have wanted to walk away leaving the bank or the government here to profit from the remainder of the equity. She couldn't very well have the money sent to her. You'd be able to trace it. From what we've discovered regarding the payout from her husband's accident, she took millions out of Australia with her. She didn't need the money from the house and must have deposited her millions in a bank that was accessible to her. Possibly in Europe somewhere. She might have seen making a donation to a charity and compensating Sonny and Chrys as a fairer way of distributing the money."

"Maybe." Rendle was considering the idea, although he was still glowering at Sonny.

"I can assure you, Detective Rendle, we knew nothing about the money. I don't know what to say about it. I don't know what I *think* about it. I'm not sure I want anything to *do* with the money."

"Let's not make a hasty decision, Sonny," Chrys said. "We need to talk it over."

***

INDIA FINALLY BOARDED a train to Aberdeen two days later, having surrendered her hire car to the company's local depot. She left Sonny and Chrys still debating whether to keep the money Hamilton had left them. One thing they had agreed on, though, was that they would use some of it to pay for Kenrick McEvoy to have a proper burial once they returned home. When India told them the hospital in Glasgow was likely to hit them with an expensive bill for their care, Chrys said the travel insurance they'd taken out for their honeymoon trip should cover it.

India left her contact details with Rendle before leaving. He'd conceded that neither Sonny nor Chrys had contrived with the doctor to claim the money that was due to be paid out over her husband's accident. In the circumstances, there was little Rendle could do about the money the doctor had transferred to their account. The transaction had been made legally. He was not optimistic that Europol was going to have any success in tracing Doctor Hamilton, who must have had support through a third party to make her escape so smoothly.

While Rendle had much to do to tie up ends in his cases and was planning on a trip to the Shetland Islands later in the week, India had the necessary information to close the files in Windsor. She was looking forward to seeing her parents again and then flying back to Australia next week. Like Rob, she had a good feeling about this baby growing inside her. At long last, they were going to be parents.

54

Buenos Aires, Argentina
February 2015

DOCTOR SOFIA RAMIREZ, a respected widow, was content with her new life. She had opened a small, private clinic in Buenos Aires, in an area largely populated with German expats and wealthy Argentinians. She knew she was safe here and believed her smooth transition to this new community was going to suit her down to the ground. She'd employed a couple of local doctors in the clinic and recently appointed one to manage it while she took some leave.

Sofia, formerly known as Greer Hamilton/McEvoy, never spoke English these days, and her Spanish was improving daily. She was already fluent in German. Greer's maternal grandmother, although brought up in Scotland, had been German born. She'd been left orphaned as a young teenager towards the end of the Second World War when her mother had died in a British internment camp on the Isle of Man. Without any known relatives back in Germany, Greer's grandmother, Giselle, or Oma as Greer called her, had returned to Aberdeen after the war, where friends, who had been running the family business in her mother's absence, took her in. Oma's father had died the year before war broke out.

Oma moved to Elgin following her marriage and was still living there when Greer was born. Oma often babysat for Greer's parents, and it was during this time that Oma spoke German to her. In her teens, Greer studied German at school, eventually taking A-level exams in the subject.

She and Lachie had moved to Berlin a few years after their marriage, remaining for twelve months, and by the end of her stay, she spoke like a local. She explained her fluency in German to her new clients by stating she'd lived in Germany for some years with no mention of her grandmother or real background.

She would have been happy to continue living in Germany, but Lachie claimed the Germans were too austere for him, and he'd applied for a job back in Scotland instead, as usual making arrangements without consulting her. She'd been tempted at that point to break up with him and remain in Berlin, which she found an exciting city. She'd been trying to become pregnant, as he'd eventually agreed she could come off the pill, and so, with some reluctance, she'd returned to Scotland with him.

Two years on with no sign of a pregnancy, she'd attended a gynaecology and fertility clinic to check there was no medical cause for it on her part. Lachie refused to have himself tested, and no amount of pleading, cajoling or arguing would make him budge on the issue. Shortly before his accident in Queensland, he'd confessed he wasn't able to father children. Although he wouldn't admit it, she suspected he'd always known and had nevertheless married her knowing she wanted a family. He could be a selfish bastard like that. She'd made the decision not to join him in Queensland, intending to seek a divorce, but when he'd had his accident, she felt she couldn't leave him then. Some days, even now, she wished she had. Life would have proved simpler, and she wouldn't have to be living under a false identity. But then she wouldn't have Dante.

Despite everything, she had her child now. A beautiful little boy, born just yesterday in the comfort of her home. She'd decided to call him Dante. Dante Tomas Ramirez. It had a nice ring to it. Her new staff at the clinic commented on how sad it was that her deceased husband—whom they believed to be Ramirez—never got to see his child. They also believed that Ramirez, who had been twenty years older than her, had lost his last surviving relatives in the Falklands War.

What had started out as a temporary measure to ensure she received Lachie's insurance payout had escalated into a complex series of events. She had intended to release Sonny once she received the money, but then Miguel had pointed out that she needed an 'incapacitated' husband for her return to Scotland to avoid arousing suspicions in Australia. Managing alone had proved complex and difficult, so she'd recruited Erik to help her, a patient she'd met at the hospital in Penrith. It was a decision she later came to regret.

Initially, she planned to have Erik masquerade as her disabled husband for the return journey to Scotland but then decided it would be better to hang on to Sonny, who was a closer fit to Lachie, and Erik was so much younger.

It was shortly before her departure from Sydney that the idea of using Sonny to father a child had first occurred to her. She'd been washing him one evening when it became obvious that, even in his drugged state, he was aroused. She'd dismissed the idea as absurd and somewhat immoral, but then laughed at herself. Kidnapping Sonny was immoral, so why not take it a step further if the opportunity was there? She was thirty-nine this year; in another few years, it would be too late. Greer had no intention of marrying again; fourteen years with one tyrannical husband was enough to put her off marriage for life. Besides, with her independent financial situation, she didn't need a husband. But she had always wanted a child.

There had been one failed attempt at becoming pregnant in Sydney, but once they arrived in Arden, intimacy with Sonny proved easier, and she fell pregnant in their first month there.

She hadn't wanted to release Sonny until she knew everything was all right with the baby and her plans were in place. A scan in a private clinic in Madrid had confirmed all was well. She'd been in the process of finalising plans for her permanent departure when those detectives had turned up—the Scottish and Australian one—accompanied by that stupid woman Chrys. The one who caused all the trouble as she was leaving.

Another week and Sonny would have healed further, and she would have been gone. She knew Sonny wasn't in the best shape after her last trip abroad, when she was away longer than anticipated. She'd had to leave him alone after Erik had fallen to his death. She'd planned to nurse Sonny back to improved health before leaving him at a hospital. But those two Australians had to stick their noses in, which meant she had to bring her plans forward a week. She wasn't sure how they'd tracked her down, but she had to make sure they would never find her again.

She'd flown to Barcelona a few times, where she liaised with her contact Miguel, whom she'd first met when she was working in Edinburgh. She'd treated him at home for an unreported gunshot wound, so he owed her a huge favour. Over the course of Miguel's treatment, she learned that he worked for the Argentinian intelligence service. It was he who organised her new identity and helped her set up bank accounts in Switzerland where Lachie's payout money had been deposited. If the Australian authorities attempted to trace the money, they would have learned that the first Swiss account was now closed with no further trail to follow.

It was after meeting Miguel that she became interested in learning Spanish. Miguel and his associates often spoke it in her presence, and it drove her mad not being able to understand what they were saying. She'd immediately purchased a course that came with a textbook and CD and set about learning it. She also attended conversation classes.

She visited Miguel daily after their first meeting, just to ensure he was healing well; his underlings collected her from the hospital. Lachie had been working up in Dunfermline at the time and was always home late of an evening. Sometimes he didn't come home at all if the bodies waiting for an autopsy were stacking up. Miguel began to relax in her company, and they often dined together if Lachie was away. When Miguel left the country some months later, he gave her a couple of phone numbers—message services, he told her—and insisted she contact him if she ever needed help. After all, she'd saved his life, and he said he would willingly return the favour.

Five years on, when Lachie died, she asked for Miguel's help. After she returned to Scotland, they met several times to make plans to change her identity, leaving Sonny in Erik's care. But then Erik had died in Glasgow, and she'd had to leave Sonny alone to travel to the continent.

Greer had detoured to Switzerland briefly on her way back to the UK, leaving Sonny in Erik's care in Abu Dhabi—where he'd travelled to, from Dubai, using his own passport. Once Miguel had obtained a new identity for her, she'd travelled back to Zurich from Spain as Sofia Ramirez to transfer her money—in cash—to a new account which would eventually make its way to a bank in Buenos Aires.

Miguel had filled her in on Sofia's background. Sofia Ramirez had existed; she was a doctor who had trained in the UK and was the daughter of an English mother and Argentinian father by the name of Perez. Sofia had grown up in England, largely estranged from her father, who had moved to Spain at the outbreak of the Falklands War in 1982 when she was only a few months old. Her parents were reconciled in Spain a few years later, but the marriage didn't last, and Sofia and her mother returned to England when she was seven, seeing her father during occasional school holidays when he visited England. Sofia grew up in Bournemouth, attended medical school in London, qualifying as a doctor, and lived there for some years until her mother died and she moved to Spain to join her father. Within weeks, she married one of her father's associates, a fellow Argentinian, a Marcos Ramirez—who, according to Miguel, Sofia had already met on previous trips to Spain and who was twenty years older than her.

Soon after Greer and Miguel's initial meeting in Barcelona, Miguel had been called out by members of his team to attend a fatal road accident involving Mr. Perez, his current girlfriend, Sofia and her husband. Perez and Ramirez were under scrutiny by Miguel's team on suspicion of diamond smuggling out of South America, and they had been tailing the men when the accident occurred on a remote country road. The car had apparently plunged into a ravine and exploded on impact, killing all four occupants.

Miguel had seen it as the perfect opportunity to acquire the new identity Greer needed. They engineered a delay in reporting the accident so that they could retrieve Sofia's body and give Greer time to catch the next flight to Madrid to be in residence when the Spanish police called with the sad news that her father and husband were dead. Miguel was there to comfort the 'pregnant widow' and dealt with the police when, overcome with grief, she had to take a pill and lie down.

It had all turned out exceptionally well for her. Sofia had never had an Argentinian passport, only an English one.

Disappearing in the hotel in Barcelona had been achieved through Miguel's ingenious arrangements.

Next came the plastic surgery in Madrid. Some minor alterations had been made to her face, and if her mother was still alive, Greer was sure even she wouldn't have recognised her. While recovering from the surgery, she'd stayed in the Perez rental property in Madrid, one of Miguel's cronies staying with her to ward off visitors. There had only been one, and he'd seen the visitor off with the tale that Sofia was still in mourning. As the real Sofia had only been living in Spain for a few months, she hadn't had time to make many friends. Although Greer had had her hair styled to match Sofia's, she couldn't let anyone who knew Sofia see her, as the real Sofia had been approximately fifteen centimetres shorter.

Once she recovered from her surgery, Miguel had hastily organised to have Sofia's Argentinian passport re-issued with Greer's new look and destroyed records of her appearance on the previous passport. She'd flown out to Buenos Aires a few days later.

Now here she was with baby Dante. He was everything she'd dreamed of. That silly woman Chrys thought Greer had wanted to kill Sonny. That had never been her intention. In fact, torn about what to do with the Glasgow property when making her plans, she had eventually decided she couldn't, on principle, leave it for the bank to repossess. There was an outstanding mortgage of just under £90,000, but the house was valued at £650k. They'd bought it for just under £320k some years before and spent a lot of money on improvements. She'd had agents in to revalue it once the more recent improvements were completed and she'd moved back in. Selling it through an agent would prove difficult with her cellar resident, so she'd approached one of those companies that buy your property for cash. Initially, they offered her £350k for the house, a four-bedroom detached property in excellent condition. There was no way she was having that. After viewing the property—"I'm sorry, I seem to have mislaid the cellar key"—they eventually settled on the sum of £425k, more than a third lower than the market value.

Greer knew they'd flip the house, selling it on to make a quick profit.

After paying off the bank, legal fees and tax, she would be left with a little over £300k. Much as she would have liked to add this money to her coffers, it would be traceable and too dangerous. Instead, she arranged for a donation to be made to Cancer Research and the balance, £250k, to be transferred into the joint bank account Sonny had with that woman in Australia. She had picked up the details from a bank card in his wallet. She would have preferred to pay it into an account which Sonny held in his name only, but Erik had damaged Sonny's other bank card in some charade at the travel agency, after which he threw it away. She didn't begrudge Sonny the money; after all, he'd unwittingly donated his sperm, which had given her the gift of Dante's life.

Tucked away in a drawer, she had photographs of Sonny. A couple were taken at Arden the day after Dante was conceived. She was sure he was conceived that night, as it had been such a special moment when they both climaxed simultaneously, and she had *felt* an immediate change in her body. She'd also removed a few other photographs of Sonny when she went to collect his passport. There had been a pile of them lying loosely in the same drawer: some with duplicates, and it was a few of these she'd removed, believing they wouldn't be missed.

She wasn't sure how Sonny had reacted to receiving the money, but it was his now to do with as he wanted.

Dante would undoubtedly ask questions about his father as he grew up. She'd have to maintain the Ramirez fiction for him, but should she eventually reveal the truth to him? She wasn't sure. One thing she was absolutely sure about, though: the truth could *never* be disclosed during her lifetime. She was confident that the British and Australian authorities wouldn't be able to trace her, and she had no intention of disturbing the comfortable life she'd established for herself. But on her deathbed? Should she leave information for Dante to find once she'd gone? Maybe.

Acknowledgements

Thanks to Judy who, as usual, was the first person to read my first draft of *The Photograph* as it came off the printer. Thanks for your scribbles over my mistakes and feedback. Thanks to Heather, who read an early edit, picked up typos and gave her feedback. Thanks also to Laura for reading an early version and giving feedback. Most of all, my heartfelt thanks to Debbie from Beaten Track Publishing who was willing to publish *The Photograph* and for the professional edit she did. It was wonderful to finally have a true professional go over my work. Thanks also to Jor Barrie for proofreading and to Bojan from PixelStudio for your cover design work. Finally, thanks to all my other friends who have encouraged me to carry on writing.

About the Author

L.E. Luttrell was born in Sydney, Australia and spent the first twenty-one years of her life there before moving to the UK. After working in publishing (in the UK) for a few years she went on to study and trained as a teacher. Since the nineties, she spent many years working in secondary education, although she's also had numerous other part-time jobs. A frustrated architect/builder, L.E. Luttrell has spent much of her adult life moving house and wielding various tools while renovating properties.

L.E. Luttrell lives in Merseyside England, but also spends time travelling between Liverpool, Wales (UK) and Australia when there is not a COVID crisis.

Follow on:

 L.E. Luttrell – Author

 @LLuttrellauthor

Go to: www.lelutrell.com and sign up to the VIP list to receive a FREE BOOK

Beaten Track Publishing

For more titles from Beaten Track Publishing,
please visit our website:

https://www.beatentrackpublishing.com

Thanks for reading!